WRITTEN

The Librarian's Coven, Book 1

KATHRYN MOON

❀ Created with Vellum

To the coven of women who carried me through this book.
These pages are for you.

CONTENTS

CHAPTER 1

JOANNA

I FELT INVISIBLE, FROZEN IN PLACE. THE CANDERFEY University campus was *stuffed* with people. They poured out of brick buildings like a sudden flood, trickling over pathways and joining friends to lounge in the grass under the massive trees of the Hand Woods that surrounded us. Most of them passed each other like strangers on the walkways. At home, I couldn't pass a neighbor without making conversation for at least five minutes. And suddenly here I was, people brushing right up against me and never saying a word.

One crossed in front of me, blocking my view of the library, and I rose up on my toes. I knew my jaw was hanging loose, making me look every bit the country bumpkin I was, but I couldn't stop staring. The building was larger than anything I'd ever seen before, and grander, with lamps glittering through the glass panes that stretched as tall as my whole house. Even from the outside, I could see them, lining the walls like invitations— my books. The university's books, really, but they would be something like mine while I trained as a librarian.

My hands squeezed around the handle of my small suitcase. I had brought so little with me. There were people passing me carrying more in their arms than I had in my possession—books and papers and goblets and wands and little potted plants and instruments and artwork still dripping fresh paint.

"Joanna Wick?"

A wind picked up and brushed my hair—now too long to stay out of my eyes and too short to do anything with—across my face and I pushed the dark strands back. My stunned gaping settled on a small woman with bright red hair braided over her shoulder and a pair of round glasses bouncing the glare of the sun into my eyes.

"I can find you a job cleaning the windows if you'd rather," the woman called from the path in front of the building. "Or you might come in."

"Yes," I said, stumbling forward to the enormous wood and glass doors of the library. My voice was practically air. All of it had been stolen out of my lungs at the sight of my new workplace.

"Well," said the woman, eyes flinty behind her lenses. "You look the part at least." Then she pushed the door behind her open and waved her arm for me to enter.

We were dressed similarly, in our long dark skirts and buttoned gray blouses and gleaming black boots. I had never seen anyone dress any different, but this woman and I seemed to stick out for our plainness here.

"It's really all I own," I admitted as a young student passed us in something feathered and flounced.

And then I was struck stupid again as we stepped into the lobby.

A library with a lobby. A giggle burst out of my mouth and I caught my breath, savoring the whispery dry smell of books in the back of my throat. Three chandeliers of candles and crystals hung above a long wooden counter that had fairies, goblins, and ghouls carved into the facade, wolves crouched and snarling along the floor. Behind the counter stood three librarians, stamping books in and out of circulation. Beyond them was one of the most beautiful sets of shelves I had ever seen, full to bursting with every shape and size and color of book.

"Am I supposed to be *here*?" I asked, starting to turn to the woman. Instead, my eyes caught on the roof above me, made of cut and colored glass, casting a scene on the black tile floor of the changing seasons.

"So they tell me, dear," she said.

I glanced at her long enough to catch the curve of a smile. And then was completely distracted by the bookshelves stretching beyond her to the left. The farther up I looked, the more stories of the library there was to see. Another wing soared up to the roof on the right, with wooden balustrades looking over the lobby.

"There are more people in this building than in my entire hometown," I said without meaning to.

The woman snorted and took my elbow leading me behind the circulation desk where the other librarians were smirking down at their tasks. She pulled at the edge of one of the shelves and it swung toward us, revealing a small room of dark armchairs and bright lamps glowing.

"Let's have some tea," she said and the bookshelf swung shut behind us.

❦

HER NAME WAS Gwen Woollard and despite her quirking lips and the dry snap in her tone, she was patient with me.

"You start tomorrow and you'll be shelving for us to start with, so there'll be plenty of time for fondling spines and sniffing pages then," she said as she led me through the stacks, orienting me with the arrangement, pointing out the places students ended up nestled together, and describing the rush hours.

Despite her words, she let me trail behind her, my eyes soaking up the sight of the shelves and their precious cargo. Had I ever even imagined there might be so many books in the world? The trip to Canderfey from Bridgeston, where I'd grown up, had taken the night and the better part of the morning, but still. I would have tried to find my way here sooner if I'd known what I'd been missing.

"These next two floors are for faculty and library staff only," Gwen said.

I had to race up a set of stairs to catch up after staring too long at a painting of a crowd of people in gossamer clothing, twining together under moonlight. The artist's subject was an

3

old fertility festival, and the canvas shimmered with life and magic, and left me blushing as I joined my new boss.

"Even then," Gwen said, pausing at the top of the steps, likely waiting for me to catch up. "Keep your eyes on the professors. They're as bad as the students, most of them. Always trying to sneak books away or cozying up in corners."

"I *know* you aren't talking about me, Gwendolyn," a man's voice purred from behind a bookshelf. I leaned around Gwen and saw him, stretched out in the window seat sunning himself like a cat. He was wearing a vivid green jacket that looked soft even from where I stood. His skin was dark and smooth, and there was silver at the temples of his short black hair. He grinned at me with full lips and a sharp smile, dark eyes flashing.

"Professor King, I absolutely am," Gwen answered, her tone biting. But her smile was easy as she added, "You're nearly late for class and if I haven't been saying that same thing for the last twenty-odd years I don't know what I've been doing."

"*Nearly* late," he agreed, rising up from the bench seat with a grace I envied. He added to me, "Don't let her bully you."

"I'm not easily bullied," I said, and his grin widened as he winked at me and passed us. If Gwen noticed the book he tucked against his side under his arm, she didn't say a word.

"Be careful," she said.

"Of him?" I whispered, glancing back at the man who was retreating down the flights of stairs.

Gwen stared at me, eyes narrowed for a long moment, her lips twitching. "Of the books," she said. "The reason the students aren't allowed up here is because this is our...more sensitive catalogue. It's a devil to keep organized and every last page is ornery and soaked in magic. They'll shift around or go missing entirely."

I wondered if Professor King had anything to do with the latter, but kept the question to myself.

"When you aren't busy elsewhere, this will be where we need you," she continued, walking ahead.

I bit my smile as one of her hands floated up from her side to brush her knuckles across the spines lining a low shelf.

"Do what you can to keep it tidy, but don't be shy or stupid about calling for help if you need it," she said, turning in place on the toes of her black boots.

"Help?" I asked, glancing at a bookshelf. It all seemed to be a smaller version of the organization in the greater library. And while it was on a scale larger than I'd ever had the imagination to fathom, it was the same system we used at home in our own little branch. It would be easy work for me.

"You'll see," Gwen said, smiling at the books. Then she turned and looked over the rims of her glasses at me. "Go on. Say it now."

My forehead knotted, not sure what she meant.

"What's been running through your head since you got off the bus," she said. "Probably since you got the letter of employment."

I took a breath and held it, staring up at the lamps above and then at the deep row of bookshelves surrounding us. There was a shuffle of pages farther off, and a quiet echo from beyond the balcony—steps on tile and whispering voices.

"Are you sure I'm right for the job?" I asked. It was a magical university, and I was...not much of anything as far as I could tell. I'd never shown any aptitude at real magic, not more than the little basic charms everyone knew. I loved books and quiet and walks. I'd applied to Canderfey's library staff on a whim, not a genuine expectation of being hired.

"Yes," Gwen said, without any hesitation. "We know what we're doing here. Soon you will too. Now let's get your suitcase and I'll tell you where to find your rooms."

THE DIRECTIONS GWEN had given me seemed clear enough while we were alone in the quiet little break room behind the circulation desk. But out on the campus grounds with classes changing and people flooding the paths that curled around massive old trees, the words were pouring out of my thoughts as they became flooded with new information. My steps slowed as I stared at the collection of towering buildings of brick and stone. A beautiful variety of people rushed around me, the kinds of people who passed through Bridgeston without stopping. Faces and clothing and lives I would only have seen glimpses of through windows.

I couldn't decide where to look. At the group of young women huddled together on the grass, painting sigils on each others' skin with blue-black ink? Or the boy who was walking up a set of stairs into a building, juggling flames through his hands while no one but me seemed to pay him any attention? I was distracted from them both by the woman coming toward me, book floating in front of her nose as her fingers were busy with small needles knitting a pair of socks.

But the walkways were too crowded for all of my gawking. A group of students, running to class with their bags beating at their hips, knocked into me, and I crashed sideways into a pair of arms full of rolls of paper and weapons.

"I'm so sorry!" I said, and it was echoed back to me just as quickly in a man's tone, low and gentle.

"It's my fault," he said. He was still standing, cast in sunlight as I scrambled on the ground to gather up the mess I'd made. There were maps unrolling and a knife that had dropped, blade down, into the dirt.

"It really isn't," I said, a nervous laugh bubbling up in my throat as he crouched down, plucking weapons up out of the grass with long, pale fingers. "I think you're meant to be walking on that path and I was too busy..." I looked up, arms full of paper and one ragged-edged axe, and my voice caught in my throat. His eyes were very blue. And he was very...lovely was the word that came to mind. Handsome in a gawky, bookish way that made my belly squirm and my cheeks heat. A shy smile grew over his face, framed by a coppery beard.

"Staring," I said. I pulled my gaze from his face, all the long narrow lines of it, and tried not to distract myself with the breadth of his shoulders or the white shirt sleeves that had been rolled up to his elbows.

"You're a new student," he said, hands reaching out to where I was starting to crush the maps in my hold.

"Trainee, in the library," I said, passing over his belongings. I had no idea how he'd managed to hold it all at once. But he was tall and long-limbed and he seemed practiced at the process as he gathered it up into a tidy arrangement. The blades and axes seemed to vanish as he arranged the bundle in his arms.

"Staff," he said, nodding. "You're looking for the housing?"

"Yes!" My breath came out in a relieved huff of laughter.

He came up to my side and shuffled everything into the crook of one arm despite the fact it had been previously overflowing both. His free hand settled at the center of my back, and I held my breath at the touch and the pool of prickling heat it created. He nodded down the path.

"Stay on this as it curves north, head west at the oak, and the housing is a row along the side street at the end. Look for the red doors," he said, and then his hand was gone from my back, plucking up a pair of glasses from his collar and sliding them up his nose. His eyes flicked over my face. "You'll find it," he said.

"I can always knock someone else over if I don't," I said, ducking my chin as I stepped back onto the walkway, letting the traffic carry me forward. I could hear his laugh following behind me—a brighter, livelier sound than I expected.

The directions weren't any more specific than Gwen's, and there were more than a few oak trees at forks in the path. But there was an instinctive tug in my belly at a great mossy old beast of a tree that arched over the path with rounded knots where low hanging branches had been cut away. At the end of the narrow road of shops and a small grocers was the side street of narrow houses pressed together with doors in all shades of red.

I found mine on the left side of the street, in the middle of the block. My heart was doing happy somersaults in my chest as I stared up at the narrow, shabby little building as if it was as grand as the library.

The iron railing leading up the steps was rusting, and whatever plant had tried to make a home in the window box was wilting. The key turned in the lock, and while the space inside was small, it was simple and entirely mine. Just ahead of the front door, a set of stairs led up to the second story, and off to the left was a thin room with a square table and two chairs facing each other. At the end of the room was an empty bookshelf, modest and plain compared to the ones I had just visited. There was a tiny kitchen at the back of the house with a smudged window, streaming foggy light in over the sink.

The bathroom upstairs had barely enough room to turn around without falling into either the tub, sink, or toilet. Still, it was clean and bright, and there was a stack of towels stuffed onto a shelf. I could take a bath and no one would come knocking, waiting for their turn.

My bedroom was as little as of the rest of the house. I could see the street through the window from where I sat down on the bed. I set my suitcase on the floor and scooted back on the mattress, springs squeaking beneath me as I moved. I rested my head against the wall and closed my eyes. For the first time in my life, I was living alone. There were neighbors next door, sharing the same wall with me, and I had no notion of their name or what they did or who their family was. I turned my head to press my cheek against the plaster and tried to imagine them in my head.

Instead, I ended up picturing two people, Professor King from the library and the man from the lawn with the gentle smile and the arms full of weapons.

I opened my eyes and chewed at my lip. Did I *have* to wait an entire day to go back to the library?

CHAPTER 2

CALLUM

I WAS LATE FOR DINNER. AGAIN.

I tried to kick the front door shut behind me—gently because Isaac listened for that kind of thing—when a knife went sliding out of...somewhere and clattered to the floor.

"Put those away before you slice your damn toe off," Aiden called from the dining room.

I winced and tiptoed to the closet door, lowering myself just enough to keep from dropping the entire mess I had taken into class with me, and doing my best to open it silently. Then I threw the entire lot in at once and snapped the door shut before anything could escape. It would all find its way back to wherever it was meant to go...sooner or later. As long as neither Aiden or Isaac went looking for their coat tonight.

I pushed the hair out of my face before taking the hall down to the dining room.

"I'm late, I'm so sor–" I stopped in the doorway.

Aiden was grinning at me from the table, lounging back in his chair with his feet up in my seat. The *empty* table. How late was I?

"I put off making dinner," Isaac said, appearing from the kitchen, steaming dishes in hand. "Feet," he said, raising a dark eyebrow at Aiden's sprawl in front of the table.

"I was holding your seat," Aiden said, not even bothering to be convincing.

"I've left the wine," Isaac mused, glaring at the table.

"I'll get it," I said. He'd left the bread and the salad as well, but I didn't mention it, just juggled it all up into my arms.

"Did either of you get to the library today?" Aiden asked as I returned. His face was blank aside from the slight wrinkle of his eyes that meant he was fighting a smile.

"I took your book back for you in the morning," Isaac said.

He glanced at me for a moment and we both turned back to stare at Aiden. He'd seemed smug when I'd walked in and he was using the slow, drawling tone he adopted when he wanted to drag a good story out. He blinked at Isaac's words and frowned for a moment.

"Why?" Isaac asked. "Did *you* get to the library today?"

"I...I wasn't *expecting* to," Aiden hedged, eyes widening. "But there was a symphony-"

"Oh, alright," Isaac said, rolling his eyes and stealing the wine from my arms before taking his seat. "Get to the point, Aide."

Aiden glanced at me and I sighed, dropping plates to the table and taking my seat so he could enjoy his dramatic reveal.

"Woollard's gone and found some ingénue from the middle of nowhere and set her up working in the library," Aiden said, grinning at us both. Isaac and I exchanged another look, both of us frowning and Aiden added, "I'm fairly certain she's even given her a set of her very own dour clothes."

"Ah!" I said, remembering the younger woman I had nearly plowed straight through on my way to class. "Tall, with hair," and I waved a hand around my head thinking of the way her hair had floated around her head like dark feathers, unsettling with the breeze.

"An artist's eye," Isaac muttered to his wine glass.

"Face like a startled little woodland fae," Aiden said, nodding.

She had seemed startled at first, those wide dark eyes staring up at me with an ancient axe in her delicate hand. And maybe a little skittish. But there had been a wry slide to her smile as she left, carrying the charm from me on her back that would see her safely home.

"See?" Aiden said, nudging Isaac and pointing at my face. "*He* noticed her too. And he doesn't notice anyone."

"I notice plenty," I said, serving myself. I just wasn't usually *interested*.

Isaac made a little 'hm'ing sound and shrugged at me. "You're picky," he said.

"But you've never been wrong," Aiden added with a toast of his wine glass to me. "Your better judgment is why we are still a lonely three-man coven without our fourth. But at least it isn't the *wrong* fourth."

I huffed softly at my plate. I don't think Aiden had ever bothered being lonely if he didn't really have to. We loved each other, my covenmates and I, but we didn't ask for faithfulness. Not while we weren't complete. And Aiden did his absolute best to search high and low for our fourth, infatuations littering the path behind him as he went.

"Is she very magical then?" Isaac asked us.

"I don't think so," I said at the same moment Aiden said, "She certainly looked so." I laughed despite myself.

She had seemed...*significant*, in a way. Or maybe Aiden was right and I took so little notice of people outside of our coven and the scene of my classroom that striking someone down on the sidewalk was what it took to shake me out of my pattern.

"She wouldn't have to be," Isaac said, more to me than Aiden. "Not with the three of us."

I hummed something that might pass for agreement and took a bite of fish. Isaac was right. Between the three of us, magic was covered. Hell, between Aiden and Isaac even the domesticities of the house were covered. We just needed the right energy to temper us together. Make something cohesive out of all of our pieces. Aiden called it a family. I had a less generous view of the word, but I did know *something* was missing in our home, happy as we were.

"See what you think," I said to Isaac. I tried not to conjure her face in my head but it was right there, staring back at me from the empty place across the table.

CHAPTER 3
JOANNA

I WAS BACK IN THE LIBRARY AT DAWN, LOADING STACKS OF returned books into the small elevators that carried them up to their respective floors, unloading them onto wheeled racks, finding their homes on the shelves, and starting over again. I found a student sleeping beneath a shelf of sigil texts and woke him up.

"When does the cafeteria open?" he growled at me.

I shrugged. "I have no idea, but it's morning."

"I *know* that," he said, and then rolled his back to me.

Three students and one professor stopped me in the hopes I had seen books that the circulation desk *swore* were not on site. I found an abandoned pen and notebook on a shelf and started myself a list titled *Books To Find*. Gwen checked on me for the first few hours, nodding at me from the end of a row of shelves, or glancing up at me as I passed the balcony on the third floor.

It was more work than any day in the Bridgeston library but it made the minutes tick faster and I had never had the opportunity to see so many titles, so many subjects, and all of them the kind of magic no one bothered with in the country. Theories and strategies and ancient traditions and symbolism. The section on domestic charms was exquisitely small in comparison to the volumes of weather magic, astronomy, shadow walking, dream travels. Concepts I had never even heard of, and words that I practiced on my lips in silence.

I had just finished re-shelving the east wing and was leaving the art and color magic section, when I stopped in front of a painting stretching floor to ceiling like a window into a scene straight out of the town I'd left behind two days before. I caught my breath, tasting soil and the dry musty scent of wheat, and stared at the stretch of the field reaching across the land to the old line of border oaks. The bristles of the stalks gleamed in the sunlight and all but shifted on the canvas with some breeze of brushstrokes. An ache bloomed in my chest and a longing for the stretch of uninterrupted sky burned at the back of my throat.

But I had only been away from Bridgeston for what felt like hours. I *couldn't* be homesick yet. Or at the very least, I hadn't been up until that moment.

"You look unhappy with that painting," a voice asked from behind me.

"It's making me think of home," I said, frowning.

I turned to see who had joined me and my throat dried at the sight of him. Was it mandatory at Canderfey to be so handsome? At least this time the man at my side was staring up at the painting instead of at me. The angles of his face were strong and broad and there was something watchful and animal in his gaze although I couldn't decide if it was predatory or merely observational. He had black hair curling down to the back of his neck and a shadow of a beard over his jaw.

When he turned to look at me I moved my stare to the painting, avoiding his eyes.

"It looks like Bridgeston," I said. "Where I'm from."

"Really? It's Hammish scenery, but I suppose there isn't much difference," he said.

I looked at him again. He had the dark hair and tanned skin and broad shoulders so common where I grew up in the southern area of Enmairian countryside. I glanced back at the painting and saw how he fit within the frame and realized all at once that it was *his* painting. His homesickness.

"You look Hammish," I said, feeling braver now. Hammish wasn't so far from home, and its people weren't so different from mine. Even if he was wearing the vivid colors and lush fabrics of the university people, he now held something familiar and safe about him too.

"Do I?" he asked, grinning. The smile, and the dimples within it, softened the edges of his face. "You don't look Bridgestony."

"Thank you," I said, and he laughed with open surprise. I blushed and added, "Not that there's anything wrong with...I didn't mean that." Embarrassed, I took hold of my cart and started my escape.

"No, no, I know exactly what you mean. I ended up here, didn't I? Before you go," he said, stepping closer still, smiling with the laugh in his voice. "There's a book I'm looking for."

"Oh, of course," I said. Of course he had spoken up because he'd needed something while I'd been busy looking at art instead of working. I grabbed up my new notebook from where I'd left it in the cart and flipped it open to my list where I'd tucked the pen. He leaned over, peeking at the words on the page, and I could smell the ink and oil from him. There was a spot of vivid blue paint behind his right ear, smudged into the skin there.

"Mmm, you'll never find those," he said, reaching out and pointing to two titles I had scribbled down for a couple of students. "People have been looking for them for ages. Lost decades ago as far as anyone can tell."

I put little stars next to where I had written *Gatekeepers; a Compendium of the Old Guard* and *Resonants.*

"It won't hurt to remember their names," I said, shrugging. "What was the title?"

I looked up and found the studious examination he had given his own painting now focused on my own face. "*Color Magic,*" he said, still staring. "By Felix Amesbury. And *Blue in Study,* now that I think about it," he said. He glanced back down at the notebook and I rushed to fill in the words.

"Thank you...what was your name?" he asked.

"Joanna," I said, finishing adding his titles to my list.

"Thank you, Joanna. Isaac," he said, holding out a large hand stained with color. I tucked my pen away and shook his hand, ignoring the heat in my cheeks. "If you find them, would you bring them to my office? Professor Metclaffe in the Burgess Building. Woollard won't mind."

"I...sure," I said.

His lips quirked and he nodded, turning and walking away. There was more blue paint at the back of his neck and for some reason, the sight of it made my stomach flip. I pressed the backs of my palms to my cheeks and grimaced when I found them warm to the touch. A little cough echoed behind me and I jumped, finding a student blocked between two shelves by my cart. I muttered a quick apology and dragged it out of the way, hurrying to move on in my work.

By the time I had finished with my re-shelving I had collected three more missing book titles. Gwen came to find me in the afternoon just as I was heading up to browse and check on the staff only area.

"Take a break. Eat something—before your eyes start crossing," she said, leading me back to the break room.

The shelves behind the circulation desk were already filling up with returns and I wondered when I would ever find the time to work in the restricted section. Gwen was dragging me back through the swinging bookshelf when I saw it, gold block letters glittering down the spine of a thin black spine. *RESONANTS*.

I pulled back and stopped in front the shelf, pulling the notebook from my skirt pocket and flipping it open. Already I could see the two texts Isaac had mentioned waiting on the shelf. I ran down the list, checking off every last title. Gwen glared at the books on the shelf and then down at my notebook.

"What a coincidence," she said dryly, looking hawkishly at me through her lenses.

It was a coincidence or, more likely, Gwen was joking at my expense. Perhaps the library had its own kinds of charms in place, bringing books back when it was ready to or when they were needed. The most it signified to me was that I needed to track down Isaac Metclaffe.

I LOST track of time in the library that evening, finishing my work and ending up nose deep in an old textbook outlining the ancient seasonal rituals. (In the country the rough shapes of the holidays were still practiced, although nothing so elaborate as the festivals and performances of history.) The Burgess Building was closed by the time I remembered where I was supposed to be so I went the next day when Gwen shooed me out of the stacks to eat lunch.

The building was swimming with students when I arrived, classes just letting out, and I felt like a fish battling the stream trying to get myself up the stairs. It cleared out enough by the second story, for the din of chatter and feet on stone to fade and for me to stop by a group of girls leaning against a railing together, paint-stained smocks still hanging over their jewel-tone clothing.

"I'm looking for Professor Metclaffe's office," I asked, trying not to shift as they looked me over head to toe with puzzled expressions.

"Oh!" one said, face softening and cheeks blushing. "It's on the third floor, down by the windows."

"Thank-" I started.

"He won't be there, though," another added. "He was working with us today so he'll still be in the studio for a while. Top floor, on the left."

I hesitated on the third floor. It would be just as easy, easier really, to leave the books in his office with a note. Gwen knew where I was and the errand didn't require me to speak to him. Or to see him. But I turned up the stairs and followed them up two more flights. The top story of the building was surrounded by windows. Even the rooms had windows facing the hall that stretched up the roof and let the light stream through every room in bright sheets.

Isaac Metclaffe sat at a canvas with his back to the doorway, the afternoon sun catching on the palette at his side. There were feathers stretched across the painting and my muscles ached with the urge to run, to flee, to escape, until I fixed my eyes on the back of the painter instead of his creation. I wanted to sit down and ask a million questions. How did he put magic into an image? Did it begin with brushstrokes or sooner, in the mixing of the paint? The stretching of the fabric over its frame?

"It's injured," I said, glancing at the painting again, seeing the way feathers at the bird's stomach were ruffled and stained, feeling a hot tear in my own gut.

Isaac glanced at me once, 'hmm'ing in agreement, and turned back to his work. Then he startled in his seat and spun the stool to face me.

"Joanna!"

I tried not to get carried away, pleased that he'd remembered my name. "Your books turned up," I said, pulling them out of the bag at my side. *Blue in Study* was, from what I could tell, a book made entirely of blue. Every shade and hue shifting from page to page, like moving liquids. *Color Magic* was a crumbling collection of browning pages and curling leather that I was too afraid of damaging to even take a glimpse of. I wrapped it up in a sheet of white paper with *For Professor Metclaffe* written at the front.

He blinked at them for a moment and then at me. "Just like that?" he asked.

"They were waiting on the circulation shelf after you left. You probably just missed them," I said. I held them out to him, wanting both to have a reason to stay and also an escape from the studying look in his eyes.

"Where did Woollard find you?" he said under his breath.

"Bridgeston," I said, smiling a little even though I felt like I didn't understand the scope of the question.

He laughed and shook himself, rising off the stool and walking up to me. "You must be the very best library clerk Canderfey has ever had because *Color Magic* has been missing for hundreds of years. Ever since Amesbury had his falling out with his favorite student."

"Maybe they finally decided to return it?" I joked.

His eyes narrowed even as his smile deepened. "What did you do? Smuggle it out of the library?"

"I told Gwen it was for you," I said, shrugging.

"You call her Gwen?" he asked, taking the books from my hands at last. "That's remarkable in itself." His finger ran over his name on the paper wrapping and a smear of russet paint followed the line.

I winced, wondering if maybe I shouldn't have lent the rare classical text to a painter.

"The others," he said, looking up suddenly. "The other books on your list..."

"They...turned up," I said, feeling the strangeness of the statement as I said it, as I watched his face shift, twitching with interest. "If you know anyone looking for them..."

"I'm sure you'll see them soon. Where did you go to university, Joanna?" he asked.

I shook my head and looked down to fidget with the strap of my bag. "No, I didn't...I'm not a witch. Just training to be a plain old librarian."

"Ohh, don't tell *Gwen* you said that. Her coven is fierce," he said, grinning.

The boyish expression on his face made me want to find a seat nearby to curl up in for the afternoon, as if it were ten years ago and I was sitting on a field fence waiting for Gregory Thatcher to notice me.

"I should get back to work," I said, turning away quickly before I could catch another flash of his smile or answer another question in a way that made him laugh at me again.

"I'm here in the studios a lot at this time," he said to my back. "I'd like it if you came back again. Canderfey has too many city people, stuck out here in the woods."

My hands clenched around the leather strap of my bag. I didn't even know how badly I wanted the invitation until it was ringing in my ears. I nodded at him, looking back over my shoulder. My eyes landed on the canvas and my chest ached as I recognized the bird in flight, copper feathers flashing at me from across the space.

"The hawk..." I bit my lip, not entirely sure what I wanted to ask.

"He'll heal," Isaac said, watching my face.

Somehow, that was the answer I needed and I left the building, hurrying as I realized how long I had dawdled with the man.

CHAPTER 4
JOANNA

I WASN'T BRAVE ENOUGH TO VISIT ISAAC AGAIN THE NEXT DAY, but I *was* brave enough to gobble down a sandwich at lunch and use the extra time to sneak back up into the staff-only library. I found a text on the pigments used to preserve a life in a portrait —ground bone and dried blood and the ashes of the body included—and the book *Resonants* which was all about the strongest tones in sound for conjuring the instruments that best formed them.

The window seat I had seen Professor King in on my first day was open and I folded myself into the corner, a stack of books I couldn't possibly work through placed in front of my feet. I was mid-explanation of the breed of tree in the northern mountains whose wood was the ideal density for the hollowness required in the bass note that brought the dead back to life, when I was interrupted.

"You're getting quite cozy with my book."

Professor King stood at the far end of the bench seat, an eyebrow raised at the book in my hands. He moved closer and sat down next to my pile of reading material, glancing down at the stack with a tilt of his head.

"That's quite the range of subjects too. Do you have much interest in the influence of ley lines on birthing cycles?"

I was beginning to resent the effect I had on the professors at Canderfey and the way I seemed to draw laughter up in them. I may have been practically magicless and from the rustic country, but Gwen had said I was where I needed to be and I *was* doing my job, even if it was simple compared to theirs.

"I have an interest in everything," I said, keeping my tone even. "And up until this week, I had very little means of finding the information."

His humor settled but the crinkle at the corner of his eyes deepened. "I have students with less ambition than you," he said. "And I'm very jealous that you've gotten a look at that book before I have."

"You must be one of Isaac's friends," I said, closing the book and passing it to him.

"Isaac?" he asked, seeming surprised by the name. But then he added, "I am. Aiden King."

He extended his hand and I took it, watching the way his hold dwarfed mine. His grip was warm and surprisingly gentle, even as he squeezed my hand once and then released me.

"Joanna Wick. Is the information in the book true?" I asked.

Aiden's thumbs were stroking the fabric cover of the book in his hands and he looked down at it, lips twisting in thought. "From what I know, they were at the time. For Wrenshaw, the author, at least. He made all his own instruments, was easily the best luthier in history. But who's to say if the conditions of the materials are still the same now."

"But the part about raising the dead," I said, leaning in to open to where I'd left off. "It seems so...like a story."

"Do you read that fast or do you just know where to look?" he asked, and when I looked up he had leaned in as well and my vision was full of his face, the prickle of stubble on his cheek and the glint in his dark gaze. He leaned away and I realized I had frozen in surprise. "Wrenshaw's wife died very young. He *did* raise her. But it didn't work out, those sort of experiments never do. I expect that portion of the book was why it was stolen from the library in the first place."

A throat cleared beyond us, and I looked up finding Cecil, one of the library clerks, winking at me before leaving a full cart at the sidewall.

I fought down my blush, probably fruitlessly, and stood up from my seat.

"I doubt it was stolen," I said to Aiden, nodding at the book. "A stack of missing books cameback at once. Probably a professor had an old collection hoarded away that just got found."

He smiled at me but his brow furrowed as if he were equally puzzled by my answer. "I'll save your seat for you," he said as I grabbed my cart.

I assumed he meant he'd be taking up the spot in the window, but when I passed by fifteen minutes later the spot was empty but for the books I collected. It wasn't until evening hit and my shift was over that I returned. The books were still waiting for me and when I reached my seat I found a charm in place, a sweet little hum of music that faded as I reached it. I thanked Aiden in my head and picked up the next book in the stack, another of the missing titles that Isaac's friends were looking for.

I hadn't answered Aiden when he asked, but the truth was I was both a fast reader and I tended to skip through pages until I found a spot that interested me. *Gatekeepers; a Compendium of the Old Guard*, another withering old book that smelled sharply of dirt and mold, had black ink drawings stamped crookedly into the page and I flipped through the pages until one of the images struck me. It was dark, saturated with ink that wrinkled the paper, faint white lines guiding the picture of a copse of trees that curled up out of the earth and a shadowy figure at the heart of them. The words below the image were blocked out boldly, little faint cracks appearing in the letters.

It Eats.

The lamps in the library dimmed in the evening, although the building was still full of people. It would close deep into the night and only for a handful of hours, open for night owls and early birds alike. The building was warm with magic and the windows on my left were cool from the night air outside. I read the story of the old god-like force of blind destruction, a being that devoured without reason, whose appetite was unquench-able. The chatter of the library fell away into a buzz that lulled me with the rhythm of the words I traced across the page with my finger.

LET ME OUT.

LET ME OUT.

LET ME OUT.

LET IT OUT.

CHAPTER 5

CALLUM

At dinner, the night before, Isaac mentioned his visit from the new librarian while I stared down at my plate and Aiden ruffled with excitement. They wanted her, I could tell, and my nerves stirred in anxiety. Would I disappoint them again? Kill another of their romances and our coven's chance for finally being settled, Aiden at last having his family. It left me wondering for the hundredth time if I was really meant to be here, sharing this home and their magic with mine.

Aiden bringing her up at our third dinner in a row was enough. He'd already decided for himself. Joanna Wick had the potential to be our fourth. His stare at me from over the candle-light wasn't subtle. It was time for me to meet her, really speak to her. And if there was no real attraction, no pull—why was there never a pull?—then I owed it to my covenmates to let them know sooner rather than later.

"I left a charm for her and her books," Aiden said, still staring at me. "She has *Gatekeepers*, by the way."

A little carrot to dangle for me. Get the stubborn ass moving in the right direction.

"I've been looking for that text," I said as if I didn't know what they were fishing for. Their shoulders relaxed in their seats.

I left for the library as Aiden cleared the table. Their watching eyes were like hands shoving me out the door.

She was asleep when I found her, with one of the most valuable, dangerous, and contentious texts of magic still gripped between her hands. Her temple was against the windowpane at her side, her lips pursed and forehead tangled. Her shoulders were drawn tight up to her ears and my palms itched, body leaning forward and wanting to follow some set of instructions I had no translation for. To wake her or soothe her or both.

I crossed in front of the lamplight and she sat up with a violent shudder and a whimpering gasp that froze my chest. I dropped down to the bench seat, hands reaching out for her even as her back stretched up against the wall behind her. A cornered animal with the whites of her eyes stark in the dim light.

"I'm sorry," I said, pulling away. "I didn't mean to startle you!"

A trembling hand fluttered into the air and then landed over her heart. The terror was bitter in the air, and a sting of bile rose in my throat, bringing back muddy fields from decades ago and the echo of magic and metal crashing.

"I...I fell asleep?" she said. The whisper in her voice of lingering sleep brushed away my memories.

"Are you alright?" There was an argument in every muscle in my body, the urge to leave, and the impulse to move in closer and offer...comfort or at least *contact*.

There was a catch in her breath and I tensed under her stare as it landed firmly on my face after skirting the space of the stacks around us.

"A dream," she said. "It must have been...I don't remember it, but it was just a bad dream." And her shoulders eased as she spoke.

Dreams were significant. A part of me wanted to press with questions, check her symptoms off against the possible causes. Nightmares were one thing, but a disturbance in dreams wasn't limited to the subconscious and if she...

"You're one of Isaac's friends, aren't you?" she asked, glancing at me out of the side of her eyes while trying to smooth her skirt and hair to erase the evidence of her nap.

"Covenmate," I said and then wished I could bite my own tongue as her eyes widened and then shuttered, face going blank.

"Of course," she said, with a wilted smile. "That makes sense. And Professor King."

"Yes." The word sat stale in my mouth with all that I wanted to add to it. That we were only three. That Aiden and Isaac had all but shoved me out the door to meet her. And that for the first time, I could understand *why*. There was a draw, an itch under my skin to be closer to her. That contact I was craving.

"This is yours then," she said, closing the book in her hands and passing it across the bench to me.

The energy around the book pooled darkly like rot and refuse in the air and I hesitated before picking it up.

"Bit of light reading?" I asked, wondering how far she had read.

"I like a spooky story," she said, tone dry and light and coaxing a smile out in spite of my nerves. "But I suppose it explains the anxious sleep."

My fingertips brushed down the spine of the book and a creeping, slithering feeling stirred at the back of my thoughts. But it was chased away as Joanna stood from the bench.

"I should be getting home, my shift ended hours ago," she said, moving to pass me.

I stood too abruptly and forced her to stop in her tracks or run into me again as she had days ago. She stared up at me in surprise, a dark curl falling down one cheek.

"Let me walk you," I said, trying not to cringe at my own clumsiness. "I'm on my way out," I added, holding up *Gatekeepers*.

"We can walk each other down to the circulation desk, how about that?" she said.

I tried to laugh off the refusal, but the sound was closer to a cough. Still, she waited for me to join her at the steps, her hand poised on the stair railing.

"I think this is the kind of building all books should live in," she said after several quiet steps down. I turned to look at her and found her staring up at the wood molding that grew up the staircase walls, rosewood vines crawling up and alien faces peering out from behind glossy wooden leaves. "Where I worked before was nice. Well, it was clean and quiet. But the town I grew up in didn't have much use for books and certainly didn't think to build them such a...shrine." I had seen women looking less seduced by Aiden at his most charming than Joanna did at the walls of the library. And her touch on the staircase was more of a caress than a steadying hold.

"How long have you been a librarian?" I asked. She looked young. Not young enough to be a student, but enough to leave a gap in our ages.

"I'm not really, yet. But I've been a clerk for a decade, about?" she said, shrugging. "Since I finished school. The librarian was working alone and I'd been doing the shelving for her for years anyway. Now she has a couple of council women volunteering. It'll do fine." There was a little wistfulness in her voice.

"Are you homesick?"

"Nooo," she said, sounding disgusted at the idea. "Not yet, at least, but..." she raised her chin and squared her shoulders, "I don't think I will be."

"In my experience you don't have to be," I said, firmly keeping home out of my head.

We reached the first floor and quieted as we passed clusters of students gathered together at long tables, studying in hushed voices. She ducked behind the circulation desk, grabbing one of the open places and reaching across to me, hand outstretched for the book.

"So you can skip the waitlist," she whispered, grinning at me.

I leaned across desk and whispered back, "I'm at the top of the waitlist."

She raised an eyebrow and pulled one of Woollard's massive reference texts up, flipping through till she found the collection of names gathered for holds on *Gatekeepers*.

"Callum Pike," I said as she skimmed past the names that had been crossed away, retired professors and graduated students from years ago.

"Callum...but this is from almost twenty years ago!" she said looking up at me. "You can't have been a student then."

"I was, I attended very young." And for a very brief amount of time. When Joanna raised an eyebrow at me I added, "I was fifteen."

Instead of shock or awe, she rolled her eyes at me. "Well

that's not fair," she said. "Wait here, I'll check this out for you and then we can walk out together."

"Let me see you home," I said, and I told myself it was a reflex. I held my breath as she chewed at the inside of her lip.

"I don't want to trouble you," she said.

The tightness in my chest eased. "Staff housing, right? It's on my way." Which was a lie. It was in the opposite direction, but it could have been miles away and not made a bit of difference.

She stared at me for another moment and then nodded, "Alright. I forgot it would be dark and I think I would be jumping at every noise on my own. Did you bring your axe with you?"

I laughed and tried to cover my embarrassment with a hand over my eyes. "I was giving a lecture on alloys in weapons being affected by ley lines. I teach warfare strategy, but I don't generally carry weapons."

"I thought as much," she said, smiling and filing away the checkouts record. "That or juggling. I'll get my coat."

She left the book on the counter for me and walked back into the room behind the circulation desk. It struck me then, seeing the sway of her hips and set of her shoulders and finding that I wanted to follow her in there, and out of the library and anywhere else she might be going. This was what Isaac and Aiden had been waiting for. That gut instinct of attraction and interest that came so easily for them and seemed all but absent in me. Except where they were concerned. And now Joanna.

I was as eager to get back to the house to tell them as I was to see her home.

She returned, a black jacket over her blouse and a canvas bag at her side, nearly overfull with the books inside. I followed her out of the library and into the cool night. I waited for the ease of conversation to return and then realized almost too late that I might have to start it myself.

"Isaac and Aiden mentioned you," I said, which was as close to a hint about the exact direction of our thoughts as I could bring myself to make.

Her face froze as she walked at my side and my stomach sank, wondering if it was a misstep.

"I think I'm a bit of an anomaly here," she said. "I feel that way at least."

"I did as well," I said, rushing to smooth away whatever awkwardness I'd created.

"Well..." she mused, her face relaxing. "You *were* fifteen."

I coughed out a laugh. "I was. But Isaac felt the same too when he got his teaching position. He said you were from similar parts of Enmaire?"

She nodded. "The middle of nowhere parts."

"The only person I know who really feels at ease everywhere he goes is Aiden," I said and she laughed. "Canderfey is full of the unusual."

Her smile dropped. "That's where I'm afraid I differ." Before I could correct her she added, "What dangerous equipment will you be carrying to your next lecture?"

I followed the subject change. Aiden or Isaac would be better at drawing her out than I was. It was enough that she was allowing me to walk with her, to spend a little more time examining this new connection and the way it thrummed with our synchronized steps.

"Oh," I said. "I keep the heavy artillery in my office. Too much of a pain to cart around."

It was enough for me to make her grin.

CHAPTER 6
ISAAC

I ROLLED THE CHARCOAL STICK IN MY HAND, SMUDGING THE black into my fingerprints. Every time I set the charcoal to paper the image grew more confused. Aiden's profile, Callum's hands... Joanna Wick's tentative smile, all scattered across parchment in fragments.

Aiden was sitting on the floor in front of me with his back against the couch, stringing and tuning his old guitar. His fingers smoothed down the fret, a whistle following, for the dozenth time that evening. I started to scribble the curve and swell of the guitar in his hands and ended with the familiar silhouette of a woman. I dropped the crayon to the paper and Aiden's head lifted at the sound.

"What if he doesn't like her?" I asked.

"He will," Aiden said.

He had probably known the question niggling at me for the past hour, only waited for the words to come spilling out to give his answer.

"This is Callum," I said, baffled by his certainty. "He doesn't like...anyone but us."

Aiden smiled at that, it was an exaggeration but it was *close*. "Exactly. And he's never been shy about his disinterest." I grimaced and Aiden set the guitar aside, twisting on the floor to face me. "He already met her on the lawn."

"…Yes," I said.

"And he agreed to go see her tonight, which means he's willing to consider her," Aiden said, shrugging.

"Or it means he's feeling guilty, thinking he's the one holding us up in finishing our coven," I said.

"Maybe. That will only go so far," he said, reaching up to squeeze my knee. "I make sure to tell him how grateful I am that he's so determined not to fall in love carelessly," he added grinning. "It saves us so much time. But I think if he's considering her, it's a good sign. It's certainly progress."

"There's a long jump between consideration and love," I said, but Aiden's optimism was infectious and I settled my hand with his, linking our fingers together. "It…it feels different, doesn't it? Not just attraction but…"

"The pull," Aiden finished, nodding. "I remember the early days with you and Callum. Constantly running into each other. Knowing where to find you without knowing why. Making up excuses. Try," he said. "Try and guess where she is now."

The answer felt ready and it wasn't the time of night or any little scrap of information I'd gleaned from the two times of meeting her.

"Home," I said. "Alone, safe."

The front door opened and Aiden and I both stiffened. He pulled away to turn back to the living room entrance, picking the guitar up from the floor and settling it in his lap as if we hadn't been spoiling hours, waiting for Callum to return. It felt like long minutes before the front door shut and his footsteps sounded on the floorboards, drawing closer. He appeared in the doorway, a little windswept and pink-cheeked, with a strange expression on his face. He looked puzzled to find us there, waiting for him. Puzzled to find himself standing in our home at all.

I waited for Aiden to start in, to quiz him about the evening, but no one spoke at all for a very long time. Aiden's shoulders were tight and he was practically holding his breath. Callum seemed to not know which way was up. My stomach was flipping giddily and I was about to launch myself off the couch and…I didn't know what.

"I think it might be her," Callum said, staring down at the carpet as if he'd never seen it before.

Aiden exhaled a shaky breath, and my thoughts went skipping out of my head one by one.

"I don't know what to do," Callum said, frowning at us both. "I don't know what comes next?"

I laughed at that and slapped my hand over my mouth, the taste of charcoal bitter on my tongue.

"They call it wooing," Aiden said, a grin stretching over his face.

Callum crossed the room with heavy steps and collapsed down to the couch next to me, his head dropping onto my shoulder.

"I think she's going to take a lot of convincing," he said, wincing. Aiden scoffed, but I had a sneaking suspicion Callum was right. Joanna wasn't even calling herself a witch, she'd never imagine fitting herself into a coven.

That, at least, I had an inkling of how to solve.

CHAPTER 7
JOANNA

THE WEEK FINISHED WITH BUSY DAYS IN THE LIBRARY AS classwork and foot traffic picked up in the narrow stacks. I landed in my bed each night with aching feet and settled into heavy, dreamless, sleeping that left me groggy and headachy again by morning. Finally, on Sunday, I woke up to the sky warming with orange light, and instead of dragging myself out, I closed my eyes and rolled over. It was my day off and for the first time all week, I was planning on staying away from the library. I came downstairs hours later to my meager supplies in the kitchen and the still dreadfully bare space of my home. In the whole week, all I'd managed to accumulate was some groceries, a lamp to read by in the evening, and a stack of books.

It was time to get outside.

I gathered up two books—one, a wishy-washy text on everyday symbolism often over-looked due to generally being coincidental, and the other a magical reference of birds and their uses in spellwork—and my broad-brimmed hat to set out for a walk. The campus was quiet in the morning, although I had walked through large groups making rowdy, colorful magics the night before, so I wasn't surprised. I stopped at the campus grocery for provisions and then found a dirt path at the farthest edge of campus to follow into the woods.

I had the book on birds out in my hand as I walked deeper

into the wilderness, sunlight mottling down through the tree branches to splash over the pages. At home, we didn't have dense woods like these but we had uneven walking paths, and I'd learned to feel my way over them with a book in front of my nose at a young age. What I wasn't used to was keeping track of which turns I took, since the flat, endless scenery of home made it easy to look out over a field and know where I was. I'd been walking through the chapter on the hawk when I heard my name and looked up, realizing how far I'd traveled and how little idea I had of how I'd gotten there.

"Joanna!" he called again, and I turned to the left, seeing a clearing of trees where the sun was flooding in to land on the drying heads of wildflowers past their season. Isaac stood at the far side, a smaller canvas set up at his side and an arrangement of tools peeking up above the weeds. He waved his arm at me. "Follow the path left and come join me."

I followed his directions like a reflex. I hadn't taken him up on his offer to revisit the studio, but there was no good reason to avoid him now. And I honestly couldn't think of anywhere I'd rather be than sitting in the sun reading, especially not with company like Isaac's.

He was sitting back at his canvas when I reached him, the scene of ringing trees and browning plants building on his paint-ing, the shadows of the woods catching in dark umber browns and blues. There was a brick red coat spread over the ground next to his work spot and he nodded at it, smiling at me with dimples in his cheeks.

"I don't have a seat for visitors but I *can* offer velvet."

"My skirt can handle a little dirt better than that jacket," I said, bending to pick it up.

"Please," he pressed. "I'll feel like a good host. If you'd like to stay, that is."

"I think I better, I was halfway to finding myself very lost," I said. "And you're making those woods look too sinister for me to feel adventurous."

He wrinkled his nose at the painting. "I agree. It wasn't my intention but the woods usually know better when I try to paint them," he said.

KATHRYN MOON

"It makes me feel like fall is coming," I said and his smile returned at that, growing as I moved and sat down on his coat, feeling the burn of the sun warming the fabric under my fingers. "You're sure I won't bother you?" I asked.

"I'm certain," he said. "No more than I'll be disturbing your reading, at least."

Which was not at all. Isaac was as studious to his work as I was to my book, and the lack of conversation was filled in with the sounds of birds chattering and the trees creaking around us. It was as easy to sit in the quiet as it was to steal glances of him while he mixed a new color or leaned back and glared at the canvas in front of him. I pulled the sandwich I had bought at the grocery out of my bag and sat half of it down on a clear spot on his side table. He hummed and took it without really seeming to notice the offer.

"Aiden and Callum spoke highly of you," he said eventually.

I had moved through my book into the subject of sparrows, and it took me a few sentences before the words registered and I looked up from the page.

"Your covenmates," I said and he nodded, watching me. "I... you suit each other."

He glanced at his painting for a moment, adding a few brush-strokes, and then looked back at me. "We do." The corner of his mouth quirked up and there was a fierceness in his gaze like he was willing me to keep speaking. Heat was rising up my neck and I couldn't think of a thing to say, couldn't imagine a reason why these men would remark on me at all.

"How did you meet?" I asked, because it seemed the only safe thing to land on.

"Callum and I were new faculty in the same year. Aiden took it upon himself to mentor us." Isaac smirked at his painting and shrugged his shoulders. "At first, I think Cal and I bonded over having zero idea of what to do with Aiden. He fills up the space he occupies and we were attempting to blend into the back-ground." He turned to me and I looked down into my lap, not sure how to speak of the man. Aiden King both intimidated me and had a magnetic pull, leaving me with the urge to soak up the brightness that poured out of him.

"But eventually you learn the gentleness in him," Isaac continued in my silence. "I was happy to find a coven so quickly. I'd pulled up all my roots leaving Hammish and it gave me somewhere to plant myself."

I bit my lip and waited for him to continue, but he was more patient than I. Or he had become reabsorbed by his art just as I had become absorbed in the story.

"And Callum?" I said, finding the curiosity outweighing the shyness.

A line tightened on his forehead between his eyebrows and he fiddled with his paint palette while I waited.

"He has a tendency to fight his own happiness," Isaac said, voice quiet and blending with the rustle of the clearing. He cleared his throat and continued, "But Aiden is determined and I am patient. And we are as settled as we can be until our fourth joins us."

My heart thrummed in my chest and then ached bitterly as my stomach dropped. They would find someone like them, someone powerful and fascinating and beautiful. A witch who would not pale behind their glow. Not a shabby library clerk from the country who could barely keep herself from staring open-mouthed at every new and strange thing she found in the world.

"Would you like to try?" he asked, standing up from his seat.

For a stupid, painful, moment I thought he'd followed where my head had traveled. Then he flicked his paintbrush in invitation, gesturing to the seat.

"I'll ruin it!" I said, glancing to the painting where the woods were growing deeper and the light stark on the canvas.

"You won't and even if you did it wouldn't matter," he said. He jumped forward, walking to where I was sitting and holding out his hand.

"I don't have any magic," I said.

His eyes tightened on my face. "That isn't true. You have charms on your shoes to keep them clean and a charm on your bag to keep it from splitting."

"That's...that's just everyday things. It's not *enough*." And I wasn't sure that I meant that in terms of the painting.

He crouched down to the ground until he was eye level with me. "How do you know? It only takes a little and what's the worst thing that could happen? You apply a bit of paint on the whole canvas that doesn't tell the viewer 'the woods are dark and dangerous today?' Try it."

It was not fair that someone should be so handsome and have a voice that sounded so warm and coaxing. I took his hand and let him pull me up from the ground. His thumb stroked over the back of my wrist and the thrill of the touch twined up my arm like a vine as he led me to the canvas. I sat down on the stool he had waiting, stiff and nervous, and he knelt in the grass next to me.

He passed me the paint palette, full of greens and grays and blues and browns with little flecks of yellow and white and red.

"It won't bite, Joanna," he soothed, holding a brush out by its handle.

"But it doesn't come with a set of instructions, either," I said.

"Pick a color, put it on the brush, apply to canvas," he said, and even without looking I could hear the grin in his voice.

"Is that how you got your teaching position?" I asked, hovering the soft bristles over the paint palette, eyes darting between the painting and the field in front of us.

"I save that speech for my problem students," he said, folding his legs on the ground, sitting down to give me space.

The painting as it was looked complete, sunlight catching at the tips of tall grass with the depth of the woods behind turning darker, like a warning. I hated to alter it in any way. I found a small smear of blue paint sneaking its way over an ashy brown and swirled them together, thinking the least obtrusive addition I could make was adding a bit more shadow near the back. My hand shook as I lifted the paintbrush, but with the first stroke of the bristles against the canvas, the action felt like a circuit connecting me to the painting. The process of painting was less choice and action than it was the follow-through of a background thought into an image on the canvas.

An image that looked less like the tree I had intended, and more like a dark figure lurking in the shadows.

I frowned and Isaac sat up, peering at the painting.

"Sinister," he said, eyebrows raised in surprise but smiling as if he were pleased. "How did it feel?"

"Magical," I said, voice tight. I cleared my throat and asked, "Was that yours or mine?"

"Some was mine," he said and his eyes were on my face as he spoke. "There's magic on the canvas, the brush, in the paints I mix. Whatever power you felt was yours."

My lips pursed and I stared at the figure, passing in dark between the trees and sending a chill up my spine.

"It gives the painting something to say," he said. "Like a story."

"I think you're being kind," I said, rolling my eyes. But when I turned my head back to look down at him he was still staring at me.

"Would you sit for me?" he asked. "I'd like to paint you."

I dropped the paint palette and brush into my lap at the question. "I...what? Today?"

"No," he laughed. "I think I'm done for the day, before the light goes. And Callum and Aiden are useless at making dinner. But I would like to, soon." He watched me for a minute, struggling to find a word to say or even to make eye contact, and then his hand settled gently on my arm. "I promise not to bully you into it like I did the painting. If you'd rather not..."

"Maybe," I said, finding my voice. "Let me think about it."

"Of course," he said.

Some openness had faded in his face, the smile going out of his eyes and I floundered for a moment. I wanted the time with him, but it was a desire accompanied by worry. Of enjoying myself too much, pretending the time meant more than friendly camaraderie.

"Would you walk me back to campus?" I asked. "I don't really know how I got here."

His shoulders eased and he stood, nodding. "I would love to."

I tried to help him with his packing, but Isaac shooed me back to my seat on his jacket. "I have a system," he said.

It looked more like 'tossing everything together in a small collapsible box.' Considering the box was smaller by far than the contents it carried, I figured it must require Isaac's magic more than any organization. By the end, all he had was a light backpack that fit around his stool and over his shoulders, and his painting in hand. He held his free hand out to me and I rose, bringing his coat along with me.

I slid my hand in his, trying not to think too much of the action, to stamp down the lightness that burned through me at the touch. He had a growing coven and it was only a friendly gesture, like two country folk together on a walk. Except then I couldn't think of an example of me holding a man's hand on a walk that *wasn't* romantic enough to start all of Bridgeston gossiping about who was getting grandchildren in the spring or whose heart would be broken before winter.

Even then, it would have been my heart broken. Isaac wasn't the type of man to stay in a place like Hammish or Bridgeston and it was a plain fact. And I...I could barely believe that I hadn't woken up back in my father's house by now, with my brother and his wife and their squalling, darling twins calling for me from downstairs.

"No wonder you got lost," Isaac said, drawing me back. "Your head's always traveling."

"Either in a book or daydreams," I agreed.

He drew me in, wrapping my hand around his elbow and pointing out scenes in the woods I had missed on my walk.

WE WERE BACK on campus in the late afternoon and the bustle of activity had returned. Not only that, but for the first time since I had arrived at Canderfey, I felt something other than invisible. Several groups of students and more than one person I suspected was faculty, paused in their tracks as Isaac walked me back to my little house on the row.

"It's more like a small town than it seems at first," Isaac whispered to me.

I didn't take any comfort in that. "I can find my way from here," I said. We were barely a block away from the street and Isaac probably could have seen me walk up to my door from where we stood now.

He didn't comment and I didn't let go of his arm so the suggestion died in the air.

I spent the rest of the walk considering what I could expect from Isaac. I knew what would be impossible, given who he was and who I was not. But it left so much room, for the possibility of a friendship at least.

"I'd make a very awkward model," I said as he walked up to my door.

His footsteps broke pace for a moment before turning to me. "I beg to differ," he said, eyes widening.

I bit my lip to keep from laughing as his face broke into a full grin. "Well, alright," I said, pulling my hand from his arm and taking the first step to my house. It gave me the inches I needed to be on eye level with him.

"Sometime soon?" he asked.

I nodded and shrugged. I didn't know when I'd really be brave enough, but now that he had offered there was a nervous little excitement in my belly to see what he would paint. To know how he saw me.

"Thank you for the afternoon, Joanna," he said, catching my hand again. And then he leaned in, with the scratch of stubble against my cheek and a soft, chaste kiss at the corner of my mouth.

He pulled away before I'd known what to do with myself and I searched his face for something I also refused to believe would be there. But he was smiling, easy and relaxed.

"See you soon," he said, releasing my hand with a last squeeze and starting off down the sidewalk.

"Yes," I managed, dumbly, after finding my throat too dry to say anything. I darted up the stairs, fumbling in my pockets for my keys as my cheeks heated. A part of me wanted to turn again, watch him walk away, and wait to see if he looked back too. Instead, I focused on turning the key in the lock and making it inside before I made a fool of myself.

An envelope skidded across the floorboards as I opened the door. I let myself droop down to the floor, the corner of my mouth still singing with the warmth of a kiss. I leant against the doorframe and picked up the envelope finding my name scrolled across the front.

Joanna,

The university has finally come through and one of Wrenshaw's last instruments—a horn rumored to gift the listener with the sensation of flight—is being delivered to my office this Tuesday. Come listen?

A. King

My head thunked back against the wood and a dull pounding started in my temples, matching the beat of my racing heart.

CHAPTER 8
ISAAC

I WAS BARELY DRIFTING OFF WHEN THE STAIRWELL LAMPS flickered on and the boards began to creak. Then they muted and I sat up, staring at the mouth and waiting. Callum's hair shone fire red in the yellow light, bobbing up the stairs as he tiptoed up to the hall in the dead of night, shoulders hunched.

"Where were you?" I hissed, whispering from my bed.

He froze at the top of the stairs, shoulders drooping further. The stair lights turned off and he shuffled to my door, the moonlight catching at the muddy knees of his pants.

"There was something on the campus," he whispered from the door. "I went...hunting. Came up with nothing. Checked on Joanna's house, the wards are good there. Then-"

"You went to Joanna's?" I asked, the surprise stealing all the quiet out of my voice.

There was a thunk and Callum dropped his bag to the floor, then huff of breath as he walked in, landing in the blue glow of light from the night. He was wrestling with his coat as if he'd forgotten how they worked. I almost snapped at him as the coat landed on the floor too, but he went straight for the buttons of his vest next and his fingers slipped in exhaustion. I sighed and climbed out from under my sheets.

"She's alright," he said as I pushed his hands out of the way and started helping him out of his clothes.

KATHRYN MOON

"Was she home?" I asked.

"Think so..." he yawned and his jaw cracked. "Didn't knock."

I screwed my mouth shut and refrained from commenting. It was maybe a misguided gesture, but I couldn't blame him and I was a little too pleased that he thought of her in the first place.

"Are you alright?" I asked, looking up at his face. His cheeks looked hollow. It occurred to me then that he hadn't meant 'hunting' as searching. He'd been using magic.

"Frustrated," he bit out in a growl, then added, "Tired. I've never felt anything like it and then...then it just skittered away. I tracked every inch of campus and then the surrounding woods and town and *nothing*."

"Are you-?"

"I'm *sure*," he said, glaring at me, taking his belt from my hand and pulling it loose. "I don't know what it was or where it went, but I know it *was* there. Can I sleep in here tonight?"

"If you don't you'll have to pick up all your things and take them with you," I said. Aiden might be a laundry chute but I was not.

Callum nodded and bumped against me as he crossed to the bed, practically falling into it.

"Did you eat?" I asked.

"Mmmhmp." He nodded into my pillow. "S'good."

That meant there was a plate of scraps sitting out downstairs because Callum never remembered to put a finished dish in the sink. I rolled my eyes while he couldn't see and kicked his clothes out of the way before following him back into the bed. I settled on my side with my back to him but after one deep sigh of breath, Callum shuffled closer, pulling me down to my back and curling himself up to my side, pressing his face into my neck and hooking his bare leg over mine. I froze in surprise and then shifted to wrap my arm around his shoulder, scratching my nails into his hair and listening to his groan. I couldn't remember the last time Callum had wanted to *cuddle*.

"Are you sure you're alright?" I asked, lifting my free arm to brush at his shoulder resting over my chest.

"Mmfine," he said, voice already scratching with sleep and he

42

settled as I squeezed him tight and set my lips against his forehead.

I WOKE AGAIN in the dark with a mouth sucking at the curve of my neck and Callum's hard length bumping against my back. His arm was stretched over my side, hand gripping at a pillow with a white knuckle grip as his hips rolled into me. He growled into my skin, teeth pinching and making me arch, and then the growl became a word.

"Joanna."

I didn't mean to but it came out all the same, a bright and sudden laugh. Callum froze and then inhaled sharply, breath panting against my neck, before rolling away. I went with him, turning to my other side so I could look at him in the dim light. His face was scrunched up tight in a grimace and he blinked one eye open at me before groaning and swinging his arm up over his face.

I stifled another laugh and bent to kiss at his shoulder, rubbing a hand over his tense stomach and feeling it twitch against my touch. "I'm flattered," I said. "But I imagine her to be much softer than any of us." Then I slid my hand down to squeeze where he was still hard and hot, stretching at the fabric of his underwear.

He snarled behind his arm as his hips lifted up into my hand.

"Don't tell Aiden," he said, words almost muffled by his arm. Then the arm was swung away and he surged up, pulling me into a messy, anxious kiss.

Callum was never what I expected; always greedier for affection, more passionate—his body always wound tight with the craving until it burst out of him. I let him pull me down, trapping my hand against him as his hips bucked and his teeth bit, lips sucking until the sleep at the back of my head was being replaced with hunger.

"Tell him what?" I asked.

Callum pulled back, head landing against the pillow and a knot between his eyes as he looked up at me. "That I...that I-"

He stopped himself, kicking his legs between us until they were framing me, my cock fitting against his ass.

"That you're dreaming of her?" I asked, rearing back as he tried to lift up and kiss me again.

"Yes," he snapped, forehead furrowing.

"That you're attracted to her?" My cheeks almost hurt with my grin and Callum's eyes narrowed dangerously at me.

"Yes."

Then his legs knotted around my hips and he surged up, pushing at my chest until we had flipped on the mattress. I landed with an 'oof' that turned into an open-mouthed moan as he lowered his head and wrapped his lips around my ear lobe. He sucked at it with a 'pop' and then moved to the corner of my jaw.

"Do you think about her here?" I asked, low in his ear. "With us?"

He stiffened and then his hips pressed hard against mine, erections nuzzling together through the thin layer of cloth until we were both panting.

"Yes," he hissed into my neck.

"Tell me where you would want her," I said and Callum whimpered, a soft whine as his chest lowered and stuck to mine. "Next to us, watching? Between us? Or like this, like I am now? Squirming beneath you as I fill you up?"

"Fuck, Isaac," Callum breathed. His eyes were huge and dark and fixed to mine as I slid my hands under the band of his underwear and started to push them down his hips. "Yes. That's what I want."

I could taste the words, the way it tore at Callum to admit them. I liked to look at my lovers, watch their faces change with every touch, but I could make an exception for this. To imagine with him, to picture her face on the pillow. I leaned up and kissed Callum, hands busy easing fabric over his stiffness, and he muttered soft begging words against my lips.

I slid out from under him and he kicked his legs free, elbows braced against the mattress and head hanging low as I moved behind him.

"Lay down, love."

Callum settled and I straddled his hips, digging my fingers

into his shoulders and working at the tension. He hissed behind his teeth, back tightening, and then sighed as I pushed my thumbs up the back of his neck.

"You'll have me asleep," he mumbled, cheek smashed to a pillow.

"So play with yourself," I said, smirking. It would do half the work for me and keep him distracted. Aiden said that Callum was like a jack in the box, coiling tighter until the strain was too much and he exploded with pent-up kinetic energy. I assumed Aiden just preferred to be the target for that energy. I had tricks for uncoiling him.

Callum's hips twisted and his hand burrowed beneath him. I watched his arm flex and twist as I moved down his back, wrestling with the knots beneath his shoulder-blades until I could see the way he melted into the mattress, eyes drooping and hand growing lazy. I stretched for the bedside table and grabbed the bottle of oil, squeezing some out into my palms and warming it before stroking it down his sides and then up over his ass, barely dipping my fingers between his cheeks.

Callum grunted beneath me. "Is there more oil?"

I added some to my palms and then took his hand to slick it. He sighed as he gripped himself again, moving smoother and a little faster.

"Tell me what you dream about. What you're thinking about right now," I said, bending to kiss the back of his neck. I spread my hands across the back of his thighs and worked up with my fingers dipping again, a little lower.

Callum was quiet for a moment. "Her eyes," he whispered. "Her hips." I hummed and he continued, "The way she looks at me out of the corner of her eye. How she teases. Like Aiden but...sweeter, dryer."

"Your knees," I said, soft so as not to pull him out of his thoughts of her. I coated my hands and fingers in the oil as Callum pushed up to his knees. "How chaste," I said. "You dream of her looking at you and that has you moaning in your sleep?"

Callum sucked in a breath as my hands went to work, one sliding up and down between his ass cheeks, a fingertip barely grazing at the puckered rosebud of sensitive flesh. The other went between us to stroke and pull at myself until I was tapping beneath him, swollen and aching.

"What do you want me to say?" he grumbled.

"Tell me how you would touch her," I said, circling his hole with my fingertip.

"I'm afraid to," he whispered.

"To touch her?" I asked, brow furrowing.

"That I'll mess up."

It wasn't as if I had forgotten that Callum had given up interest in anyone but me or Aiden, only that I forgot that meant he hadn't been with a woman in over a decade. Or anyone new.

"It's not so different," I said. His ass was twitching in my direction, my middle finger just resting at his opening with him nudging back, impatient. I pressed in, just to the first knuckle and Callum released himself to rise up to his elbows, pushing back and fitting my finger deeper.

"Like...right now, I'm thinking about how her legs would look wrapped around your hips as you filled her up," I said, pumping my hand for him and watching his mouth fall open, face grimacing down at the mattress. "Think about how warm she'd be, how wet we could get her."

I pushed my index finger in, adding to the stretch and he buried a cry into the pillow, one of relief. His hips rolled, dipping into the fantasy of a woman, and a whimper echoed from his mouth.

"I need this faster, Isaac," Callum said through gritted teeth.

I tested him, adding a third finger but his face only relaxed and he gave easily. I pulled my hand free and then held him open, his hips holding still while I rested the blunt head of my cock against his entrance.

"I want to taste her," Callum whispered. "Have her soak my tongue." And then a moan broke free as I pushed in an inch.

"I want to know what she sounds like, crying out for you," I said, holding still.

Callum's shoulders tensed, the lines of muscle in his back standing out in shadow. "Want to feel her softness."

"Good," I said, and I entered him another inch, swallowing at the hot grip of him. "And?"

"Damn it, Isaac," he hissed but I held still, rocking away as he tried to push back against me. "I want to suck on her breasts...*oh*." He breathed deeply and continued, "Pull her legs up around our hips and fuck her fast, play with her clit. Bite at her neck."

My hips were settled against him and his head was rolling back and forth. "Would you leave a bruise?" I asked. I wanted to mark her, in secret spots for our eyes only.

"Only if she wanted me to," Callum said and he looked back over his shoulder to smile at me. He'd left hickeys on my neck back when we'd started courting and it'd been free gossip for the campus for weeks. "Please, Isaac."

I slid my hands up and down his sides and then took his hips in a hard grip. "Picture her there."

"Tell me," he said, and our hips rolled down together.

"I want to watch her face as she comes for us," I said, drawing back and surging forward and feeling the first sparking beat of pleasure in my groin. "Watch her take you in her mouth and make you fall apart."

Callum lifted his head from the pillow and one hand braced itself there, leaving room for another face to nuzzle against.

"Her skin," I said, finding a rhythm with the words, with the sound of Callum's breaths and the hiccup of a whine at the back of his throat. "I want to mark it too, to claim her. Fill the bed with the smell of her like... like..."

Like cookies my mother had made on rainy days. The spice of cinnamon and the thick halo of sugar in the air. I groaned as Callum conjured it around us, the cloud of sweetness and spice. I wondered how she would smell with us inside of her.

I pressed my belly to Callum's back as my hips bucked and his rolled forward into nothing. My hand found Callum's already folded around the sheets as if he were holding hers, and we knotted our fingers together and braced ourselves. My other hand stroked down his chest and then wrapped itself around his cock. His pulse was throbbing against my palm and his voice was breaking in the air.

KATHRYN MOON

I left wet, licking kisses over his spine, my breaths sobbing out on his skin.

"Fuck, Isaac, I won't last," he growled and jerked in uneven, desperate hitches and thrusts.

There was a spike of white-hot, dizzying sensation running up my own spine. I released his hand on the bed and wrapped my arm around his chest and we fell hard into the bed, gasping and groaning together as we fell apart. Callum burst and spilled himself over his stomach and the sheets and my hand and I buried myself deep and held on tight to him, my teeth grasping at his shoulder.

His arm wrapped over mine and he caught his foot around the underwear, lost somewhere in the sheets, and drew it up to wipe as much away as he could.

"We're going to have to do better than that for her," he mumbled.

I snorted against his skin and left a soft kiss where I had bit. I moved to pull away and one of his hands landed on my hip to hold me still.

"Not yet," he said. So I curled myself around his back and kissed his neck and behind his ear. "Don't tell Aiden, yet." The words were slurring with sleep and I rolled my eyes a little, my own head feeling heavy and drowsy.

"It's all going to work out," I murmured, and Callum sighed and shifted, either to nod or to drop off into sleep.

48

CHAPTER 9
JOANNA

AIDEN SAT ON A BENCH IN FRONT OF AN UPRIGHT PIANO WITH a long pipe-like instrument, as tall as my waist and narrow in his hands. The wood gleamed red as he polished at the metal fixtures running up the long body that twisted back around itself. Sunset streaked in from the window at the far end of the room, glinting like gold on the pedals and tuning clamps and curving over his broad shoulders like a heavenly silhouette.

"That looks like a weapon," I said, standing in the doorway of his office.

"I would take serious issue with anyone who tried to use it as such," Aiden said. His eyes traveled openly from my boots up to my face, expression easy and eyes slanted with interest. "Thank you for coming."

"I'm flattered you asked," I said, which was true. I was baffled too, and flustered, and nervous. I felt like I hadn't stopped blushing since Isaac had left me standing on my stoop on Sunday, and Aiden's gaze—somehow both casual *and* thorough—was no help.

"Will you come in and sit?" he asked, nodding to an armchair waiting at the desk on the opposite side of the room as his piano.

"Why *did* you invite me?" I asked, finding that words came easier if I didn't have to look directly back at him.

"I like an audience," he said. I caught his grin as I sat in the chair. It was too big for me, Aiden was broader and taller by far, but I fit nicely when I curled up in the seat.

"And you've scared off all the other potentials?" I said.

He laughed. "Some of them, yes. Others, I've simply worn out my welcome."

"Settling for a little country librarian," I teased.

He hummed at that, glancing at me out of the side of his eyes, and the sound was almost a growl for how low it was. "At the very least you'll be a university librarian soon, Joanna," he said.

I ignored the flutter in my stomach at the way his voice purred over my name. That was only how he spoke. And I was spending too much time with these men, searching in the conversation for an invitation that wasn't really being issued.

Isaac was bad enough, but at least he had the charm of home on his edges. Aiden was the kind of man I would never have imagined meeting because I could never have imagined a man *like* him. He was style and charm and art in an exquisitely perfect package. Flirting aside, and his interaction with Gwen had made it clear he did plenty of that, I had no chance of keeping his interest past the novelty.

"What's it called?" I asked, nodding at the horn in his hands.

"Ah yes, the Wing Horn," he said, lifting the instrument up off his lap and holding it vertically in the air. Everything from the height and gleam and warm tone of it suited him. "Wrenshaw was a little romantic and he was constantly building new pieces, trying to make it impossible for anyone to really learn his tech-niques. At least until he published. There are a few Wing Horns of his, each one a different manner of flight, supposedly."

"Have you heard any before?" I asked.

"Once, at a concert my parents took me to when I was young," he said. He was more interested in the Wing Horn now than me, and I settled deeper into the chair, happy to watch him handling the piece while ruminating. "It *did* feel like flying to listen. Dizzying and fast and like the floor fell away right from under where we sat. Then my mother told me to close my eyes and...the music just soared and took us with it."

His face softened as he spoke, shedding the smirk that lingered at the corner of his mouth and the tight focus that left me squirming. The catlike cunning and handsomeness transformed into something open and gentle and the sight left me warm, cocooned in the chair that smelled like spice and the sharp pine of wood polish.

"Would you like to hear?" he asked. The quirk in his grin returned with the glint in his eye, but this time instead of wanting to shy away from it, I answered it with my own.

"Please," I said.

He held my gaze for a moment, eyes darkening, and then slowly lifted the horn up to set the reed to his lips in a kiss. The first note rose, sweet and coiling through the air, and the room spun without moving. I closed my eyes as the sound deepened, reverberating around me and against my skin. There was no seat beneath me, no worn fabric beneath my fingertips, just the glow of the sun falling in through the window and stretching out to stroke at my cheeks.

Aiden spun the single note into several, rising and falling and flurrying around each other. Something like a breeze brushed through my thoughts. I pictured the lane at home that stretched flat and straight through the county and without pulling at the image it began rushing beneath me. The music built and I flew higher, watched the pattern of the fields organize themselves into a quilt of my hometown, all while the wind wrapped itself around my waist and limbs and carried me off like a leaf or a bit of cotton weed.

I was partway between woman and bird and speck of dust on the air, losing the sense of having a form or thoughts and feeling; only *flight*.

Too soon, *far* too soon for my liking, the whirlwind settled. My shoulders were heavy and the roots of my hair ached as I remembered them. There was a soft chair beneath and it felt as hard as landing from a great height. I opened my eyes and the smell of fresh air was replaced with wood polish and dry pages. The sun was shifting lower and casting shadows in the room.

Aiden waited for me to speak, eyes soft on my face.

"Like...floating," I said, then added, "Is there more?"

His laugh was like gravel after the pure notes of the horn. "That's it for now. From me, at least. I'll write you something," he said. "A flight suite."

He could find a better use of that time, I was sure, but I didn't want to argue. I could enjoy the idea of the offer without building expectations.

"I do, however, have a recording I think you would like," he said. He grabbed a case that had been leaning against the piano and started to pack away the horn.

"I should go," I said, but I didn't move to get up out of the chair.

"Stay a little longer," he said, looking at me over from over his shoulder which I had been busy watching shift beneath his jacket. "Or I've dragged you all the way up here for a few bars of music."

"And a few moments of flying," I said, laughing.

His grin turned wicked for a moment and then settled. "My favorite recording and I'll walk you home."

"Everyone is always offering to walk me home," I said. "I must look easily disoriented."

"You *look* like good company," he countered, crossing the room to rifle the contents of a shelf, heavy with records. "And maybe a little bit stubborn."

"The last part's true. But alright, I'll listen."

He had already pulled the envelope off the shelf and turned to the gramophone. I had seen one before in the Bridgeston pub, a rickety old thing that skipped and hissed through the limited collection of stomping tunes the town agreed on. Aiden loaded the record into the player with quick, practiced precision. Even if I had been determined to leave he would have had the music playing before I'd made it to the door.

"I hope you like water," he said, dropping the needle. He came to join me, sitting on the floor in front of the chair and then leaning back, resting his head against my knees.

There was a hiss of static and then we were swimming in music; piano keys bursting into bubbling notes, strings sweeping tidal waves into the room around us, and a low groaning tuba in the background dropping away the world and leaving the ocean beating beneath us.

My fingers reached down and grabbed onto Aiden's shoulder to steady myself and he rested his cheek there. His own hand reached back and wrapped around my ankle as we were swallowed up in sound.

⬧

"YOU MUST BE JOANNA."

I was standing on a ladder, arguing under my breath with a group of divination texts that insisted upon organizing themselves by year of publication instead of the last name of the author. And I thought to myself, *must I be Joanna?* Because it seemed as if 'Joanna' had a great deal going on in her life and I wondered if it might be nice to be someone else.

"The new librarian trainee," the voice behind me added.

That, at least, I could not argue. I twisted on the ladder and looked down to find one of the most fashionable women I had ever seen. And beautiful, or at least polished to the point of being inarguably perfect. She was tall, enough so that she barely had to crane her neck to look up at where I stood on the ladder, and statuesque in sapphire blues and charcoal silks that sang against her brown, glowing skin.

"What can I help you with?" I asked.

Her facial features were large and well made-up, and her black hair was piled high, lustrous and smelling strongly of roses. But in spite of all that there was something straightforward about her and she looked less amused by me than most people on campus.

"Gwen sent me for The Arcanary," she said, pointing to a book near my hand. "But I suspect now she sent me up to meet you since we've been gossiping about you."

I turned away to cover my surprise, grabbing The Arcanary as an excuse. She was waiting, her expression even and patient, when I turned back.

"What is there to gossip about?" I asked.

"Oh," she waved her hand in the air and then grabbed the book I held out. "It depends on what you're interested in. For some, it's where you came from. And for others, it's the company you keep," she paused at that, and I suspected she had a little interest there too. She grinned and then shrugged. "Personally, I'm fascinated to know what you can do."

"Most days I'm lucky to manage alphabetization," I said, my voice clipping.

"Who could blame you, with this lot?" she asked looking at the shelves around us.

"Hildy?" Gwen appeared from around the corner. "There you are. And Joanna, of course. Why are you still here?"

Hildy leaned towards Gwen as the other woman approached, and Gwen's arm wrapped around her waist. I noted that no matter how Gwen dressed—a lot like me—*she* never looked drab. Even next to all that silk and embroidery and perfume.

"Just because you work the extra hours doesn't mean you're paid for them, now mark your place and come with me," Gwen said to me. She looked to Hildy and added, "The others are waiting."

"I was going to stay and read," I said. I wasn't the only one who hung around outside of their shift and I hadn't gotten in trouble for it before now.

"And then go home and eat, what? A tomato and cheese sandwich?" Gwen asked, raising her eyebrows. "Come have dinner with us."

I pulled my notebook from my pocket and came down the ladder steps, writing down the shelf I had stopped at and *needs rearranged to author's last name NOT publication.*

"The other library staff?" I asked, tucking the notebook away.

"Book mice?" Hildy laughed. "Nooo. Dinner with our coven."

"Don't say no," Gwen said as I opened my mouth in surprise. "Or I won't offer again, and you'll miss very good cooking."

"Oh yes, you must come," Hildy echoed.

I swallowed down my excuse and made to follow the two women down to the lobby. "Gwen...how did you know what I was planning to eat?"

"I'm clairvoyant," Gwen said.

"She spied in your lunch box," Hildy said, winking at me over her shoulder.

Downstairs, waiting for us, or at least for Gwen and Hildy, were the others. A man, straight and thin as an arrow who was as elegant as Hildy and as sharply focused as Gwen with moon pale skin and short black hair. At his side was a petite person, beautiful and fae with catlike green eyes and wispy blonde hair brushing high, golden cheekbones. They ignored gender entirely in body and dress, and they looked like a magical creature's best impression of a human. Canderfey seemed the place for that kind of thing and Gwen was probably too matter of fact to care.

"Joanna Wick," Gwen said, gesturing to me. "My covenmates, Hildy Samanta, Tatsuo Ito," she said, and the man stepped forward to shake my hand. She finished with the most curious of the group. "And Bryce Gast."

Bryce smiled at me and it was toothy and edged and left me more certain than ever that they were not strictly human, and neither male nor female. But it was Tatsuo that walked at my side through the campus, while Bryce walked to the front to lead our party.

"How are you settling?" Tatsuo asked, with his hands folded together at his back.

"Alright, I think," I said slowly. The library was enjoyable at least, it was everything else that left me not knowing which way was up.

"Do you enjoy your work?"

"I love my work," I said, happy to have a simple question. "It's the only thing I've ever really wanted to do."

"*That* is a blessing," he said. "I have yet to decide what I enjoy in work."

Hildy looked over her shoulder at that and they smiled softly at one another.

"What have you tried?" I asked.

"Oh, aura healing, astrology, herbalism, phrenology, predictive hallucinations..."

I started to laugh as the list went on, not certain whether or not he was teasing me but enjoying the variety all the same. Tatsuo's smile deepened in response.

"What are you trying now?" I asked, interrupting the list after 'beekeeping.'

"Writing," Tatsuo said, raising his eyebrows at me.

"What kind of writing?" I asked, taking the bait.

"Trance writing, it's a wonderful process for working out the subconscious," he said. "You should try it."

"I'm not sure I'd like what came out," I said and Gwen snorted ahead of us.

"It's only words," Tatsuo said with heavy sweetness and Gwen eyed him over her glasses.

We reached the neighborhood at the north edge of campus where permanent faculty lived. The houses were beautiful, tall and broad and colorful, built for covens and families rather than individuals. There were gardens in the front yards already planted with bright orange blossoms hearty enough for the coming chill of fall.

Gwen and her coven lived in a sprawling cornflower blue house with cream shutters and a porch wrapping from the front steps all the way to the back of the house. The yard was surrounded by a tidy hedge and the view through the windows into the house was obstructed with pale blue lace curtains. It had the look of Hildy about it, but even Bryce, wild and quiet, seemed settled and comfortable as they walked up the steps to the front door.

Tatsuo and I made to turn up the walkway to the house and my eye was caught by another, down at the end of the block. A red brick beast of a house, narrower and taller than the others around it, sat glowing in the sunset. I couldn't see much, just bay windows curving out into a trim yard, and several chimneys stretching up into the sky, one of them spitting a little trickle of smoke. I turned away at the first pang in my chest. There was no reason to feel it, but I was certain that was their house, Isaac and Aiden and Callum's.

Tatsuo had walked ahead without me and the four of them waited on the porch for me. A perfect set, elegant and powerful with a fascinating, delicate, ferocity. Tatsuo and Hildy had their arms around each other's waists and Hildy's knowing smile had been replaced with something fragile and private. Bryce's hand was in Gwen's, possibly an effort on the latter's part to keep them patient while they waited on me.

I hurried up to the steps, begging my mind to quit wishing for something I was not meant for.

CHAPTER 10

JOANNA

THE NEXT MORNING I FOUND THAT SOMEONE ELSE HAD managed to organize the divination shelf I'd been working on, and this time had managed to make it stick. I was a little jealous and a bit disappointed in myself for not handling the work myself. It was as if I was being shown proof that even training as a simple librarian, here in Canderfey I failed to measure up. It put a fire in my belly and I finished my shelving on a tear of speed and set to bullying the books to rights in the restricted section for the rest of the day.

I caught sight of myself in a window near the end of the day —hair in a mess sticking at odd angles around my head, my hands and white shirt smudged with dust and old ink, and my cheeks red with exertion. I remembered that I had agreed to see Isaac, to sit for a sketch, after I was done at the library and I wondered if I couldn't sneak home first. Not that I had much better to wear or any chance of fixing hair that refused to do anything other than what it liked. I tried anyway, combing my fingers through tangled curls as I turned away from the window and found Callum Pike waiting for me at the end of the aisle, eyes wide and startled.

"You look like you've been in an argument," he said.

"Only with books," I answered.

"The rumors are true?" he asked, coming closer with his arms full of books. "They rearrange themselves."

"That or you professors are playing tricks on me," I said, narrowing my eyes at him.

His cheeks pinked and my stomach churned. "I used to sneak up here as a student," he said, looking around. "Woollard always caught me, dragged me out by the earlobes."

"She does that to me sometimes too," I said.

Callum laughed and it was a surprised noise, like I had caught him in a trap of humor he hadn't expected. I thought of the way Isaac spoke of him and wondered if a laugh was a rare sound from Callum.

"Isaac mentioned he'd be seeing you later, for a portrait," Callum said, stepping closer. Closer than librarians and professors really needed to stand, but farther than my skin ached to have him.

"I'm afraid I will be the first person to fail at being the subject of a portrait," I admitted.

"You'll do better than me," he said, grinning like the sun. "He has yet to manage it and we've known each other for over a decade."

From the back of my thoughts came the image of the hawk, wounded and screaming and still soaring, and I realized the color of the copper feathers matched Callum's hair, that the glaring green eyes of the painting were fixed to my face now. I wasn't sure how right he was about that claim, but I couldn't find my voice to correct him.

"I look forward to seeing it, either way," he said and this time I realized I had been the one to step forward, searching his expression for the hawk in the painting.

"I've never been very good at being looked at," I said, which was a thought I hadn't meant to speak aloud, but there it was and it was true.

"You'll have practice," he said.

I was getting practice right now and it made my heartbeat pound in my ears and my skin felt charged and sensitive to the air against it. And I didn't feel shy or embarrassed under Callum's gaze at all. If anything, I felt like I was stretching up to him, trying to catch more of that sunlight feeling. That being looked at should only be the precursor to being touched.

"Joanna," he said, and his eyes flicked down to my mouth where my lips were parted and catching a breath.

The books shifted between us, pushed aside and he had done that trick again; the one where what he was holding seemed to fit itself away. But I was distracted by his now free hand reaching up to cup my jaw and lift my chin. I blinked and my eyelids felt heavy as I watched him bend his head to mine, nose brushing across my cheek before his lips settled over mine, slanted and pulling gently.

It was a kiss, but it felt something like the flying of Aiden playing the Wing Horn and something like the burn of connection while painting with Isaac's brush and canvas. And something like lifting my face up to the sky to feel the scorch of the sun on my skin.

I was on my toes, hands reaching for something to hold onto, when Callum nipped at my bottom lip and heat burst in my belly, and the world—and good sense—returned to my head.

I yanked myself away, steps tripping backward and my hands clapping over my mouth.

"I'm sorry!" I said, and my eyes searched the library around us, seeing no one. The relief was a heavy, queasy feeling in the moment.

"No, Joanna, I-" he started, face torn and twisted with deep lines digging into his forehead.

"You have a *coven*," I hissed and watched him swallow his words, expression falling. "And I have no right-"

"You have every right," he said. His hand reached out for me and I fell back a step. My stomach twisted as he winced, but his shoulders set straight and he fixed his eyes to mine and said, "We want you. In the coven, with us. I shouldn't have pushed but..."

He trailed off as my head shook, back and forth in the rapid beat of my heart pounding. I closed my eyes, covering them with a shaking hand as bone-deep disbelief battled with the pathetic part of me wishing for the words to be true.

"I'm not a witch," I said, and my voice was dry in my throat.

"You are," he said, but I heard the uncertainty. "Surely there must be something...all the librarians at Canderfey can do something."

I lowered my hand and looked up at him.

I swallowed. "But I'm not a librarian. And I probably won't be. I can barely keep dust off the shelves."

It was something in his expression, the way his eyes darted over the shelves like he was scrambling for an answer as he said, "We'll...think of something."

"Is this a joke?" I asked, flat and low. My stomach sank. Outside the bells for the hour echoed over the campus.

Callum's face went blank with surprise. "A joke?"

It had to be. It made more sense that they were *laughing* at me than that...that I could be of actual interest to them. The knots in my gut hardened to pits.

"The three of you finding the *least* likely person to ever- ever be *worthy* of you," I spat, feeling triumphant in anger, in seeing his face sharpen at my words. "And then you all chase her around the campus. What did you want? To seduce me? You could have done it without the charade of sweetness. Or is me being foolish enough to fall for the fantasy part of the fun?"

"Joanna, stop. None of that is true," he said. But the sweet, earnest bend of his voice was paired with the tight anger in his face.

I *still* wanted to believe. It was in the shake of my hands and the way my heart seemed to thrash inside its cage and the stupid tears gathering at the corners of my eyes. With all the self-disgust I could muster I stared at Callum and said, "I want you to leave me alone. All three of you."

I had to push past him to get to the stairs. It was after five and I was free to leave the library, and I burnt on the inside knowing I would not even want to come back the next day or the day after. He didn't grab for me, but his voice pleaded my name as I edged around him and without the tangle of his expression the tone curled around me, drawing at my weakness. I whimpered as the tears spilled over and I ran to the stairs, steps skidding.

"Please, wait," he whispered, words cracking.

I ignored the stares in the library, grabbing my bag and

rushing out onto the lawn as classes let out. It was easier to be invisible, head ducked down, in the crowd of students busy with themselves. I thought I would make it to my house and I knew the walk well enough to follow it with my eyes on the ground, but I forgot where else it would lead me.

"Joanna," Isaac said, a gentle hand on my elbow and a kiss on my wet cheek as I was pulled to a stop. I looked up as he drew back and his wide smile fell. "What's happened?"

"Get away from me," I whispered, but it could barely be heard over the tears in my throat and the crowd around us.

He heard it and the reaction was as sudden as if I had struck him with my fist. But it smoothed away and he huddled in closer, broad shoulders blocking me from the bustle around us.

"Please," he said, head lowering almost to mine. "Please tell me what's wrong."

"Callum kissed me." I hadn't meant to say it, but it was easier than shoving Isaac away in all this crowd. Than making a bigger idiot of myself at this university than I already had managed to.

Isaac's eyes lightened for a moment but they searched my face. He didn't look triumphant or angry or jealous. He just looked...concerned.

I didn't want Isaac to be a liar. More than the others even, I wanted Isaac to be a friend to me. An honest one.

"We can go into my office," he said and I looked over his shoulder. I had walked directly past the Burgess Building on my way home. "I was getting you flowers," he added, lifting up a bouquet of crimson roses. "For the portrait."

They would outshine me by far, I thought, almost spitefully. I had always been a little unsure of myself, even in Bridgeston. I was humble like my neighbors but more interested in the world outside our village than the others. I'd built up a fantasy in my head of finding myself in Canderfey, of growing into someone new, but instead I'd only been seeing how little I measured up. Suddenly I hated this place, and these men, for upsetting the fragile truce I'd maintained with myself, for pulling me out of my books and giving me something real to compare my own life to.

"I only want to help, Joanna, I promise," Isaac said, gray-blue eyes aching like a storm cloud about to burst.

If Isaac was a liar, he was the best of them. I didn't want him to be that. I didn't want to be the person I saw myself as either.

I nodded and whispered, "Alright."

His hand at my elbow slid down to my hand and I followed him up the stairs of the arts building. I kept my eyes fixed to his back as chattering students curved around us until we were up to the third floor. Isaac held the door open for me and left it open by an inch behind us.

He had a corner office with windows on two walls and it looked as though he had converted the small space into another studio for himself. Smaller easels took up more room than the minuscule desk pushed into the corner next to a closet door. The room smelled like him and felt inhabited by him and against my better judgment I could feel the tension easing out of me. He pulled the desk chair out for me and grabbed a low stool for himself after putting the bundle of roses together in a short, black vase. He pulled the stool close until our knees were almost touching, and then he simply waited.

"He said that you want me in your coven," I said, watching him.

"That's true," he said, without any hesitation. He smiled a little and then added, "Although I think we agreed to talk to you about it as a group. After some time."

"Isaac, that's not how it works. You need a witch."

"We do," he said nodding.

I raised my eyebrows, waiting for him to catch up, but his smile only flickered back. "I'm *not* one," I said.

"I think you might be," he said. "I haven't said anything to the others yet. Because you deserve to know first, of course."

I released something between a laugh and a cough. "Do you honestly think I could have missed it somehow? I'm twenty-seven years old."

"Are you?" he asked, smiling. "I guessed about that."

"Isaac," I said, feeling something like panic rising up in my chest. I had been so angry with Callum, at the very idea he suggested. Certain that it *must* be a trick or a lie. It didn't seem fair that it could feel silly and sweet here with Isaac. "I don't

KATHRYN MOON

understand. If you aren't sure that I am a witch, how can you even think of me being in the coven?"

"I haven't thought of anything else since meeting you," Isaac said and my heartbeat paused for a moment, as if to listen. "Neither have the others, I think. Aiden could care less if you had magic or not, honestly. Callum just assumes you must."

"I don't," I said, trying to press the words to him, into his head. Because it hurt more to think he might really want me when I was so unfit to be in a coven, than it did to think he was making fun of me.

"What did you say to Callum?" he asked.

I looked down into my lap, fidgeting with my bag where it sat. "I thought you were all making fun of me."

"Oh, Joanna." He jumped off the stool he'd been sitting on and came to kneel in front of me, lifting my hands from my lap and fitting them in his own. "It's not that. I swear to you. We may have been clumsy, but I promise we were sincere."

I blinked a new bout of tears away, staring out the window and Isaac waited at my feet, thumbs making patterns over my knuckles.

"If you were a witch," he started, soft and slow. "Would you accept our invitation? At least consider us?"

I chewed at the inside of my mouth for a long minute, and then looked to him. "Yes," I whispered.

He beamed at me, lifting my hands to kiss them, before standing up from the floor and crossing to one of his easels. He brought me a stick of white chalk. "Take this," he said.

I took it, forehead furrowing in confusion at the leap between my confession and this.

"I don't want an art lesson right now," I said.

He grinned and pulled me up from the chair. "It isn't an art lesson, it's a magic lesson," he said. He dragged me a foot over to stand in front of the closet door.

"I'm not sure I want that either," I mumbled.

Isaac's hands were warm around my waist as he stood behind me, and he pressed a kiss to the back of my neck. His breath was in my hair and his hands squeezed once on my sides before releasing me and stepping back.

64

"Write on the door," he said, and then after I'd stared at him for too long he added, "With the chalk."

I frowned at him and then lifted the chalk up to scribble on the door. *This is sil-*

"No, no, no." Isaac rushed forward to grab my hand and stop the sentence. "Not that."

"But it's true," I said, raising my eyebrows.

He opened his mouth to respond and then shut it again, glancing between me and the door. "Wipe that off and...and write 'door'," he said.

"That's even sillier."

"Joanna," he said, voice dropping. He was at my side, our shoulders brushing and we were close enough in height that I would only need to twist and lift on my toes a bit to be kissing him. His eyes flicked down to my lips and I thought he would do it, but then he looked to the door. "It will only take a minute to humor me. And if I'm wrong it won't change how I feel or Callum feels or Aiden feels about you."

I wasn't sure how to explain that while I returned their feelings, I wasn't *prepared* for them.

I sighed and reached up, smudging the chalk away with the heel of my hand. "Door," I said, writing the word out in clear, square letters.

"Now, 'to'," Isaac said.

I wrote *'to.'*

"Now think of a place it might lead to, *other* than the closet," he said, giving me a significant look. "And then write that place."

Like an escape route, I thought. And then I wrote *'my bedroom.'*

He smiled at my work, all four words of it, and then we stared at each other.

"Now what?" I asked.

"Now you open it," he said as if it should be obvious. And his eyes were bright and his grin was twitching, waiting to grow brighter.

I looked at the door blankly. "Isaac, I've read about portals and you don't make them with chalk and a few words in a tidy hand. There's...runes and preparation, and meditation and-"

"Open the door, Joanna," he said, lips pressed to my cheek.

CHAPTER 11

AIDEN

"I've bungled it!"

The front door slammed shut and I looked up from the violin I'd been sanding, just in time to watch Callum storm into the living room, fists in his hair as if he were trying to pull the whole lot out at once.

"Bungled what?" I asked.

"Joanna," Callum sighed, collapsing into an armchair. His face was crashing down to the floor with a weight that dripped down his whole body. "I've ruined it. Again. Aide, I'm so sorry. You and Isaac are better off without me. You'd have a prop-"

"Don't be an idiot," I said, cutting him short. "We're all but useless without you. Now tell me what happened."

"She thinks it's a joke," Callum whispered, head dropping to the back of the chair. "Worse, she thinks *she's* the butt of it. I went wrong somewhere and now..."

I set the violin down on the low table in front of me and brushed the sawdust away into nothing before standing. Callum looked as though he were halfway to coming up with a spell to disintegrate himself. It struck me suddenly. Callum looked *awful*. Over a woman.

"You like her," I said, trying and failing not to grin.

He groaned and rolled his head to glare at me, but it melted quickly into an agonized twist of his expression. "I want her," he said. "You're right. She's...she feels like she should fit, right here," he said, gesturing to the space between us.

I crossed the room and bent over him, kissing his forehead. "You haven't bungled anything," I said. He was still glaring up at me, but that was fair since I was probably still smiling. But a lovesick Callum? That was new. And worth a little good humor. "Not alone," I added. "We went about this wrong. We'll approach her together. Invite her to dinner. Be the decent gentleman we are rather than cornering her from all sides like a pack of starving wolves."

"I *feel* starved when I look at her," Callum whispered.

I laughed at his grimace. "About damn time, Pike. Now, where did you leave her?"

"She ran out of the library," he said, and his nails were nearly digging grooves into the arms of the chair. "Told me to stay away from her. All of us."

My eyes widened at that. "That's... What did you do to her?"

"Kissed her," Callum said, and I congratulated myself at not laughing at the announcement or the way his bottom lip was threatening to pout.

"I see. Well, we better go get Isaac before we find her," I said.

"Should we?" Callum asked. "Find her, that is. Wouldn't it be better to...give her space?"

"Maybe, but I think Isaac has a better read on her emotions. And they were supposed to meet today so he'll be worrying. Come on. No sulking, yet," I said, grabbing his elbows and pulling him up from the chair.

"Wasn't sulking," he muttered, but his feet dragged as he followed me.

CHAPTER 12
JOANNA

MY HAND WAS ON THE DOOR HANDLE WHEN ISAAC'S OFFICE door swung open and Aiden and Callum ran in. It was the first time I had ever been in their company all together and the effect was immediate. I felt settled and excited at the same time, grounded and light. I knew that something inside of me, deeper than my thoughts or the nervous anxiety that twisted me up in knots around them, had made the decision for me. I wanted these men. I wanted the magic that would make me worth being with them.

"Ah," Aiden said, upon seeing me.

Callum behind him froze in his tracks and then stared down at the floor, and I knew I owed him an apology for what I'd said.

"It's good that you're here, but it's important that you don't interrupt," Isaac said to them. And then after turning to me and then back again, he added, "We'd better close the door."

Both men stepped inside and shut the door behind them, but Callum hugged himself to the wall as if he were scared to come closer. The anger I had seen in the library was turned inwards and I wanted to leave the little closet door project behind to speak to him. Isaac caught my eye and shook his head slightly.

"Just to know," he said to me.

I twisted the handle and swung the door out, still staring back at Isaac, prepared for his disappointment. But the sunlight from the street outside my bedroom window hit my cheek and I looked through the doorway, mouth falling open. Inside of the little narrow closet door was my creaky bed with books and nightclothes tossed on the covers, and my small case I had traveled with against the wall, and my tiny dresser. And the window overlooking the street on a part of campus that couldn't even be seen from the Burgess Building.

"That's... What is that?" Callum asked. He was suddenly behind me, next to Isaac staring through the door.

"My bedroom," I said, words dumb on my tongue.

"No, the magic," he said, and all of his reserve from moments ago had been replaced with studious curiosity. "It's not a portal, it's more...refined?"

"It's a door," Isaac said shrugging.

"How much did you help?" Aiden asked.

"I gave her chalk," Isaac said. "Drawing chalk."

"And directions," I added, edging closer to the doorway. Isaac snorted behind me.

"Can I- can I walk through?" I asked.

"Wait," Callum said, stopping me with a hand in my path. "Let me."

He had to bend to fit through the door and he stepped inside with enough caution that I half expected the door frame or my bedroom to collapse in on him. But nothing happened. And standing inside my bedroom, studying every surface, Callum looked more confused than ever. Also, a great deal taller. A half thought at the back of my mind pointed out that he wouldn't even fit in the bed.

"How?" he asked, turning back to us, staring across a few feet of floorboards and more than half a mile of the campus.

"She wrote it," Isaac said, a hand settling at the small of my back. He looked down at me and said, "Just like you wrote 'books to find' and texts that had been missing for hundreds of years suddenly reappeared."

"Or a shelf that stayed organized," I said under my breath. I had always made lists and directions for myself. But they had always been mundane things. A need for a sunny day, a list of ingredients for the market, a return date on a book.

And no one in Bridgeston had missed a due date in all my time at the library.

"And that haunting you added to my painting is yours too," Isaac said. "My students won't even look at it. I thought it would be a good test. Painting and writing have more similarities than most fields of magic."

"I didn't know writing was a field of magic," Aiden said, joining Isaac and me in watching Callum squint and frown at the wall around my bedroom door.

"Runes, sigils," Callum said.

"But just words?" Aiden tossed back.

Callum only covered his frown with his hand, scratching at his beard.

"I imagine giving you a rune would be like giving you a hammer," Callum said to me.

"I never used one, I thought..." my voice tangled in my throat. "I didn't know..."

And then I was nearly crying again for an entirely different reason. Aiden's arm wrapped heavily over my shoulder and I leaned into his side.

"You're a witch, love," he said, and then kissed the top of my head.

Callum stopped his pacing upon seeing my watery gaze and I tried not to laugh as he looked between Isaac and Aiden with a bit of panic on his face.

"Do you mind if we leave the door here a bit longer?" Isaac asked me. "We can go inside and have..."

"Tea," I said nodding, blinking away the tears that had risen. "Or will we be stuck between the office and my bedroom?"

"One way to find out," Callum said. And he looked excited to do so.

I expected to feel something upon crossing the threshold. A push of air or some kind of friction, but it was as if Isaac's closet had always led to my room. And when we were all inside, which only furthered the point that my bedroom was far too small for any one of the men let alone all three, I shut the door behind us. And like nothing, it was *my* door. Wider and taller than the closet's and in a different shade of wood.

"It's a surprisingly elegant construction," Callum said and it took me half a beat to realize he didn't mean anything to do with my house.

I turned the handle again, and this time the door swung in on my room, and waiting outside was the small little alcove at the top of the stairs.

"*That* is magic," Aiden said from behind me and the tone of his voice warmed the back of my neck.

The first floor wasn't much better in terms of fitting the four of us. I only had two chairs at my little table and when Isaac tried to join me in the kitchen to help with the tea we may as well have been dancing for how close we had to stand together. When I put the kettle on the stove Isaac wrapped his arm around my waist and leaned in to whisper.

"Do you need more time? Do you want us to go?"

I reached past him to the counter, leaning into his side to grab the tea tin. He didn't lean away, only brushed the tip of his nose along my jaw until I settled back and started prepping the teapot.

"Yes," I said. "And no. I want to talk."

"Alright."

He moved to go and I reached out, tugging him back by the pocket of his vest. Our lips bumped clumsily together, and I wished for half a moment that I planned instead of acted. But then Isaac hummed a pleased little sound and pressed into the kiss for a soft, sweet moment. I was blushing and he was smiling as he pulled away, squeezing at my waist and then leaving me to the tea.

There was chalk in my pocket, the stick Isaac had given me to write on the door, and I reached in to play with it a moment, thinking of the men waiting for me in the other room. Then I pulled it out and looked down at the dark wooden countertop.

There are four...

I paused for a moment chewing at my lip before continuing.

There are four identical chairs in the dining room.

"Joanna!" Aiden shouted.

"It worked," I said, as the tea kettle started to whistle. I tucked my grin against my shoulder as Isaac peeked his head back into the kitchen, an eyebrow raised.

"Sit," I said.

"Glad to know you're handling that well," Isaac said, smiling back at me.

I had mismatched china to serve the tea in but I at least had four cups and I carried them out to the table. There was an open seat across from Callum and Aiden took two cups out of my hands and passed one to him.

Then he turned back to me and said, "Have dinner with us."

It was somehow both more and less than what I had expected him to say. Although I didn't think I'd have an easier time answering if he'd asked for me to join the coven as plainly.

"I..." I had spent so long trying to avoid familiarity for a reason that no longer existed and now I couldn't think of a word to say. I'd been so angry barely fifteen minute ago, with myself and Canderfey and them, and now it was all just evaporated into a little magic and confusion.

"You're a witch," Aiden said. "So the argument against our request to court you is void, right?"

"Don't push," Callum muttered, looking up from where he'd fixed his eyes to the cup of tea.

Aiden raised his eyebrows at the other man in answer and Callum turned gray and looked back down at the table. Aiden winced and he and Isaac communicated in silence for a tense moment. Here was another thing I was afraid of, not fitting into the space they shared together. Not being enough.

But there was something I could say in this moment. Something important.

"I owe you an apology," I said and Callum looked up frowning, glancing at the others until he met my eyes and realized I was speaking to him. "I was...confused, but I shouldn't have said those things or run off."

"It was my fault," he said, voice tight. "I shouldn't have..."

Kissed me. Although the twist of his face implied something much less innocent and sweet than what occurred.

"It's alright," I said.

I had just kissed Isaac in the kitchen. And it had been clumsy and simple and made the blood in my veins sing. If it had been Callum and his slow, smooth caress just now instead of an hour ago before everything had been turned inside out...before *I* had been turned inside out, we wouldn't be grimacing and apologizing to one another.

Callum swallowed and the subject died.

"Come to dinner, please," Aiden started again, this time more gingerly. "Isaac will cook, so you don't have to worry. It's...dinner, that's all, I promise."

"No," Isaac said. He reached over the table and tangled our fingers together. He looked at Aiden and then Callum before back to me. "We should be clear. Joanna Wick, our coven wants to court you. Please come have dinner with us."

My heart was pounding in my chest and I could feel the heat on my face and the way my feet pinned themselves to the floor, half ready to take flight. The invitation, the weight of it, and pointed intentions behind it had felt so impossible as recently as the morning.

But I had thought about the possibility of them. Had wished for it. Imagined myself in a life where I might have expected such a thing.

"Are you sure?" I asked, barely a whisper.

Aiden was beaming, smiling too hard to speak and Isaac's dimples were growing deeper as he joined him.

"We're sure," Callum said, eyes fixed to mine.

I took a shaky breath and swallowed. "Dinner would be lovely," I said.

CHAPTER 13
JOANNA

THE MORNING OF THE DINNER I TRIED TO GO FOR A WALK. Just a small break away from the campus to clear my head and gather my thoughts about the upcoming evening. But when I got to the path it shimmered a fiery orange-red and my feet stopped in place. Posted to the nearest tree was a small poster reading *Paths Out Of Order; please refrain from exploring the woods at this time.*

I laughed at first. How could a path be out of order? Was it a prank from the students? But it would take a serious effort to close the paths with magic. I could ask the men later.

I thought of going to the library instead, but it was full of people and my coworkers would probably want an explanation for why I was pacing the stacks. Instead, I headed north past Gwen and her coven's neighborhood, into the downtown of Canderfey proper.

The streets were full, the town up earlier than the campus on a Sunday, but my anonymity here was better, and I could stroll and window shop in peace. I found a shop entirely filled with tea, and another solely dedicated to beauty and bath tinctures. At the shop at home there had been two kinds of tea, and one kind of soap. I spent a good hour sniffing jar after jar and coming up with reasons to buy new tea and a small collection of washes that probably wouldn't even fit in my bathroom. I was walking back to the bus stop, debating between walking home for an hour or riding for ten minutes, when I stopped at a shop window full of dresses.

An evening gown stood on a mannequin, the black fabric gleaming red where the sun hit it, with the skirt pooling over the floor like blood. It looked like liquid on the frame of the body, sliding down the shoulders and over the breasts and hips. There was black pearl beading at the shoulders and down the collar, and fine seams down the bodice and it was the most beautiful thing I had ever seen. But I could only imagine myself slouching wrong, tripping over the hem, and wrinkling the skirt with the way I sat.

Hildy passed the window behind the dresses, turned away from me, and talking to a woman who was considering a petal pink dress on a hanger in her hands. She had mentioned her shop while I'd had dinner with them and while I'd imagine something *nice*, this was... Well, it made much more sense when it came to Hildy, I supposed. I doubted there was anything inside for me, but I wanted to say hello.

And I wanted to touch.

Hildy looked away from her customer as the doorbells chimed with my entrance. Her eyes lit up and her smile turned from professional to friendly for a moment. She nodded at me and I returned the greeting before she went back to work. The shop was bright and well lit, the colors of the garments hanging shining against the cream and white stripes of the satiny wallpaper. A table sat in the center with several elegant hats, feathered and topped in silk flowers, as well as a collection of gloves and their glowing pearl buttons running up the arms.

When faced with the dresses in person, each one an individual work of art formed out of decadent fabrics and lace and delicate embellishments, I found myself keeping my hands knotted up in front of me. And when faced with the price tags, handwritten on heavy card stock with the dress's details, I found myself swallowing heavily and averting my eyes. Hildy was finishing with her customer, wrapping up the pink dress in black tissue paper when I finally found a corner better suited to me. Simple dresses and skirts with clean lines out of rich fabrics, and tidy blouses in light silks.

"That's Gwen's corner," Hildy said, as the bells rang and we were alone in the shop. "I started carrying them when I realized I was never going to trick her into lace."

Most of the pieces were in neutrals but my fingers were wrapping around the hanger of a dress the purple-red of cherry juice. It had short sleeves and a full skirt and while it was nicer than anything I'd ever owned or worn, it was still simple by the university standards.

"At least you like color," Hildy said.

I glanced at the tag and decided it would be safe for me to touch. It was a soft, light velvet and it felt downy under my fingers.

"Can I try it on?" I asked.

"I would've wrestled you into it," Hildy said, smile bright.

I knew in the dressing room, as soon as the fabric slid over my shoulders and with the first *snick* of the zipper, that I was going to go home with the dress. The fit was close, just a little loose around the waist and shoulders, and the skirt swished like music around my calves as I twisted in place.

"It's perfect for you," Hildy said. While I knew it would be a sale for her shop, I could tell the words were those of a friend.

I bit my lip and stared at my reflection in the mirror. My hair was a mess and my boots were a little scuffed but I looked good. Pretty, maybe. Less like a book mouse and more like...

"I've just found out I'm a witch," I said, staring at myself in the mirror.

"Just?" Hildy asked, and she was fussing at my waist, fitting the fabric tighter. "We've known since Gwen received your application."

She was grinning to herself and I frowned at her thinking. A slow sinking weight dropped through me.

"My *application*," I hissed, grimacing. My *written* application. Describing why I would be a good fit for the position.

"Ohh, don't fuss," soothed Hildy before taking pins to the fabric at my shoulders. "Gwen saw it right away and it's not as if she couldn't have turned you down with a little de-charming. But with that talent? Who would?"

"You must all think I'm an idiot," I said. My fingers were playing at the folds of skirt at my waist and found their way into a pocket and I twisted in happy surprise, nearly getting myself stuck with a pin.

"There are plenty of strange magical talents," Hildy said with a shrug. "Sometimes they get overlooked, other times they get shoved into a more familiar field of study. You probably would have ended up in the arts if anyone had noticed sooner. *I* almost landed myself in carpentry for goodness sake. Can you imagine?" She made a disgusted face over my shoulder, nose wrinkling in annoyance. "As if carpentry has any of the subtlety of tailoring."

"Think of the wood shavings," I said, teasing and laughing at Hildy's horrified expression.

"You're better off," she said, patting my shoulder. "Who knows if there'd be anyone to really teach you. And now here you are, likely ruining all the romantic hopes of half the students on campus."

I blushed and stared at her as she put away her pins and began to unzip me from the dress. "Gossip travels fast," I said.

Hildy grinned and shrugged. "I have a shop-girl in the arts who had a lot to say about your picnic with her favorite professor this week."

I ducked back into the dressing room, a smile creeping up my cheeks as I remembered Isaac rescuing me from the library for lunch in the grass together. There was a last burst of summer in the weather and the lawn had been full of students and professors. I knew we had been seen, but I hadn't imagined there being anything worth gossiping about. I didn't think anyone else could tell the way we'd made excuses to have our fingers brushing, or the way Isaac wrapped his hand around my ankle as we sat opposite each other, eating in quiet.

"They're very lucky men," Hildy said from the other side of the curtain.

"You don't think it's unlikely? They could do...more than *me*." I almost hated to put my old clothes back on after wearing the dress for only a handful of minutes.

"I'm not sure that they could, darling," Hildy said sweetly. "And it's not as though there haven't been attempts before. But from what I know, which is quite a lot, they've never all been interested in the same person before. Callum Pike is notoriously standoffish. If he wants you in the coven, then that makes you more qualified than anyone. Do you want to be?" she asked as I came back out with the dress, pins still in place.

It hadn't even occurred to me to tell her not to fit the dress. And I couldn't bear to not buy it now.

Hildy was watching my face, waiting on my answer, as I passed her the dress.

"I'm having dinner with them tonight," I said. It was one thing to say it to their faces, that I wanted to be with them, that I wanted to try. It felt like a much riskier thing to share it with others. If the relationship failed, if they changed their mind, did I really want others to know I had thought it possible in the first place?

"Give me ten minutes and I'll have this ready for your dinner tonight," Hildy said. She ducked into an office and a billow of magic, bright and spiky like the tips of tailoring pins, trickled out for a moment.

I thought of what she had said about Callum. He had wanted me, for a moment in the library. I knew that much. What I was less sure of was if he still did after my outburst. He had said the words while we all sat around my little dining table, but they didn't take down the walls he seemed to place between us after the kiss. If I had already ruined things, would he say so? Or was he going along now for the sake of his covenmates?

I wished I could have rewound the week and gone back to the moment in the library. Accepted the kiss or at least not made such a fool of myself refusing it. But it didn't seem like the kind of problem words on paper would fix.

"Here you are," Hildy said, returning from her office with a box wrapped in gleaming cream paper. I joined her at the counter to pay and she pulled a small jar of red lip stain from her pocket. "And this is for you from me. I stash them everywhere so it won't be missed."

And I didn't have any at home, but of course, Hildy could already tell that.

"Thank you," I said, as earnestly as I could. The dress and makeup would feel like a kind of armor to wear at the dinner tonight. A costume of the woman who *could* imagine herself with the three beautiful men.

"Oh," Hildy waved her hand at me dismissively with a small smile on her face. "Just come back. Give me a reason to bring in some colors Gwen wouldn't touch."

We kissed cheeks in parting and I took the bus home. When I closed the entry door behind me and took off my boots I found an idea brewing. I had washed the countertop in the kitchen earlier in the week, erasing the words I'd written. And with them went the two chairs that had materialized. I found my rescued notebook and pen in my bag and open them to write in *my boots are like new again*.

They shone black by the door.

CHAPTER 14
JOANNA

AIDEN WAS WAITING FOR ME ON MY STEPS WHEN IT WAS TIME to leave.

"I would have found the house on my own," I said, a bottle of wine in hand as his eyes raked over me.

"I wouldn't have had the pleasure of walking with you," he said, grinning. "You're stunning."

I couldn't think fast enough to answer that and his grin grew. Hildy had thought further ahead for me than I had. I had no good coat to wear with such a beautiful dress, but she'd enfolded it in the box in a heavy black and gold wrap for me to wear. After dabbing on the lip stain and draping the wrap over my shoulders I barely recognized myself in the small bathroom mirror upstairs.

"There's a minor security fuss in the woods outside of the campus. Callum was fretting, and I was happy to take the excuse to have a little time alone with you," he explained, sobering.

"Did he want to cancel the dinner?" I asked, hunting for a clue about Callum's changed feelings.

Aiden barked out a laugh. "He wanted all three of us to come get you," he said.

I locked my door and came down the steps and Aiden took the wine from me. He tucked it inside of his jacket and it disappeared.

"I can't do that," I said, frowning at the place where the wine had vanished.

"Callum could teach you," Aiden said.

"Callum?"

"He taught me," Aiden said, taking my hand and leading us down the block. "He said he found it in a dusty old book, but I think he made it up. I've never seen anyone else do it."

"How does it work?"

"Something to do with making a very small space bigger," he said with a shrug. He patted at his ribs and said, "It's still here. I can feel it against me like it's in a pocket I can't see. I lose things this way occasionally because I can't find the pocket again. I just don't tell Callum that or he'll repeat the whole lesson all over again and he's a beast when he's lecturing."

I tried to fight my laugh and failed. In all my interactions with Callum, he had been gentle and direct. Even while we'd been hissing at each other in the library. 'Beast' was not the word I would ever choose for him.

Aiden smirked at me out of the corner of his mouth. "Oh, just wait. You'll see. He's chomping at the bit to learn more about what you can do."

I chewed at my lip and he watched me. I could make doors, chairs, shiny shoes. I could influence a job application.

"Are you nervous about the magic or the dinner?" Aiden murmured, bending his head to mine as we passed students on the common lawns.

"Both," I answered just as quietly.

"We'll follow your pace," he said, squeezing my hand. "Tonight is only dinner. A significant one, for us certainly, but just dinner. Conversation. Isaac will show off his cooking, and I'll probably corner you into listening to more music." I smiled at that and Aiden's brow furrowed as he continued, "And Callum... well he's more scared of you than you are of him."

"That doesn't sound promising," I said, looking up at him. "I think he's upset with me, about the way I spoke in the library."

"He's upset with himself," Aiden said, without any doubt. "He's out of his element. Isaac and I are inclined to find it amusing because it's so rare. But he's sincere."

"You don't think he's just going along? For the sake of keeping the peace?" I asked.

Aiden's grin stretched, wicked and excited. "Not at all. And if you worry, you should talk to him. He'll make himself clear."

It was a slightly cryptic thing to say, but we'd just reached the neighborhood, passing Gwen and Hildy's house, so I let the subject drop.

"How long have you lived here?" I asked as Aiden pointed out the house, the red brick I had seen before.

"Since I got my position," Aiden said. "About eight years before Isaac and Callum started at Canderfey."

"You lived alone that long?"

Aiden's usual smile faded as he nodded, staring up at the house. "I didn't think it would be so long," he said. "I thought I'd start working and meet my coven and we would have a house ready." He looked down at me and said, "That was twenty years ago."

He looked up at the house as it seemed to grow larger the closer we stepped. I tried not to sink under the weight of the declaration. Twenty years of waiting, considering the possibilities. Twelve for Isaac and Callum. I didn't know a lot about covens, not expecting to ever find myself in one, but it was common knowledge that most people found theirs not long after coming of age. Aiden's expectations had been realistic if not a little eager. Twenty years was a long time.

His fingers were stroking the back of my hand and I knew he had said the words with good intentions, but they left me wondering again. Was I here because the wait was too long and I appeared at the right time, strange and unfamiliar?

"You're fretting, Joanna," Aiden said as we turned to the red brick tower house at the end of the street. It was at least four stories tall with something strange and unfamiliar in every window. Every window but the one at the center front.

"I am," I admitted, staring at Callum Pike stretched out in a window bench with a book in his lap. He looked up and jumped from his spot, the book landing with a flutter of pages on the cushion.

"Tonight is only dinner," He repeated, lifting my hand up to kiss at the knuckles. "And there's no majority vote on this. We'll respect any decision you make. But I may try to influence it for my own interests," he added, grin returning.

The front door swung in—an enormous, elaborate door with a stained glass window depicting a rich sunset landing with the stars and moon winking out at the top of the door frame—and Callum stood waiting for us on the step. He was dressed tidily in cool grays and blues, but his reddish hair was sticking out at odd angles like he'd be mussing and pulling at the strands.

"I...Isaac's been waiting," Callum said, and then he winced. Aiden snorted and gestured me ahead of him.

Callum moved out of the way at the last moment, busy blinking at me as I approached, but it was me that held us up at the head of the hallway as I stared down the length of it. Someone, probably Aiden, plucked the wrap off my shoulders and I let it slide away as I soaked in the vibrant jewel blue walls covered almost top to bottom in paintings and photographs.

"You'll have plenty of time to explore," Aiden said behind me.

"Don't lose my wine," I volleyed back, and he laughed. I started at the closest painting, as small as my hand and covered in bright red raspberries that sparkled sweetly on my tongue. I studied another of a small gray house surrounded by pine trees that eased away the tension in my shoulders. I made it as far as a thunderstorm, snapping wind and wet cooling my cheeks, ignoring Callum and Aiden behind me all the while, when Isaac appeared at the end of the hall. His shirt sleeves were rolled up and he had a towel thrown over his shoulder. His long hair was pulled back and trying to escape.

"Hello, love," he said, as I met him halfway. "I like your dress," he murmured in my ear as he leaned in to kiss me, brief and gentle. The heat returned to my cheeks.

"These aren't all yours," I said looking up at a portrait of a sour old man that, incongruously, made me want to laugh.

"No, only a few," he said.

"He likes to give *his* paintings better light to be seen by," Aiden said, passing us in the hall.

KATHRYN MOON

"It's part of my collection," Isaac said. "Will you help me in the kitchen?"

"Yes please," I said. I looked behind us, but Callum had already disappeared, probably back to his book in the window.

The kitchen was at the back of the house and it also left me stunned. I had never seen a kitchen this large. Tall, multi-paned windows let in all the evening sun. The stove was at the far side taking up most of the wall aside from a door leading to a greenhouse. There were pots hissing and steaming on the top of it and something glowing in the belly and someone had opened a window nearby to let the cool fall air in as relief against the heat.

"I mostly wanted some company," Isaac admitted as I stopped at a wall where racks of herbs hung to dry.

"Make me useful so I don't fidget," I said. He laughed and dug a spoon out of a pitcher full of utensils, passing it to me.

◦✺◦

DINNER WAS EASIER than I expected. Isaac's cooking was too good to ignore with lots of talking and when my words did dry up Aiden had plenty to say. The word 'coven' was never uttered. Callum disappeared after the dishes were cleared from the table and my gut twisted as I realized. He'd been across from me again during the meal and I'd caught him smiling and felt him watching. I'd wanted to believe that the stiffness was fading, but the avoidance was as clear as ever.

I was standing at the kitchen counter, tracing my finger around the rim of a wine glass when Aiden's hand landed on mine, still damp from washing dishes in the sink.

"Go find him," he said.

"He's *supposed* to be drying," Isaac said, glaring down at the plate he was toweling off.

"I don't want to force this," I said.

"Just nudge a little," Aiden said. "He'll be holed up in his office on the third floor, 'researching,'" and he said the last word with a sarcastic wiggle of his eyebrows.

"Tell him to quit being an ass," Isaac added.

Aiden took advantage of the distraction and my laughter to

duck down and press a kiss below my ear that brought goose-bumps out along my neck. "Go on, you'll both feel better. Second door on the left."

The stairs were at the heart of the house, a round flight that twisted up with dark wood steps and glossy sage green paper and yellowy lamps glowing. I hurried up to the third story to a harvest yellow hallway. There were two closed doors on the right end and three open doors on the left.

The first was a bathroom with bright green and sparkling white tiles that looked cleaner than my own and had a tub big enough for me to go swimming in. The second doorway revealed a bright room with a massive bed, unmade with white sheets printed with charcoal smudges. Isaac's room. The last was an office that looked more like a library. Callum had his back to me, bent over a desk at the far end of the room in front of a window, but I was busy staring at the full walls of bookshelves, bursting with pages. They were stuffed into every available inch, stacked in front of and top of each other like it was a puzzle to see all the different ways they might fit together.

I forgot about knocking completely and walked in without an invitation. "How do you keep track of them all?" I asked, going to a bursting shelf and seeing no rhyme or reason to the arrangement.

There was a clatter at the window and when I looked over Callum was half out of his chair, it tilted dangerously on the back two legs.

"I'm sorry," we said together at the same time. But at least he smiled at me in the pause that followed.

"I don't," he said. "But I usually...I have a charm for getting the book I need to pop out."

"Do you have a charm for making the shelves bigger too?" I asked counting the shelves up to the ceiling and realizing that they didn't make sense in terms of the size of the room.

"Sort of," he admitted, standing and putting the chair back to rights. "Don't tell Aiden, he's fussy about not stretching the house."

"He hasn't noticed?"

Callum shook his head. He took small steps to approach me,

as if he was afraid of making me run. Maybe Aiden had been right.

"He has his own office and... You're very observant with magic," he added.

We stared at each other for a quiet moment until I'd managed to steel my nerves.

"Do you want me to leave?" I asked.

He looked around the room, brow furrowing and half shrugged. "I don't mind you being here."

I bit my lip and debated leaving it at that. But I needed to know before I enjoyed the evening any more than I already had, before I found any more beautiful places in the house that made me crave spending time here.

"Do you want me to leave the house, now?" I said. "I can tell Aiden and Isaac that this isn't-"

"What? No!" He rushed forward, eyes wide and nervous.

"If I am here for them and you really aren't...you don't want me..." I tried to dig the words out, but they jammed in my throat.

"Joanna, it isn't that at all," he said, and his own voice was tight. "I sent you running in the library, I don't want to make another mistake like that. Aiden would have my head."

I looked down at the floor at the reminder of what my being here meant to Aiden and what that must mean to Callum.

"It isn't about him either," Callum said, quiet and close.

"The library wasn't your fault," I said, looking up. "I had spent so much time trying not to think of any of you this way, and I had a very strict list of why it was impossible."

"It's not," he said firmly.

But I could see the battle in him, the strain in his muscles. Only this time I knew what he was resisting. And maybe I could fix it by telling him that he wasn't going to scare me off or set me running again, but there was an easier solution than that too.

I rose up on my toes, hands braced behind me on the edge of a bookshelf. I brushed my cheek against his beard, kissing at the bare jaw just past the coarse hair while his head ducked lower. A sigh stroked along the skin of my neck and we held still for a breath together. His hands wrapped around my waist as my mouth searched out his and with the first stroke of the kiss, he pulled me tight against him. I gasped, lips parting and Callum was there filling in the spaces.

I released the bookshelf behind me to hold onto his shoulders as my toes scraped against the floor. He groaned as my fingers tightened and the sound vibrated against me, under my hands and into the kiss. Teeth dragged over lips and tongues followed to soothe, and with every quick clamor for breath we wrapped up tighter in each other's arms. My heart was pounding and the beat was echoing in my blood and down into my stomach and sinking lower still until I was twisting in his hold trying to find friction.

My back hit the bookshelf behind us and Callum's fingers dug into my hips as I stepped wider to make room for him against me. I was surrounded by him, my head tipped back and eyes squeezed shut as his mouth pressed wet kisses down to my jaw, nipping at my throat. I whimpered and his thumbs circled over my hip bones as he shifted closer. I could feel him against me, stirring hard and as restless as every inch of my skin was feeling.

"Glad you two talked."

I jumped at the intrusion and tried to scramble away, but Callum just straightened slowly and soothed his hands up my spine.

Aiden was grinning at us from the doorway, eyes sparkling as he bit his lip. He looked as if he *hadn't* just dined on a beautiful meal, but was now staring at one. Callum was still stroking at my back, settling my surprise and embarrassment. I looked up and found his face relaxed, with a small smile nearly hidden at the corners. But I didn't doubt that Aiden could spot it as well as I could.

"Are we expected downstairs?" Callum asked as I tucked my heated face against his chest.

"Well, you were, but I can make excuses," Aiden hedged, a laugh at the back of his voice.

"Give us a few minutes, Aide," Callum murmured, fingertips drumming softly at my back.

I heard the floorboards creak—and why couldn't I have heard

them *before* being caught—and Callum pulled back slightly so he could look down at my face.

"Are you alright?" he asked.

I opened my mouth to joke and then swallowed the words, not wanting to interrupt the tenuous affection of the moment.

"Not used to being caught by anyone other than the town gossip," I said after a beat.

Callum's smile stretched wide for the first time I had seen in a week. "You still haven't," he said.

I laughed, head falling back and he took advantage. Ducking down and kissing at my throat, by my ear, his nose nuzzling until my laughter skidded away. I ended up back against the bookshelf again, but the kisses were slow and sweetly lazy instead of building. Callum's hair was rumpled from my fingers when we eased apart, and I left it that way to make Aiden and Isaac smile.

We turned down the stairs hand in hand and Callum led me midway down the hall to a rosy orange room where Aiden was seated at a massive, glossy, black piano. The music was airy, skipping and trilling, and I watched his hands for a moment wondering how hands so large could play so lightly. Isaac was sitting cross-legged with a sketchbook in his lap, in the middle of a long brown couch. Callum joined him, leaving a gap between them just large enough for me. They were ready as I approached, Callum twisting and reaching out to settle me against his chest and Isaac, dimples sharp in his smile, pulling my legs up to drape over his. Aiden's playing deepened and all the nervous tension in me fled away.

I would let myself enjoy this, this impossible thing, for the evening at least.

CHAPTER 15
JOANNA

"WE REALLY SHOULDN'T BE DOING THIS," I WHISPERED. BUT I didn't get up from Isaac's lap, tucked away together in a corner of the staff library, and I didn't pull my arms from around his neck.

The coven had found ways of keeping me company for over a week now; bumping into me on campus or appearing in the library in the evening to walk me home. Isaac was especially good at finding excuses. I was especially good at playing along with them.

"I could argue," he said, trailing kisses up the side of my jaw before continuing, "that you shouldn't be loitering in the library so late."

"I've got a better reason than you," I said, grinning and tapping my forehead to his.

"You *had* a better reason. Now you're canoodling. Woollard hates canoodlers." And then he kissed me, fingers digging into the short hair at the back of my neck. I swallowed my groan and wondered how easy it would be to get a massage from Isaac. Probably very.

"I caught Woollard canoodling last week," I whispered against Isaac's lips and he pulled away, eyes wide with surprise. "She and Bryce were having lunch together in the lounge."

"You're on first name terms with Gast too?" he asked, eyebrows raising.

"We didn't speak much, but I had dinner with the coven a couple of weeks ago."

Isaac swallowed, leaning back, his head thunking against the wall.

"What?" I asked, and bent to kiss the corded muscle at the side of his throat.

"They may as well have offered you an invitation into their coven," he said.

I made a rude sound and rolled my eyes. "They already have a finished coven."

"That doesn't mean you couldn't have a place in it if you wanted," Isaac said. His smile quirked at the corner and his arms wrapped tighter around my back as I mulled it over. I suppose I had heard of a coven of more than four, although generally only in stories. "They're a better offer than we are," he said watching my face. But he didn't look nervous as I glared down at him.

"I think Gwen was just being friendly," I said. "They all were. Even Bryce, who terrifies me."

"Bryce terrifies everyone but their own coven," Isaac said. "*Gwen* terrifies everyone but her own coven for that matter. I'll warn Aiden and Callum of our competition."

"Don't you dare," I said, bending and nipping at his chin until he was grinning. "Aiden will take it as an excuse to come around here and start harassing Gwen...and *me*."

Isaac laughed beneath me, stretching up for a smooth, pulling kiss that was sure to lead to another...

And then the library *CRACKED!* all around us, one enormous groan of wood and screech of glass and iron.

The lamps went out with a spitting noise and an electric burn in the air. Isaac jumped up, arms like a vice around me, and twisted us so I was behind him. He seemed to grow, shoulders broadening and back tightening and I stood on my tiptoes to see, but the library was shadowy beyond us. Isaac's hand sought mine behind his back and I gripped it tight, holding my breath in the following silence.

"Do you want to stay-?" he started.

"With you," I said.

The air turned muggy and warm around us as if a thick

coating of mist had crawled over shelves and risen up from the floor. It was cloying and dusty in my mouth, like candy left out too long to the air and it scratched down my throat as I swallowed. Below us the library took a collective gasp, every book seeming to shudder on its shelf and a great moaning came from dozens of voices like a chorus.

"Students," I whispered, and my heart was rattling in my chest like a wild animal.

Isaac's hand squeezed mine and I guided him forward through the weave of shelves to the dark stairs. We were running down the flight, just reaching the landing, when a terrorized scream whipped through the air. The sweet fog was sliced and the sound cut at my ears and Isaac stopped in his tracks, pressing me back against the wall. My free hand gripped at my skirt and I felt the chalk stick waiting in my pocket, a thought clamoring forward.

Isaac released my hand, turning, and took my face clumsily in his hold. A kiss landed high on my cheek, over the bridge of my nose, and then hard against my lips.

"Stay here, go back upstairs, climb out the window," he rushed, the words as quiet as he could make them. "I'm going down, but I need you to get out, alright? Get help, but get out safely, Joanna."

A part of me wanted to protest, but the other part was slipping my hand into my pocket, a plan racing to piece itself together.

"Be careful," I whispered.

"Callum will be on his way," Isaac said as if it were a promise of rescue.

And then he let go of me and in four steps he was lost in shadow. I didn't run. I crouched down to the ground, feeling at the floor for the edge of the stair carpeting, for the stretch of clean wooden floorboards. I pulled the chalk from my pocket and it almost glowed in my hand, pure and white. There was another scream from downstairs, another cracking groan of wood and the floor shook against my knees. I set the chalk to the wood grain, squinting to try and see in the dark.

THE LIBRARY I scratched out in blocky, jagged letters, and then the glass roof in the lobby screeched, plates grinding together, and there was a high sprinkling sound. My arms ached and the chalk slipped in my fingers and my breath was short as if writing the words cost me physical effort. *IS* came with my vision spinning in front of me.

"Joanna!" Callum's voice, deeper and harsher, came ringing out from the heart of the library.

"Callum. Here, quickly!" I heard Isaac's voice and let my eyes fall shut with relief. I forced my hand to shape the *A* on the wood, messy and crooked but solid. A headache like an axe split through my skull and I found myself breathing through my teeth, ignoring the shouting from downstairs.

For every letter I managed another symptom rose up, my skin breaking into a thin sweat or my stomach cramping or the walls seemed to bend forward to crush me. *SAFE* looked like a child who was only just learning their letters had written it. I got as far as *PLA-* and then I was on the floor on my side with my hand as hot as flames, fingers twitching and burning where I squeezed the chalk. I twisted out a *C* with tears streaking out of my eyes and the shouts from the lobby banging like the beat of drums in my ears. But with the last four scratches of chalk on the floor everything released like a great pop of pressure.

The front doors banged and the walls and floor rattled in response, shallow and harmless now. The lamps flickered back to life, dim but warm and yellow. I could hear the sobs of students downstairs as my head cleared; still throbbing, but at least not feeling *stabbed* at every second. The floorboards rattled again, now with a clamor of steps running up the stairs, familiar voices echoing with my name in the mix.

I pushed myself up to sitting, my arms wobbling and my breath short, with the white words scribbled on the floor at my side.

THE LIBRARY IS A SAFE PLACE

Isaac and Callum came skidding and tripping around the corner of the staircase and Callum grabbed at the other man by the scruff of his neck before he crashed to the floor, right into my work.

"Don't mar the words," Callum barked, all the edges of his

face sharpened into something ferocious and unfamiliar to me. He looked up the steps where Isaac and I had come from, eyes narrowed as he held still for a long moment.

Isaac landed at my other side, arms pulling me in by my shoulders and tucking my face under his chin. He smelled like ash and copper.

"Witch," he murmured into my hair, turning the word into something reverent.

Warm hands wrapped over the tops of my knees and I shifted, Isaac loosening his hold, so I could see Callum kneeling in front of me.

His gaze was sharp on my face, studying me in fast flicks of his eyes. "Are you alright?" he asked.

"It's-" my voice scratched and I swallowed, mouth dry, before trying again. "It's never hurt before to write. Did it...was that happening to you too?"

Isaac's hands were soothing my hair away from my face, his nose pressed to my temple, as Callum stared back at me.

"Some," he said, and the strain in him eased as he rested in front of me. "It would have targeted you when it felt the spell start."

"I asked you to run," Isaac said, tipping my chin up to see the worry digging lines across his forehead and between his eyebrows, jaw ticking with tension.

"This is big magic," Callum said more to himself than to us. "That may have contributed to the strain."

"It's my library, and I had an idea," I said to Isaac, and then looked to Callum to ask, "Is it a ward?"

Callum shook his head, staring at the words. His fingers were tracing circles over my knees, drawing up a sweeter trembling feeling in my skin. "Wards can't kick something out once it's already in. Although it will act as one now as long as it isn't erased. Can you stand?"

As soon as I moved, they were lifting me up. My legs felt shaky and weak, but I was fairly sure that if Isaac took his arm from my waist I would stay standing. Not that he seemed about to.

"I can manage," I said. "What happened downstairs? Was anyone hurt?"

Their faces were grim and Isaac looked away, swallowing and paling almost to green.

"I'm going back down to take care of it," Callum said. "Isaac will take you home."

He lifted his hand from my elbow up to the back of my neck, bending to kiss my cheekbone and then lingering there as I argued. "I'm staying to help, there's going to be...sweeping. Or something. I heard glass breaking and..." I swallowed, thinking of their faces and what they hadn't said. Someone *was* hurt. "I want to help," I added, quietly.

"You've helped," Isaac said. "And you're exhausted."

"I'm *not*."

"You're aching," Callum said, hand sliding down to my back and leading us to the steps. "And still shaking."

"Alright, *listen*—" I started. There was a hiccup in my voice but I was ready to have this fight.

But then Aiden came thundering up the steps, the whites of his eyes wide and his warm dark skin turned gray. He had me scooped up in his arms before the others had time to let go of me. And then he was pulling Callum and Isaac in by their shirts too until I was smashed between the three of them in an embrace. The knot in my throat released and tears spilled out of my eyes. I pressed them into Aiden's shirt.

"They said a librarian had been killed," Aiden croaked from above.

"*What?*" I asked, squirming. I found Isaac's eyes, as wet as mine and still creased with worry. "...Who?"

"Cecil Pincombe," Callum said, voice nearly muted against my hair.

My stomach turned and now I was sure my legs would not work.

"When we get downstairs, don't look," Callum told me. "Keep your eyes down until you get outside."

I opened my mouth to answer, but I couldn't think of a word.

"Woollard arrived. Gast is outside, guarding," Aiden said. "They've gotten the students out and to medical."

"Gwen," I whispered, although I wasn't sure that anyone heard me. I was set back on my toes, but I didn't feel them beneath me and between Aiden and Isaac they had such a tight hold on me, it didn't matter. Callum stopped at the bottom of the steps.

"I'm warding the stairs until Gwen can do something to preserve your words," he said. His hands framed my face and his head bent, filling my liquid gaze as he pressed a long kiss to the center of my forehead. "You saved us," he whispered.

Not Cecil Pincombe, I thought. Callum's words felt like a bad joke.

And then I saw Gwen, over Isaac's shoulder, standing in front of the library doors and looking half lost. There was an explosion of charred books at her feet, mixed with wood and glass shards. Overhead, most of winter and part of spring had been torn out of the stained glass ceiling. I tugged my way out of Isaac and Aiden's hold and rushed across the tile to her.

I saw it out of the corner of my eye. Just a piece, unrecogniz-able and bloodied, near the circulation desk—now a shattered, torn thing, raw wood exposed and smoking like coals. And in the midst of it, what Callum didn't want me seeing. Smeared like waste at the belly of the room.

I fixed my eyes to Gwen and she turned at my approach, overturned and scorched bookshelves all around us. The other two night-staff were standing behind one, out of sight of the circulation desk, arms around each other as the younger woman cried.

Gwen stared at me as if she didn't recognize me. But then she blinked and said, "I told you there's no good in staying after your shift."

I paused in place at that, hearing footsteps catch up to me, and Gwen covered her face with her hand and shook her head.

"Excuse me," she whispered, and twisted herself toward me, turning away from the giant wound in the library. "I'm glad you're safe."

"What can I do to help?" I asked.

"Joanna, you need to rest," Isaac said, arriving behind me.

"He's right," Gwen said, taking my hand to squeeze it. "I'll need my staff tomorrow morning. Tonight I need him," and she pointed past us all to where Callum was striding across the tile, head up and shoulders straight. He looked ready for battle and I wondered how well he knew his subject. He was too young to have served in the war, but if he'd been in an army...

"I want your best wards, Pike," Gwen growled.

"You have better now," he said. "Joanna wrote on the floorboards. That's why the library is still standing."

Gwen reeled back for a moment before falling forward, small arms snaking around my shoulders. My poor bones ground together in her grip, but I was grateful for the hug all the same.

"Oh, you silly girl," she muttered in my ear. She released me before I could answer, smoothing at her skirts and lifting her chin. "Hildy should be able to fix it to the building. Joanna, go home and rest. I've got plans for you in the morning."

My objections faded with the exhaustion that was building like a brick wall in my body. I wobbled and Isaac was behind me.

"Walk with them to the house and then come back?" Callum asked Aiden.

"Bryce can walk them home and then fetch Hildy," Gwen said. "I need your help now before more faculty arrives."

No one argued with Gwen. Callum's hand brushed at my back, leaving a tingling warmth before he was striding over to where the rest of us refused to look. Aiden pulled me into another bone-crushing hug and I took a deep breath of him, and then Isaac was pulling me outside.

Bryce was pacing the grounds in front of the library like an overgrown wildcat and froze as we approached. Isaac spoke to them as I swayed in place and then we were all walking. Or Bryce and Isaac were walking and I was floating along despite feeling like a lead weight.

"Did Callum charm me?" I mumbled to Isaac, and he pulled me into his side.

His hand spread out over my back and he hummed. "He has a tendency to do that."

"I think it's all that's keeping me upright at this point," I said. Although the cold air kept my eyes open at least.

"I was going to carry you, but I thought you might be mad,"

Isaac whispered and then, even quieter, added, "Bryce would do it if you asked."

I snorted and it turned into a cracking, panicked laugh. Isaac squeezed me and Bryce glanced over their shoulder at us.

"We're going the wrong way," I said, suddenly realizing we were walking in the opposite direction as the campus staff houses.

"Sorry," Isaac said. "But Callum would have a fit if you weren't with us tonight...we all would, really. We have a guest room you can use. And the four of us won't fit in that little house."

Thinking on it, I didn't really want to be alone in my house either. And their home had felt warm and beautiful and magical and safe. "I want to use that massive bath of yours," I said as we got close to the house.

Isaac's lips brushed my temple. "That can be arranged."

Bryce took a deep sniff of the air as we reached the house, back tight for a long moment, their lips parted slightly. Then they relaxed, turning to us and nodding.

"Thank you, Gast," Isaac said. Bryce passed him with a sideways glance and then stepped up to me and left a dry hot kiss on my cheek. There was a funny smell in the air as they left and Isaac pulled me inside.

"What is Bryce?" I whispered as the door closed behind us.

Isaac grinned, weary but bright, and looked at me. "Would you believe me if I said a dragon?"

"Yes," I said.

He chuckled and shrugged. "It's only a rumor, but I believe it too."

We were smiling at one another and then my chin was wobbling and my eyes were stinging. Isaac's smile sagged and I was folded up in his arms with my hands clutching at his back.

"What was it? In the library?" I whispered against the skin of his neck where I pressed my face and the tears that were spilling.

"We don't know yet," he rasped. "Callum's been tracking it, but this was...it's bigger than he thought. We'll figure it out. Everything will be okay."

Except that someone had already been killed.

CHAPTER 16
JOANNA

IT OCCURRED TO ME, WATCHING ISAAC FUSS WITH THE FAUCETS of the tub—his shirtsleeves rolled up to his elbows—that I'd never seen him look nervous before. He was fidgeting and his knee was jiggling and he hadn't looked me in the eye since we'd walked into the bathroom. I was too tired to be nervous or self-conscious, and still too shaken to be alone. We had stood together in the entrance for a long time before he'd remembered my request for a bath.

When Isaac cleared his throat for the third time, sitting on the edge of the tub, I started to unbutton my blouse.

"Will you join me?" I asked, deciding I could settle the matter.

He looked up from the water filling the tub and blinked at me, and then at the peek of my plain gray slip.

"Are you sure?" he asked, rising.

"Yes," I said, tugging my arms free of my sleeves. I winced at the smell of my clothes, the sour sweat and bitter burn of the events of the library.

He crossed the tile as I left my shirt on their sink counter. His hands folded around my bare shoulders and I sighed at the touch as he bent and kissed the skin next to his thumb. "I don't want you out of my sight," he said, almost a whisper with the roar of water behind him. "But if it's pushing or..."

98

"I'm asking you, Isaac," I said raising my hands to wrap my fingers around his wrists. "I want you here with me."

He lifted his head and we were kissing, something between comfort and desire. I found the buttons of his shirt with my fingers, which were still shaking, and his hands circled the waistband of my skirt, content to hold me there for a long moment before releasing the zipper. Our lips parted and we watched each other as we finished, him shrugging out of his shirt and letting his pants fall to the floor as I pushed the straps of the slip off my shoulders and tugged it down my waist.

Isaac was built like the men at home, with wide shoulders for tossing hay bales in the wagon and narrow hips to suit their wives' tastes. But he was refined too, as if he had studied the chiseled statues of men in art and become one himself. His eyes were pale as they tracked the path of the slip down to the tile and then traveled up again, slower, to my face. He was wearing a faint smile and nothing else and I mimicked him. Studying the cut lines of his stomach, the dark hair between his legs, and the length of him stirring there. His legs were lean and strong and I imagined fitting him between mine, the way we might twist together.

"Come here, love," he said, words rasping like a touch on my skin.

It was only a step or two and then he was warm against me, our stomachs and chests brushing together and my breasts aching at the contact. Our gazes locked, noses bumping and I twined my arms over his shoulder. His hands spanned my back and traveled down to my waist and then over the swell of my ass, cupping underneath. I could feel him growing against me at the same lazy pace of his smile.

"The tub will overflow," I said. There was a dull ache left lingering at the back of my head, and now a pleasanter one growing in my belly.

Isaac's smile stretched and quirked, and then he lifted me up in his hands and carried me over to the tub. I bent my legs up as he climbed in, and we both hissed at the heat of the water before sinking down, letting it flush our skin. Isaac stretched a leg out in front of us and switched the water off with his toes as I settled at his side. The heat and steam clung sticky but warm enough to burn away some of the fog in my head.

"I can't tell if I've just been seduced or vice versa," Isaac murmured, scattering kisses over my nose and forehead.

"Haven't even gotten that far," I said, and he made a small choking sound in surprise.

I turned in the water, stretching my legs out to bob behind me, and studied the planes of Isaac's stomach and chest with my fingertips and the line of his jaw with my teeth and lips. He gave me a moment's head start before gripping at my hips to guide me over him, then pushed my knees apart with his. His hands skirted the backs of my thighs, traced a line behind my knees that had me squirming closer, my breasts resting just below his chin and the sensitive skin of my sex teased against the narrow trail of hair leading down from his belly.

His head was resting back against the rim of the tub, eyes closed and teeth gleaming in a narrow smile as I scratched the back of his neck and tried to soothe the growing itch in my skin with small shifts of my hips. As if I could find the satisfaction and keep it secret from him. He nuzzled his face down into my wet skin, nosing at the arch of my breasts while his palms squeezed me closer, right below my ass

Just as I thought I might start to beg for more, his lips parted and his mouth latched onto my breast above a nipple. The pull drew deep into my skin and down into my belly, making me throb and cry out while his hand slid forward, fingers teasing where I wanted them most. I tugged at his hair in response and he released me, a red mark blooming on my skin where his mouth had been.

"That's better," I said, looking down at him, as he set his chin on my breast bone to gaze up.

"What would help?" he asked, hand cupped between my legs and fingers pressing in softly against my folds.

"More," I managed, ducking down to swallow his laugh.

There *was* more but at an idling pace as we floated in the tub, hands and lips mapping a terrain of touch, guided by hitched breaths and hums of pleasure. Isaac's hands traveled more than I wanted them to, always returning back to my core to build me up and then move on again before they had finished their work. I repaid him in kind, but he seemed too patient, too happy to be turned weak and moaning at my explorative touches and then denied again.

"You're teasing," I said, panting slightly. Isaac had me arched back over the edge of the tub, tracing his tongue below my breast and across a rib as his thumbs stroked right at the inside edges of my hips. The pressure was beautifully stirring and yet nowhere near enough to satiate me.

"Tell me to stop," he said, and I could hear the grin in his voice. He rose up on his knees, his cock brushing between my legs where I wanted him and our stomachs sticking together.

I braced myself up on my elbows and we stared at one another for a long moment. His lips had just started to twitch, and he was about to pull away when I called the game to an end.

"No more teasing," I said.

His eyes darkened and then he was pulling me up out of the water and out to the bath mat. "Do you want to see your room or mine across the hall?" he asked.

Guest room, I thought, correcting him. But I busied myself by fitting closer against him, nipping up his throat to his ear and feeling him groan against me. A warm towel wrapped around us both, doing a perfunctory job of drying away the water, and then he had me scooped up in his arms.

"Closest," I managed, still tasting his skin.

The hall was cool and we were half laughing as he crossed it in a great rush. A door swung shut behind him and then my back was on a soft mattress and I was pulling him down with me, our bodies pressing heavier together without the buoy of the water around us. His skin was hot on mine and his kiss was deep, tongue seeking and stroking and licking. My legs were hanging off the bed and my hips were arching up, nudging and begging against his.

"Joanna," he groaned, and an arm burrowed beneath my back to hold me tight against him. His pelvis pressed to mine and my head fell back with a sigh, relief and need pooling together at the pressure. "We should slow..." he started, mouth panting wet breath against my neck.

"Not for my sake," I whispered. He chuckled, but his back shook under my hands for a long time after the sound.

The library, I thought, and I placed a hand between us and pushed him back. His face was dry, but the lines were deep on his forehead.

"We're safe," I whispered.

His breath came out unevenly and he pressed back down, lips just barely set to mine. "I want you to remember what you did tonight the next time you're thinking you don't belong with us," he whispered. "We would not have made it out of the library without you."

I didn't think that could be true and I wondered what he had seen. What the destruction I had seen the end of had looked like in action. I was ready to pull him down to my side, to curl up together and let the night be made of up of a different kind of closeness, when his fingers found my center again, one digit dipping in while his thumb swirled over my clit.

"Is this better?" he asked, pushing up on his free hand to look down between us to where he was touching.

My breath caught in my throat as I tried to answer him.

"I need you," he said, and when my head rolled to the side he pressed a kiss at the corner of my jaw by my ear. "If you'll have me."

I laughed at that, turning my face back and pulling him down to me, sucking at his bottom lip and fumbling a hand between us to wrap around his cock. My hips were rolling into his touches, a fluttering heat building in my core and spreading out like waves lapping under my skin. His mouth traveled down my neck, pausing at my pulse and groaning into my throat as I squeezed and slid my hand over him.

I'd had lovers growing up, but they'd been brief relationships with couplings to match—sweet but often bumbling and awkward too. Isaac pressed a second finger inside me, crooking them gently and the stretch and angle was better than anything anyone had tried before.

"I-Isaac, *yes.*" My legs stretched wider, feet bracing at the edge of the bed and Isaac's thumb swirled again as his head ducked down and his lips wrapped around my nipple.

With a pull of his mouth and a deep stroke of his fingers, my body was turning loose and tight all at once, my mouth falling open and broken words falling free. The tug at my breast vibrated with Isaac's hum, the rhythm matching the pump and twist of his fingers, the circling pressure of his thumb, all of it a rising pulse building in my bloodstream. I was rocking into his hand, begging without instruction. When Isaac pulled back, his teeth scraping at too sensitive skin, and the pressure broke apart. My fingers clutched at the sheets and my voice cracked and a spiraling flying feeling flooded through me.

Isaac's fingers pulled away before I wanted them to and then he was pushing in, smooth and deep, while I was still flying from the high of bliss. My feet lifted and wrapped around his back to hold him tight and still against me, studying the full feeling as I adjusted to the gentle burn of him inside me. The hair at his groin brushed against my swollen clit and I whimpered as he ducked down, kissing at my closed lips.

"Beautiful," he murmured, and his arms framed my shoulders, fingers digging into my curls.

My skin was still at a simmer, limbs soft and relaxed and I loosened the grip of my legs around his hips. I skimmed my fingernails up his back, scratching lightly and hiccuping a moan as he shifted deeper.

"Your turn," I said, kissing at his chin.

His eyes narrowed and a smirk curled at the corners of his mouth at that but instead of speaking, he sipped at my lips. His hips rocked in shallow, soft thrusts that stirred the remains of my orgasm. My thighs squeezed and I rolled in closer, trying to stir him into action but he only kept his pace and alternated slow teasing kisses with pulling away to nuzzle and watch my face.

"What are you thinking?" I asked, grinning and sliding my hands to clutch at his ass and try and gain control.

He grinned back. "You've had very lazy lovers," he said.

Which was true, I supposed. And with little spikes of heat growing in the stretch and push of where we were joined I could guess his aim.

"What if I wanted to watch you fall apart this time?" I asked. I scratched up his spine again, a little harder, and noted the way his hips kicked in response. But he was watching my face and caught the flash of aching pleasure that snap sent reeling through me.

"Trust me, love," he said, breathless and half-laughing. "You will."

He drew back farther that time, thrusting in deep and quick. My back arched and my eyes slammed shut and there was something like a chuckle or a groan from him. One hand slid down from my hair to the base of my spine and he lifted me there, holding me just so, every push landing his hips against me. I could feel the head of his cock high inside me, tapping at a spot that left stars in my eyes and my brain turning to liquid.

"Isaac," I said without meaning to, voice high and pleading.

"Does it feel good?" he asked, and at least he sounded strained too.

"Please don't stop. Please."

He hummed and then his other hand came down to my hip, fingers fitting between us just so. Not teasing or scraping but only pressing.

"I would do anything you asked, Joanna," he whispered in my ear and I moaned. "Especially that."

I couldn't answer, the feeling inside of me was deeper and tighter than before and it stifled any thinking but the need to hold tight to Isaac. My fingers dug into his shoulder and my legs crossed at his back even as he plunged with longer, deeper thrusts. I was cresting higher, but I could not break, only cling and I didn't have the words to beg for relief. Isaac was pouring sweetness into my ears, praises that were turning into pleads as his strokes broke rhythm. His fingers rubbed, gentle and quick, between my legs and I shattered.

He kept his promise. My eyes opened as I came down, feeling melted and made up of sparks of stirring satisfaction. Isaac was arching above me, a shout on his lips as he buried himself deep, a burst of heat in my belly. His forehead was knotted but his eyes stayed open and fixed to my face, gaze dizzy and sweet, throat bobbing as he swallowed. His forehead dropped to mine as he sagged, the weight and heat of him a comfort for the moment. I kissed his cheek and the corner of his mouth.

"Are you alright?" he asked.

I giggled and pressed a hand over my mouth as he opened one eye to check on me. "Seems like a silly question," I said. I wasn't sure I'd ever felt better. Drowsy and a little sticky with sweat, but practically incandescent.

He rolled us, taking me against his side and pulling us up to the head of the bed. I hummed with the aftershocks. His arms wrapped around me and he peppered kisses over the shoulder resting on his chest.

"You'll stay with me, like this?" he asked.

I blinked my eyes open. His were shut, his face relaxed and tilted to me. I stretched up for a kiss and his lips pursed back.

"I'm not going anywhere," I said, and then added, "I don't think I can walk."

"Sore?" he asked, brow furrowing.

"Turned to jelly."

His smile burst forth and his eyes opened at that. "Aiden and Callum will probably check on us when they make it back."

I hummed and snuggled into his chest.

"They might crawl into the bed," he added.

I thought that over for half a minute, but my clothes were too far away to worry about modesty and I was too tired to really care. Isaac twitched the covers over us and then nothing mattered.

When I stirred in the night there was a dark arm stretched over Isaac's stomach, warm hand resting on my waist, and a lean body pressed up the length of my back. Callum was snoring softly into my shoulder, arm wrapped over my lower belly. He and Aiden smelled clean and they were safe and I had never felt more comfortable sleeping next to someone, let alone plural.

CHAPTER 17

JOANNA

I woke up to the door creaking open and sat up with a start. The bed was empty around me and a bleary glance out the window revealed the sky, pink with morning. Isaac stood in the doorway, a tray of food and coffee in his hands.

"Wha' time is it?" I rasped. I stretched under the sheets and smiled at the gentle ache still left from the night before.

He came in, setting the tray on the bed and laughing as I scooped the coffee cup up straight away. "You've got almost an hour before you need to be at the library," he said.

"Where's Callum and Aiden?" I asked, squinting at the dent in the pillow to my right. I was sure they had been there at some point.

"They cleared out a bit ago," Isaac said. "To get ready and... and we weren't sure how you would feel, given..."

"Given I was sex dizzy last night?" I asked, smirking behind the cup as Isaac's eyes flashed for a brief moment, scanning over my bare chest.

"Yes." He scooted forward, bracing his arms on either side of my waist and leaning in, kissing at one shoulder and then the other. "We don't want to rush you."

"I don't want to be rushed. But I didn't mind them joining us to sleep." At Isaac's beaming smile, I added, "And if you hand me that shirt I wouldn't mind a kiss good morning from them."

Isaac grabbed a white dress shirt from the foot of the bed, and I pulled it on over my head, the shoulders hanging loose. I guessed it was probably Callum's if the length of the sleeves was any clue, and I rolled the cuffs up three times. As if Isaac had called for them, Aiden peeked his head in through the cracked door.

"Hello, you," he said. He looked exhausted and his gaze was less playful and more relieved as if he'd needed the reassurance of seeing me again.

I reached a hand out for him and he glanced back into the hall and then came to me. He took my hand and I had to tilt my head far back to catch his kiss on my lips.

"Morning," I said, looking up and searching his face.

He smiled, an attempt at cheer, but there was stress in the lines at the corners of his eyes. "Any chance of convincing you to take the day off with me?" he asked.

"No." My lips twitched in a smile and his followed, even as he rumbled in his chest.

"Worth a shot," he said, sighing and pecking at my lips again.

Aiden stepped back and Callum was hovering in the doorway.

"Thank you for the shirt," I said.

He looked at me, some combination of interest and wariness and hunger until I could feel the heat in my cheeks. "Anytime. I'm heading out early to scout the campus. I'll see you later?"

I nodded, chewing at the inside of my lip. I wanted to jump out of the bed and pull Callum back to join me. But he was already disappearing down the hall.

"Before you go getting any ideas about what he's thinking, he practically arm-wrestled me to crawl in beside you last night," Aiden said, a hand reaching down to squeeze at my shoulder.

"Eat up," Isaac said, nudging at my knee under the blankets. "We'll walk you to the library."

❦

FOR THE FIRST TIME, I walked into the library that morning and it was truly *silent*. I stopped as the doors swung shut behind me, and stared at the wreckage. It looked worse by the light some-how, the destruction stark and clear. They had done a thorough job of cleaning the night before—the air was sharp with it—and all the dust and shards were swept away. The desk was in pieces with bared teeth, jagged wooden spikes where it had been shat-tered. I had done my best the night before *not* to see what the scene really looked like, but either I had failed or I had too vivid an imagination. I turned my face up, trying to avoid my grue-some vision, and saw the gaping maw of the broken ceiling. The sky was visible through the tear, and magic shimmered like a temporary pane of glass.

"Oh!" The voice was soft. I looked to my left and Alice Batting, another clerk and a recent graduate was standing between two shelves that had been pushed upright again. She stared at me with wide eyes and then glanced at the desk with me.

All at once, she was flying across the room. My heart thudded in my chest and then I had a set of arms wrapped around mine, pinning them to my sides, and a puff of white-blonde hair in my face. Alice was crying into my shirt—Callum's shirt—and squeezing me tighter with every breath. I searched the balconies for a rescue and found my coworkers peeking out from shelves and...smiling.

The doors swung open behind us and I twisted in Alice's grasp.

"Oh, alright Batting," Gwen said. "Back to work."

Alice released me with a watery smile and then dashed back to the stacks. I stared at Gwen, baffled. She had dark circles under her eyes and her dress was wrinkled and stained, but her hawkish gaze was sharp as she looked back at me. Hildy was at her side although I almost hadn't recognized her without her finery. But she looked ready to work and there was a group of men bringing in a cartload of wood behind her.

"You don't look well-rested," Gwen said to me.

I ignored my blush rising. I may not have gotten a lot of sleep, but it was *good* sleep. I had no complaints.

"I'm fine, do you know why...?" Why Alice had hugged me

when we'd barely spoken before? Why the others were still watching me?

"They know what you did last night," Gwen said, and we backed away to give the workers room to move. "You'll have to put up with everyone liking you now."

"Nicely done, darling," Hildy said, greeting me with a kiss to the cheek and a muted smile.

Tatsuo and Bryce were bringing up the rear and Gwen nodded them in our direction. Tatsuo and I hugged while Bryce sniffed at my collar and grinned toothily at me.

"What needs doing?" I asked Gwen.

"Plenty, but I have something specific I'd like to see if you can help with." She led me to the long tables, now stacked with books, some of which were partially burnt or torn in half. "Normally I have a strict policy against our books being marked up. But I'll make an exception if you can fix them," she said.

I picked up a book, *Orientation and Alignment*, that still had its cover and only looked a little dusty.

"Open it," Bryce said, voice light and low like the late echo of a bell.

I flipped it open and found blank pages filling the spine. "Ah," I said.

"Yes," Gwen said. "Those especially concern me. Tatsuo is familiar enough with the catalog to let you know if you're on the right track."

"Do you have a pencil?" I asked, chewing at my lip and drawing up a chair.

❧

Be whole worked to put the torn books back together but it didn't fix charred edges or empty pages. *I am unburnt and fireproof* did the trick for the former but I had yet to find a solution for the latter.

My pages are full brought uninterrupted gibberish that Tatsuo read loudly and with great solemnity. Or in one case, a book stuffed with feathers and dried flowers and leaves. Bryce, who had taken it upon themself to guard me—either from danger or grateful coworkers—snatched that up and pulled each piece of refuse free, taking experimental whiffs.

I am restored and *My text is returned* brought nothing but my erase marks inside the covers.

I was practicing phrases on a piece of paper like the words were a puzzle. Was *I contain my original text as it was printed* too wordy? I grabbed the book Bryce had picked clean like a carcass and tested the words in pencil and waited.

"Ahh," Tatsuo said, watching small captions appear at the bottom of the open pages. "Yes, that's actually a compendium of natural materials in flight work. It's primarily illustrated."

I sighed and sagged in my chair. "Hence the feathers," I said.

Tatsuo and Bryce nodded. "Hence the feathers," Tatsuo said.

I looked at Bryce. "Maybe we could just paste them back in with the captions?" I suggested weakly.

Bryce snorted. "Ate them," they said.

I blinked at that. Two warm hands cupped at my shoulders and I tilted my head back to see Callum standing over my chair, eyes peering through his glasses to my words in the book.

"It isn't working," I said to him, chewing the inside of my lip to keep from pouting.

"It is," he said. "It just isn't doing what you want it to."

"Same thing," I muttered.

Callum's thumbs kneaded into the back of my neck and I resisted the urge to purr. "Come on," he said. "Take a break, I've brought lunch."

I made to stand, but Bryce growled out, "Ask nicely."

I wasn't sure they were joking, even if Tatsuo was grinning, but Callum only rolled his eyes. Then he turned fully to me, a bright smile on his face.

"Joanna," he said. "Would you please join me for lunch?"

Bryce made a snuffling sound that might have been a laugh and I ducked my head to hide my bright cheeks.

"I'll organize these into text only," Tatsuo said as I stood. "This new spell should suffice for those. We'll plan for the others after your meal."

I thanked them both and then took Callum's waiting hand.

"Do you mind eating as we walk?" he asked as we reached the doors. "There's something I want to show you."

"I need a walk. I'm not used to sitting while I'm working."

People stared at us on the grounds and I kept my eyes on the sandwich Callum passed me from his bag.

"It's because of the library," Callum said glancing between the gawkers and me.

"It could just as easily be because I'm with you," I said, looking up at him. His hair was reddish in the sunlight, his smile nervous, and it gave me a good reason to quit staring at the ground. "It happens with Aiden or Isaac too."

"People like to gossip," he said, shrugging.

"It is a long time," I said, thinking of Aiden's decades of waiting.

Callum was quiet for a stretch, and then he released my hand. I thought for a moment I made a misstep saying anything, but he only wrapped his arm around my waist.

"Worth the wait," he said, so quiet I almost didn't hear.

But it made the nerves in my stomach swoop and spin dizzily, uncertain if I was scared or delighted by the finality in his words.

"Are we...I thought the woods were restricted?" I asked as I realized we were headed to the edge of campus, trees turning dense ahead of us.

"They are and we won't go far in," Callum said. "But Isaac called me out when he saw what was happening."

Before I could ask, Isaac appeared from behind a massive tree trunk in a dark wool coat. His expression, knotted and dark, eased as he spotted us and he jogged over. I accepted the kiss as he reached me, smiling and feeling the night's light sweetness as it lingered. Callum was watching us as Isaac stepped back, looking almost shy. Isaac smirked at me and then pulled Callum in as well, the taller man's eyebrows raising for a moment before his eyes fell shut and his shoulders relaxed. They parted slowly, gazes full of a familiar kind of understanding and I ignored the warm twist in my belly at the sight.

"I didn't think you'd listen to me," Isaac said to him, cheeks dimpling.

"She's safe with us," Callum murmured, eyes soft and sleepy

with affection. "And you're right," he said before turning to me, "You've been living outside of serious spellcraft so long, it's better to share as much as we can with you."

"I don't know that I'd call this spellcraft," Isaac said, tone darkening. "Come see."

I followed with Callum, lifting my skirt to avoid catching it on briars as the forest brush turned wilder the farther we walked in. Fall had caught up with the woods, the colors dimming and the smell of growth gone musty and wet. And, somehow stranger, a stillness had fallen. There were no other sounds, no other movement, than ours as we traveled.

"This is far enough," Callum said and there was a touch at my elbow as if he thought of holding me and then reconsidered.

I stopped and stuck close to his side and Isaac backtracked to us, framing me at my right.

"Do you see it?" he asked.

I looked up at Callum, expecting him to answer but his eyes were fixed up, wary and distant, and I realized he was keeping an eye out for any danger. Any sign of what had come to the library. Isaac nudged me and I looked back into the woods. Was it the silence? Was there some kind of familiar scene here that I should recognize? I hadn't walked this part of the woods before, at least not as far as I knew. And it was Isaac that had noticed the change which meant...

"There's no...green," I said. It sounded stupid as it came out of my mouth, but I was staring at an evergreen tree that was a dull slate gray. I thought of home and walking in winter and even on the grayest of days in the deepest of snow, there was still a little life. "And no animals," I added.

Callum stirred next to me, turning to Isaac, "Is it...?"

"Complete," Isaac said. "Not a single spot of green, up until about four yards from the campus. It's like this for miles around. The west end is still good."

"You shouldn't have gone in that deep," Callum said.

"I wasn't alone," Isaac said, and they watched each other for a moment before Isaac smiled. "If you mean I shouldn't have done something dangerous without *you* just say so."

"Mmmph." Callum shrugged and I bit my lip to keep from laughing.

"Is it all dead?" I asked, stepping up to test a little under-growth sapling. It bent and stretched under my hands, still young but without any of its lively green.

"No, just absent of color," Isaac said. "A significant color. Life, healing, growth, safety."

"And the animals?" I asked.

"That I didn't notice, actually," Isaac admitted with a twist of his mouth, studiously avoiding Callum's gaze.

"I'll come back with Frost, look for tracks to see if they moved to a new territory or..."

Or if they'd gone the way of Cecil Pincombe and the circula-tion desk.

I swallowed and cleared my throat. "I should get back to the library soon."

They walked with me, Callum sharing more of the sand-wiches with Isaac and the pair of them with arms or hands settled around me. It was a solid, safe feeling, and this time I didn't mind the looks from others on campus. I don't think I even noticed them.

"Come back and stay at the house tonight," Isaac said as we reached the library doors.

"I need to get back to mine first," I said. I needed fresh clothing and also to restock on the spelled anti-fertility tinc-tures, especially if I was going to be a nightly guest with these men. Even if falling into bed with Isaac had been born out of a need for comfort, it was certainly something I planned on repeating.

"Just don't eat dinner before you come in," Isaac said. "If I have to cook for Aiden and Callum you deserve to have some too."

Callum looked as if he was fighting words at the tip of his tongue, but in the end they both kissed me goodbye and I entered the library alone.

Gwen and Hildy were overseeing a repair on the desk. It looked patchy and temporary for the moment, and the loss of the art of the original left my heart aching. Tatsuo was missing from my tables of books, but Bryce was still perched on their stack, picking a bone clean from lunch.

They snapped it as I arrived and sucked on the marrow, teeth gleaming a grin at me as I sat.

I raised an eyebrow. "You'll have to do better than that to scare me," I said and Bryce huffed out a laugh.

I stared at my paper, scribbled with tests of words, and thought of the woods, all the green taken right off the plants. Like words off a page. A bone picked clean...

Words cannot be eaten, I wrote.

"Oh!" Tatsuo shouted, sitting up from behind a table stacked with books. He had one in his hand and twisted it to show me the pages, full of tiny, perfectly lined print. "You've solved it!"

CHAPTER 18
JOANNA

I WAS FINISHING AT HOME—THERE WERE LETTERS FROM MY sister-in-law and the new librarians in Bridgeston to answer— when there was a knock at the door. I opened it and narrowed my eyes at Aiden.

"I *do* know the way to the house," I said.

Aiden only grinned and bent, pressing a kiss to my lips with his soft mouth. I chased the touch without thinking and he chuckled, the low sound ringing in my bones, a thrill low in my belly.

"I wanted to show you a shortcut," he said. "May I come in?"

I stepped back to make room for him and laughed as he crowded in close, arms snaking around me. The door shut behind him with a low, abrupt, hum at the back of his throat. And then I was scooped up, my feet hanging free and Aiden's face pressed into my neck, breathing deeply. I wrapped my arms over his shoulders and tucked my face down into his shoulder.

"How are you?" I asked as the moment stretched.

"Better now," he mumbled into my skin, making goosebumps break out over my arms.

I felt unusually small and light in his hold, and I settled myself more comfortably since he didn't seem interested in setting me down.

"I'm exhausted," he added after another deep breath.

"I almost fell asleep on Bryce Gast today," I said.

Aiden looked up at that, our faces so close I almost went cross-eyed looking back at him.

"Gast let you?" he asked, eyes wide.

"No, they whacked me upside the head with a pamphlet," I said, and the tightness in my chest eased at Aiden's roar of a laugh that shook us both.

"Are you alright?" he asked, kissing my cheek and then my jaw before settling back at my neck and taking a long breath.

"I think so?" I said, and he kissed my throat. "I haven't really given myself a moment to think. And now I just feel...sort of like it was years ago instead of hours." My head was foggy and my body was heavy, and I felt caught between senseless giggles and tears.

"Take a nap with me at the house," Aiden said. I smiled, noting the way Aiden forgot to *ask*. At least he made the orders sound more like suggestions every time.

"Alright, but we should get going or there won't be time. Even with a shortcut," I said.

"Ah yes, that's the other reason I came. Do you feel up to a little magic?" He set me back on my feet, hands rubbing at my back.

"Of course," I said. "I've been writing all day, but I haven't felt anything like I did last night."

"Good, now grab your things and find me a closet," Aiden said.

I knew before he had to tell me what the idea was, and I drew the chalk out of my skirt pocket when we made it to the tiny pantry door.

"Will you even be able to fit through?" I asked, glancing at Aiden's chest. Even if he turned sideways it might be a squeeze.

"Don't be smart, just get us home," he said with a mocking glare.

Door to Aiden's bedroom I wrote on the outside of the door, biting my lip at his use of 'home.'

I opened the door and my jaw fell loose as I stepped inside. The room was scarlet, with an enormous, dark four-poster bed staring at me from the opposite end. The windows were curtained with heavy black material that matched the drapes on the bed, and the only light came from a small golden lamp on a bedside table. There was a glossy blood-red leather armchair holding a guitar and a dark armoire with one door open and revealing Aiden's collection of clothes that would have had Hildy swooning.

"Scoot," he said from behind me and I stumbled deeper into the room, the toes of my shoes catching on a dense, patterned rug.

I was so dazzled by the room, the color and heat and intensity of a beating heart, that I missed watching Aiden squeeze himself through a too-small door.

"I told Callum he could come and look at the portal after we arrived, but since you picked my room and the bed is right here, I think we'll just see if he notices," Aiden said. He passed me, shrugging out of his suit coat and hanging it up in his armoire, along with the tie fixed around his neck. His shoes were toed off next and then he shuffled over to the bed and fell in with a creak of protest and a flutter of sheets.

"Coming, darling?" he asked, face down in the mattress.

I snorted, setting down my small case by the armoire where it would be out of the way and then untangling myself out of my boots. I touched the wallpaper which was stiff and shiny, something like a crest pressed in a matte pattern over every inch. I looked at the art on the walls, certain Isaac had painted the series of constellations that glittered inside of gleaming black frames. I dug my toes into the carpet and felt guilty for even stepping on something that felt like velvet.

"City boy," I murmured, looking around.

Aiden rolled over on the bed, propping himself up on an elbow and staring at me.

"Isaac calls me that," he said.

"But you did, didn't you?" I asked, fingering the crystals hanging from the lamp at his bedside. "Grow up in the city? In the south?"

"Yes," he said, sounding a little wary.

There was more I could say. That the contents of this bedroom probably cost more than my entire house in Bridgeston. Mine and my neighbors. That I had never seen a room like it before. Never met anyone like him before.

"Where can I leave my things?" I asked, not wanting to muss the place. I unbuttoned my borrowed shirt and pulled it free from my skirt.

"Are you undressing?" he asked, eyes brightening.

"I'm not napping in my clothes; they'll get wrinkled," I said.

"Leave them next to my guitar."

I folded them up, standing in my slip, and then went to join Aiden in the bed where he'd moved over to make room for me. The mattress dipped like a cloud under my knee and I froze. Aiden watched me, barely stifling a laugh.

"C'mere," he said, and then he grabbed my hand and pulled me down into silk and feather down.

I held my breath as the bed settled around me like an airy hug and then caught Aiden's grin in the corner of my eye.

"Isaac keeps his bed like a country boy," Aiden said. "I prefer a softer touch."

I wiggled into the mattress and it shifted and curved around me until Aiden's patience ran out and he wrapped his arms around me, pulling my back to his chest.

"Plenty of time to test the give later," he mumbled into my hair.

I covered his hands with mine and he tangled our fingers, his knees drawing up to curve behind mine. Aiden's heartbeat was at my back, the soft puff of his breath in my hair. And the house around us was quiet but active, the creak of floorboards not far off as someone came down the stairs. I was more comfortable than I'd ever been. And *wearier* too. But that wasn't a cure for what happened when I let my eyes fall shut.

The dark of the library and the choking heaviness that had hung in the air. The scene of the circulation desk out of the corner of my eye, blurry and indistinct but no less gruesome. Something small and torn in a puddle of red.

So I kept my eyes open and studied the pattern of the wallpaper until it became abstracted. A red face sneering, and something in flight in the spaces between. Aiden huffed and held me tighter and my eyelids were heavy, but there was nothing good behind them. So I found Isaac's constellations on the wall and matched them with the familiar pieces of the night sky you could see over fields at home.

"You're not sleeping," Aiden rumbled, and I shivered. "Tell me what's wrong?"

"Too much in my head," I answered and he released me a little, pulling at my hip to turn me on my back until he was hovering at my side.

"Would you feel better alone? You have a room here-"

"No," I said quickly, twisting again and draping an arm over his side and propping my head up with the other.

"Then tell me what's in your head," he said, stretching his neck forward to kiss the center of my forehead.

I closed my eyes and this time the backs of my eyelids were simple and dark so I held still. "It's just...nothing has stopped since I got to Canderfey," I said.

"With us?" he asked, and I held him to me before he could try to move away.

"No, well that's only a part of it. I never really left Bridgeston before, not far. Canderfey is new. The kind of place I *knew* existed, but didn't really believe because it was so...outside. And all the people here. And the magic." Aiden's fingers traced up and down my spine and the drowsy peace that followed made it easier to speak. "And yes, there is you and Isaac and Callum, a coven. But there is the fact that I'm a *witch*. A real one. Every time I write something and it works I almost don't believe it. And then...last night—" my voice choked in my throat and Aiden held me tight. I caught my breath and let the handful of tears that had gathered slip out.

"Last night was new for all of us," Aiden said. "Well, for Isaac and I, at least."

I thought of that, thought of Callum prowling through the library like a soldier.

"Was Callum in the Enmaire army?" I asked.

Aiden sighed, a big deep breath that ruffled the top of my head. "Callum was in the war."

I blinked at that. "That can't be right, he's too young." The

Red War in the North was nearly twenty years ago and Callum couldn't have been more than a teenager.

"He was too young," Aiden said, voice flat. I thought that if I pressed I could learn more, but it sounded as if it hurt Aiden to speak of it, and I imagined the same would be true for Callum.

"He doesn't like to act the soldier," Aiden said. "Still, it comes out in ways. Over-protective, quick reactions...gut instincts. He's born to it and it suits him, even when he hates the fact."

"That's why I always seem to have an escort now?" I asked, thinking of the way someone seemed to be conveniently placed to walk me to my next destination at any moment.

Aiden hummed in agreement and then added, "And why you'll be talked into staying for dinner and the rest of the night as often as he can manage it. Mind you, I don't disagree with him."

I frowned against Aiden's chest, chewing at my lip. I had a few thoughts about that, but they deserved Callum's ears, not Aiden's so I'd hold onto them for now.

"We just want you safe," Aiden murmured, kissing the top of my head.

I pulled back to look up at him and raised an eyebrow.

"With us," Aiden added, his smile growing. "Happy...satisfied."

He was grinning now and my cheeks ached with resisting the urge to join him. He pulled me up, my slip rucking up my hips as he moved me closer, resting his forehead against mine. He was shifting us in small movements, bodies brushing together until I was on my back, pinned into the decadent mattress by his weight. It was simultaneously tender and carnal, the feel of him pressing me down, surrounding me.

"Do you want to rest?" he asked, and his head bent to mine, lips stroking over mine and then pulling away as I chased them.

"This feels restful," I said, which was a bit of a lie because this felt *stirring* and left me wanting more. But it was certainly better than lying in a bed and staring at a wall.

"Oh good," he said, dipping down again, body stroking mine with the movement and hitching my breath in my chest.

I wriggled underneath him, spreading my legs to fit him between. His body was thicker than Isaac's and the stretch in my thighs traveled up my back and down to my toes as he settled closer. We both took heavy breaths, mouths open against one another.

"Been waiting to kiss you since the day you arrived," he said.

I smiled at that, thinking of him in the window seat. The shock of him to my system, someone so beautiful and teasing. "You have kissed me," I said.

He lifted his head, eyes wrinkled in the corners with his smile. Then he sank back down, taking my lips in a long draw, clasped between his. His tongue flicked out, tasting, and then he dove back in, our hips grinding together as I struggled to find purchase in the kiss. But with every stroke of his mouth and caress of his tongue, I was being swept into a current—a vocabulary of touch well beyond my experience.

His hands framed my face, holding me to him, fingertips stroking along my jaw. Every whimper he drew out of me, he answered with a melodic hum that travelled into the kiss and down into my belly, creating a thrumming warmth. It was magic, a melody made for pleasing. I couldn't answer it with a written word so instead, I wrapped myself around Aiden, clinging and accepting until I had to pull away to breathe. His mouth moved to my neck and I gasped, the music just as strong on my skin as it was on my tongue.

My hips writhed against his and he was stiff and heavy against me. His palms were spread beneath my shoulder blades and he slid down, teeth scraping at my collarbone and releasing a low note that reverberated down between my legs. I cried out and clasped the back of his neck trying to hold him there, to keep the vibration in my bones steady. But he traveled again, soft kisses over my chest as he held a quiet, sweet tone.

"Kisses shouldn't be rushed," he said.

He kissed the gap between my breasts, cheek rubbing against me and stubble snagging at my slip. I caught my breath for the half-beat between one note and the next.

When his lips wrapped around a silk-covered nipple I sang with him, off-key and broken but it did nothing to stop the tremor running through me. Aiden grinned, pulling away and looking up from my chest with a wicked gleam in his eyes.

"That's cheating," I said, voice low.

"I warned you I'd try to influence you in our favor," he said and then he blew softly on the wet spot he left over my slip.

I shivered, tilting my head back to hide my face. Aiden traced the low collar of my slip with his tongue and then sucked on the unattended breast. I held him to me as he started to hum again and I groaned in chorus. He held himself off me then, giving me nothing to seek any badly needed friction from. But every tug of his mouth around my pebbling nipple was an echoing tug inside of me. He reached around a hand to my front, fingers gently pinching in tandem with his mouth. The song burrowing in my skin was turning high and ringing through me, carrying out of my own lips.

"Please, please," I whimpered.

"Patience, darling." Aiden kept up his work, never really touching below my waist, but building up a throbbing beat there all the same. My legs were quaking on the bed as I begged for a release I would have thought was impossible, not with so little stimulation to only my breasts.

He tugged at my slip and it scraped over my skin, exposing me to his hot breath, tongue lashing over one tender nipple while his thumb swirled over the other. My legs stretched up and knotted around his back, tugging him down to land heavily on me. Aiden growled into my skin and the trilling, wavering tension broke in me, music flooding my ears and spiraling out from my aching core.

Aiden kissed his way back up, peppering a warm wet path up my chest and neck and across my jaw. His hands stroked at my thighs, holding me in place. I clutched his jaw in my hold and brought him in for a lazy, licking kiss until he was purring into my mouth.

"S'dinner time," he murmured, pulling away. And there was no apology for the smug smile on his face, although I couldn't really blame him.

"I'm not hungry," I said, reaching up to attend to the buttons of his shirt. My stomach betrayed me with a growl and Aiden laughed.

"You are, and so am I," Aiden said, and he kissed me once more. "Also, I don't want to be interrupted and I suspect if I keep you here too much longer we will be."

"You don't want..." I trailed off biting my lip and righting the collar of my slip, damp fabric sticking on my skin. Aiden raised up and I could see him, stretching at the zipper of his pants.

"Of course I want you to strip me naked and have your way with me," Aiden said, grinning and easing the knot of nerves in my stomach. He settled at my side, hand soothing down my hip while the other brushed the loose curls out of my face. "But I'm patient. The part I was most anxious for was knowing you existed. The rest is icing."

There was a knock at the bedroom door at that moment and then it was opening, Isaac smirking at the pair of us. He glanced down briefly at my chest, eyes darkening, and then looked at Aiden.

"Callum's hunting for you," he said. "And dinner is ready."

I squirmed out of Aiden's hold and pushed my slip back down my hips, rising from the bed.

Isaac stayed leaning in the doorway. "I have a robe," he said to me. "It'll be more comfortable and no one will mind."

I paused at Aiden's armchair. It would be nice not to have to get dressed again. Isaac shrugged as I thought it over.

"Yes, please," I said.

We were leaving Isaac's bedroom with me wrapped in green velvet when Callum came thundering up the stairs and nearly ran into us.

"Where's the portal?" he asked, eyes wide behind his glasses.

I was about to answer when Isaac gestured to me and asked, "Are you completely blind?"

Callum rolled his eyes, stepping forward and sweeping an arm around my waist to plant a swift, fierce kiss to my mouth.

"You're beautiful," he said, words mumbling into my lips. "Where's the portal?"

Isaac made an exhausted sound and started down the stairs as

I laughed and kissed Callum again. "Aiden's bedroom door," I told him as he released me.

"You have ten minutes to be downstairs or you forfeit your right to second helpings," Isaac called from a flight down.

I stood at the top of the stairs for a beat, watching Callum race to the door, and debated joining him. But I was starving and Aiden was just emerging from his room, looking as rumpled as I'd left him if not more so. And I wanted those second helpings.

CHAPTER 19
JOANNA

STUDENTS TRICKLED BACK INTO THE LIBRARY AS THE WEEK went on, suddenly turning up with overdue books as if it might be a consolation to those of us working. Construction continued on the front desk, as well as the glass roof, and for the first time since my arrival, the library was loud with activity. Isaac walked me to work before his classes. Callum brought me lunch and did research in the staff section. Aiden appeared at the end of my shift with some excuse for me to return back to the house with him. He had a new piece of music he wanted me to hear. Isaac was trying a new recipe. Callum wanted to test different writing utensils with my magic. I pretended not to see through the orchestration.

It all felt very regular. Or it did in the moments where I made sure to not look toward the woods that had gone gray. Even the sky hanging over the tops of the trees had lost its color. And now grocers were keeping smaller stocks of food because the fresh would turn to rot overnight.

So I had bought a bag of apples and commandeered the kitchen from Isaac to bake them in dark sugar and whiskey for dessert. We had gorged ourselves on them before they went to waste. And then Callum had disappeared up into his office. Like he did every night.

Just like every night after falling asleep with Isaac and sometimes Aiden, I would wake up and find Callum curved against my back, an arm wrapped possessively around my stomach.

"Do you want to see your room tonight?" Isaac asked. He had dragged an armchair over from the corner of the front room when I'd settled in the window seat with a book. And while I knew he'd pulled out his sketchbook, it was easy to ignore the scratches of a pencil on paper in favor of studying runes and sigils.

"Sick of me stealing your pillow?" I asked in answer, flipping a page but not seeing it.

The room, the guest room as Aiden had first called it, came up often. And always referred to as '*your* room' like there was a permanent place for me here. Everything they said to me offered that, and every time it was offered I felt a swell of panic. That this was a dream that could be snatched away. That they would realize their mistake in bringing me into their fold.

I glanced over at Isaac and he was looking away, a frown on his mouth and a guarded tightness around his eyes. *Just take the stupid room*, I thought to myself. But there wasn't a room in this house I hadn't loved upon finding it, and I knew that would be the case now. But it had only been a few weeks, and things between us so rarely felt real. It was too perfect for me to feel comfortable grabbing onto, and in spite of their insistence that I belonged I didn't see where I fit yet.

"I need to go find Callum," I said, which was true, but it had been just as true days ago. Now was only convenient because I needed the escape.

Isaac nodded but didn't look back. I rose and crossed to the doorway and he caught my hand on the way, linking our fingers and holding me there.

"When you're ready," he said, meeting my eyes with something fierce and tender in his, "We can take my damn pillow with us."

He smiled a little and I dove down for a kiss to thank him for his patience. He held me there for a long, sweet, stretch and I was practically ready to accept the room *and* the coven when he released me.

"Good luck with him," he said, kissing once more at my cheek.

I blinked and then remembered. Callum. I had used him as my excuse to break the tension and now I suppose I had to follow through. It was overdue anyway.

I took the stairs up to the third floor, hearing Aiden practicing from his studio on the second. Callum was squinting down at a text by the dying sunlight from his office window. A pile of books on the floor surrounded his desk chair like a protective wall.

"You need a lamp," I said.

He glanced over his shoulder at me, a furrow on his brow easing with his smile. "Write me one."

I pulled the chalk—now kept in a little cigarette case Aiden had found for me—from my pocket and wrote on the edge of a bookshelf. *Callum has a lamp on his home desk.*

"Ohhh, not *that*," Callum said, and he pushed his chair away from his desk. It was gaudy, a more elaborate version of the crystal one in Aiden's bedroom. "Anyway, there's nowhere for it to plug into."

It is always lit. And so it was. Callum's face went wide with surprise.

"You should have been more specific to your tastes," I said.

"You could fix it with a word," he muttered, prodding at one of the hanging crystals and sending prisms of light dancing over the books around us.

"I'm thinking I'll spend next week at my own house," I said, pretending to study the books on the shelves.

"What? Why?" Callum asked, voice sharp. "What if we…need you?"

"For what?" I asked, laughing. I pulled a small paper bound text on defensive glamouring and disguise from the shelf and flipped aimlessly through.

He was quiet and then I heard him pushing books aside. "Aiden or Isaac will want to stay close—"

"Aiden or Isaac, but not you?" I asked, turning on my heel to face him.

He winced and raked his hand through his hair. "No, of course, I—but—"

I took pity on him and abandoned the teasing offense. "Just say it, Callum."

He froze and swallowed and his fingers swept through his hair again, tangling at the ends. He sighed and dropped his arm. "I'd like it if you stayed with us as long as we're dealing with this threat. Or...or with Gwen and her coven. If you'd prefer. As long as I know you're safe."

The suggestion of staying with Gwen caught me by surprise, I'd give him that. I'd expected more insistence and less...genuine worry.

"I'd rather stay here," I said, smiling.

His shoulders dropped with relief. "You mean that?"

"I do, I was just sick of the play-acting, Callum. You can be honest with me, I promise not to argue for the sake of it," I said.

I had meant to say more, but the words were lost as Callum surrounded me, arms clutching and lips hard against mine. It was an urgent, hungry kiss and in half a breath I was answering it in kind, my fingers clawing at his shoulders. I felt like I was trying to climb him, force our bodies closer, close enough that I could feel his heartbeat against my breast and pounding through my blood. His hands grasped my hips, holding me tight to him and pinned against the shelves.

"I promise to be better," he whispered, pulling away just long enough for me to gasp. I wanted to answer him, to tell him I didn't need *better*, that he could simply be less skittish around me.

But he wasn't skittish now. He was consuming, his tongue stroking against mine, hands traveling, gathering up my skirt so my legs could cling around his waist. I severed the kiss as my nose smashed against his glasses and broke away laughing, pulling them off his nose. Callum barely noticed, intent on sucking kisses along my jaw. His hips jerked between us, fingers digging into the soft underside of my thighs and the glasses went clattering to the floor. There was too much fabric between us and with every aching groan from Callum I needed him more. I wanted to soothe him as much as I wanted to satisfy myself.

"Put me down," I rasped and Callum stepped back so fast I nearly fell to the floor.

"I'm sorr—" he started.

"Don't you dare say it," I said, raising a finger in his face. I dropped my skirt to the floor and pulled my shirt over my head too fast, a button popping and dinging against a book.

Callum stared dumbly at me for a moment and I smiled shakily back, reaching out and plucking his vest buttons loose. There was a sudden hot shimmer and then Callum was bare and I had a second to see him, the long narrow lean of him, muscles corded, and the tangle of scars down his right hip before I was back in his hold. I swallowed his groan; tangling my hands between us to pull my slip over my head. And then he covered my cry as his fingers slid into my panties, fondling at my skin, dipping inside of me and spreading the wetness he found here. I pushed the last scrap of clothing between us off my hips and Callum lifted me from the floor.

I grabbed the shelf above me for balance, laughing and kicking one leg free of my underwear to brace it against a stack of books. Callum hitched my other leg over his hips, fingers guiding himself into place and then he filled me with one swift stroke. I cried out at the stretch and the suddenness. But it brought with it an immediate flutter of relief, like I'd been waiting hours for him instead of minutes. I felt full to bursting, Callum fitting so deeply, pressing into places I'd never found before.

"Oh gods, Jo-Joanna," he muttered, the words were winded. His lips snagged over my earlobe, breath puffing against my skin.

One of my heels was pressed to his ass, holding him still inside me.

"I didn't mean to rush," he said, a whine at the back of his throat and I nuzzled into his cheek.

"I want you to," I said, and I squeezed experimentally around him. His mouth fell open with his moan, and he stirred, hips twitching. "Please, Callum," I said. I kissed his cheek as his hands braced me. My foot stroked down the back of his thigh and I rolled my hips into his, our breaths catching.

His belly quivered against mine, all the tension in his body built up. And then his lips latched onto mine like an anchor and he drank my ragged cry as he gave in, drawing back and surging in again. It was a harsh, heavy rhythm, our bodies slapping noisily together and Callum's hands tight enough on me to leave fingertip bruises. But every push threw stars into my eyes and a hot flutter mounting in my belly.

Books rattled on the shelf behind me and I pulled away from his mouth to giggle and gasp, a moan falling free with every hitch of his hips into mine. Callum's forehead was knotted, mouth open and he looked so desperate and lost. I wrapped an arm around his shoulders, tangling my fingers into the hair at the back of his neck.

"You feel so good," I said, kissing over his brow.

He grunted into my neck, hips snapping. It was a deep, full pleasure, but not the kind that would send me over the edge. Still, I didn't want him to stop. Having Callum turning needy and wild in my arms was a heady enough feeling on its own. As his thrusts became more urgent and the groan held tight behind his teeth turned into an aching, begging sound I only wanted more. I raised my legs higher around his hips and squeezed him with every buck and twist, watching with hungry eyes as his back arched and his cries tore free.

"Joanna," he gasped, gaze fixing to mine. "Joanna—I want—"

"I want to watch you," I said softly, nails scratching into his hair and thighs clasping around his hips. "You're beautiful."

He cursed and the bookshelf dug into my back as his even thrusts turned erratic and sharp. My hand above slipped, bringing two smaller books crashing down to the floor. I was grinning as Callum was grunting, face pressed to my neck as there was a warm, slippery feeling bursting inside of me. His arms twisted up around my back like a fierce hug and for a long moment, I could feel his legs shaking as he leaned into me, with soft little thrusts. Then he straightened, face leaning up to glare at me, and he pulled us away from the bookshelf, a few more texts tumbling down.

"Where are we going?" I asked as we wavered in step for a moment.

"To find my dignity," Callum muttered, taking me over to his desk chair.

"Callum, you don't need—" I said with a small 'oof' as I landed in the seat, the leather cold against my skin.

Callum kneeled at my feet, cheeks still flushed from his orgasm, and a light smile replacing his glare. "I forgot how that felt, if I'm being honest," he said, hands stroking over my thighs, and then sliding between to touch where I was still aching and now dripping as he said, "Being in a woman. But I *did not* forget how to please. And that's all I want, Joanna."

His hands parted my legs, drawing me forward in the chair to make room for his shoulders. He kissed up the top of my right thigh, and then across my belly and back down the left, all while his hands cupped and petted at my swollen folds.

"I'm a mess," I said, squirming under his touch but my knees were falling open for him and his hands were already stirring up sparks in my skin.

"Whose fault is that?" he grumbled, and then his hands slid away and he pressed a tender, open kiss to my clit, tongue flicking out. My fingers dug into the arms of the chair and I held a whimper at the back of my throat. "I want to hear you, Joanna," he said.

He licked a stripe up my center, the hair of his beard prickling at my skin and I let my gasp carry up to the ceiling. His hands scooped under my bottom and pulled me forward, nose nuzzling at the top of my lips as his tongue dipped and swirled. It was a teasing, sweet touch, tickling up the pleasure he had brought to a simmer with his cock. He alternated sucks over my folds with probing licks and gentle nibbles until I was bucking in his hands, now desperate for the pounding pressure. He kissed and soothed and stroked while my whimpers built into sobs.

"Callum, please, please," I chanted, hips rolling towards him even as he backed away, keeping the same delicate touch. "I need *more*."

He pressed a long, closed-mouth kiss over me, hands stroking at the outsides of my thighs as they crept towards his shoulders. Then his tongue pressed flat, mouth wrapping around me as he sucked and licked. My back bowed as the pressure broke, sweeping slow through me like warm syrup while Callum kept lapping and kissing. I was a trembling puddle in the chair as the aftershocks eased. I hissed, eyes popping open, as he dipped a finger inside of me.

I looked down to my lap, where Callum's cheek was resting against my thigh, lips still shiny. His finger pumped gently, pressing deeper and then easing back again.

"Can you take more?" he asked, thumb brushing over my clit and making me twitch and draw back.

"I...I don't know," I said. My body still felt glowy and soft, but every touch was on the edge of too much sensation.

He smiled, beard scratching at my skin. "I think you can."

A second finger joined the first, twisting and he lifted one of my legs onto his shoulder. He sucked a ring around my over-sensitive lips, stirring up warmth and making my legs shake and my toes curl, all while keeping a shallow rhythm at my opening. I unclenched my hands from the armchair, dipping my fingers into his hair, body relaxing under his ministrations. There was a hum in my ears and it wasn't until Callum looked up from between my legs, eyes smiling, that I realized the sound was coming from me.

"Feels nice," I said, voice slurring with the lazy heat flowing through me. I didn't know if it meant I would come again, but Callum seemed in no rush and it was too nice a feeling to want it to end.

"You taste sweet," he said, tongue flicking gently over me.

I snorted at that and his eyes darkened, fingers delving deeper suddenly and then crooking up.

"Oh!" I shouted at the swelling feeling inside of me.

"I'm not teasing," he said, still stroking inside of me as I squirmed closer, wanting more and less, lips parted on a soundless cry. "I want to keep the flavor of you on my tongue."

And then he was laving at me again, tongue firm and seeking out all the places he had already discovered, but now with intent and purpose. I was riding his hand and mouth, a cracking, pleading noise rising up from my throat. My hands held him tight to me and he groaned against my skin, the sound echoing deeply and making me writhe. I called out his name and his touch grew firmer, tongue pointing and lashing at my clit. The pleasure was spiky and burning and seemed to stretch from toe to head through, one long bright heat content to leave me hanging.

"Come for me, Joanna," Callum said, the words heavy in my ears. "Let me hear you."

And then his lips wrapped tight around my clit pulling and pressing, and his fingers pushed high against me. My legs lifted up around his ears and my belly clenched and I tugged tight on Callum's hair even as I drove my hips against his face, stars bursting behind my eyes. He moaned into me again and all the tension in me splintered as I fell apart and my body trembled into a limp puddle in the chair.

Callum rose slowly, easing my loose fingers out of his hair and settling my legs back from his shoulders. He kissed a slow wet path up my stomach and his arms wrapped around my back as I let out a small, helpless sound that was meant partly in thanks. I felt almost wounded with how thoroughly undone I was, but the tender hold of him around me soothed away the sting and I snuggled into his chest.

He draped my arms over his shoulders lifted me from the chair and I grunted. "No," I said.

He chuckled, holding me to him as he stood up from the floor. "No?" he asked. "I'm taking you to bed."

Oh. I wasn't sure what I had thought, only that I knew I was officially used up for the night. I nodded against him and wondered if it was really possible to *hear* someone's smile. Or if I was just that tired.

He carried us to Isaac's room where Isaac and Aiden were facing each other on their sides in the bed, the sheets low enough that I knew they were naked too.

"I hope you two are satisfied for the evening because Joanna here is done," Callum said, sounding a little too smug. I pinched at the skin under my hand, but he only shrugged and I caught him grinning.

"We heard," Aiden said and my cheeks blushed hotly.

"Come here, love," Isaac said, rolling in my direction and pulling back the covers.

Callum settled me on the mattress and I pulled him down

with me, wanting to be surrounded. I got my wish, Isaac pulling me to his chest and Callum sliding in tight behind me. Three hands stroked down my side and I hummed again, eyes drooping.

"What was all the crashing about, though?" Aiden whispered as I sank into slumber.

"Books," Callum said, and then I was asleep.

CHAPTER 20
CALLUM

I woke as Joanna twisted next to me, rolling away from a now empty spot and cuddling into my chest. I squinted in the dim light and found Aiden and Isaac rising out of bed.

"Where're you going?" I whispered. My hands were helping Joanna, soothing at the bed warm skin of her back and pulling the sheets back to cover us.

"Groceries, errands," Isaac said, hunting his dresser for clothes.

"It's your turn to come up with an excuse for her to stay here," Aiden said, low voice almost growling in an effort to keep quiet.

"She's staying," I said. "We talked last night."

"For good?" Isaac asked, and both he and Aiden had paused in dressing.

Joanna made a small sound of protest, hands clutching at my skin, and I wrapped my arms around her, marveling in how she settled at the touch.

"Until it's safe," I answered. Aiden's expression fell but he nodded. "But...don't you think? She might...after some time?"

"We hope so," Aiden said softly. "The day she doesn't skirt the subject, I'll feel confident." Isaac and I both frowned and Aiden came around to the bed, bending down and kissing the center of Joanna's back. He smiled at me and leaned in for a real kiss. "She will," he whispered before leaving the room.

Isaac kissed us both before leaving as well. "Let her sleep," he said, but his expression looked as if he didn't expect me to follow the advice.

And a part of me was tempted to wake her—slowly, with lips and hands—if only to have a chance to perfect my efforts from the night before. Mostly to have her in my ear again, her begging words and the pretty broken twist to her voice as I did something right.

But I didn't want to interrupt the sleepy cling of her on my chest so instead, I half-dozed with my fingers in her hair and her toes against my calf. I turned my face to her and took long breaths, the salt and sugar of her filling up my lungs until I was drowsy. She whimpered in her sleep and her back tightened so I stroked my free hand down the length of her spine and pulled the sheet up to her shoulder. Her forehead was knotted so I loosened the tangles in her hair and brushed it out of her face. And when she shivered I rolled us so she was in my warm spot of the bed.

She stirred then, breath hitching and fingers tightening on my sides. There was a half-second of terror in her eyes as they fluttered open and then it faded just as quickly and the frown on her mouth curled up into a smile.

"Morning," she murmured, eyes falling shut again as she relaxed back on the mattress.

"Morning," I said. "Bad dream?"

Her mouth pouted with a sleepy frown and she twisted, leaning into my hand that was stroking down her side to her hip.

"No dreams," she said shaking her head.

"No nightmares?" I asked.

Her nose wrinkled and her hands uncurled from between us, circling to my back. "No. I don't remember dreaming in...weeks. S'like...like I'm not even sleeping. I'm awake and then I'm waking up again. Almost doesn't feel like rest."

All the drowsy lazy pleasure of the morning stilled as she spoke, turning dull and muted as my thoughts started catching up. My brain was cataloging away the warm maple color of her eyes in the morning, and the deep peachy pink of the tips of her breast, in favor of recalling the weight of dreams. And the forces that had the ability to take them away.

"Hmm, I lost you somewhere, didn't I?" she said, smile creeping up on one side of her mouth. A hand appeared between us, one finger reaching up to stroke between my eyebrows. "What did I say?"

"How long have your dreams been missing?" I asked.

There were psychic drains, like parasites, that might take on a host. But that wouldn't explain the woods or even the attack on the library.

"Weeks," she repeated, shrugging. She looked at me for a moment and then thought again. "Since...since that first batch of books turned back up."

"The night I walked you home," I said, stiffening.

"I suppose...probably."

I jumped out of the bed, hearing her laugh my name as I hurried to the door and into the hall. *Gatekeepers* was on my desk by the window of my office, buried under a stack of books. I grabbed my pants out of the pocket of space I'd left them in and tripped my way into them on my way to the window. Soft footsteps padded behind me and Joanna was at my side, wrapped in Isaac's green robe and peering over the arm of the chair.

"You think what was in the library, what's taken over the woods, also has to do with me not dreaming?" she asked. "I've gone without dreams before."

"You said it felt like you weren't even asleep," I said, pushing the other books aside and pulling forward the fragile old beast of a nightmare text I had left stinking up my desk.

"Out like a light," she said softly. "That's significant?"

"Dreams are often a warning system. Something has stolen yours." I flipped through the pages with clumsy fingers. Nails scratched gently into the back of my hair and I paused to shift the book in her direction.

"I skipped ahead," she said, still combing her fingers into my hair. She brought her free hand down, turning in halfway through the pages and flicking ahead to land on a wavery illustration of a figure in the woods. "It eats," she said, pointing down the words beneath the woodblock print.

"Sounds..." I trailed off, the vision of the library coming to mind. A maw of darkness throwing silhouettes in eerie relief. The librarian who sent a cowering student across the room to safety and then splintered in a metallic grind of light.

"Like a boogeyman," Joanna said. She was perched on the arm of the chair and I looked up at her, puzzled. "You know... don't go into the woods, or you'll get eaten up for being a rotten child. What?"

"Nothing. Is...is that what parents say to children in the country?" I asked. "Isaac made it sound rustic but—"

Joanna grinned. "My mother was northern. Every misbehavior was threatened with death or kidnapping by a monster of some sort."

I swallowed and looked back down at the book in my hands. Her mother was northern. Did she know about my part in the war yet? Would Isaac or Aiden share that with her, take the burden out of my hands, or would they leave it alone as my business? I would never share it with another soul if I thought I could. Even Joanna. *Especially* Joanna.

"It does say it consumes everything but dreams seem like a light meal," Joanna mused, tracing her finger over the page of the story.

I shook off my thoughts, leaning into Joanna's side—as if her closeness might burn away old stains from my past, as if I could keep them from her indefinitely.

"Dreams could be powerful," I said. "From the right person. Stronger than a desk or—" I broke off, feeling her tense at my side. "And this story looks a little familiar."

"That illustration looks familiar," she mumbled, leaning in as well.

"You've seen it before," I said, just to tease.

She ignored me, pulling her fingers from my hair and making me regret my joke. She lifted the book out of my lap and held it back from her face.

"That looks like Isaac's painting," she said. "The trees and and the meadow. The one I..."

"Painted a shadowy figure in the background of?" I asked as she trailed off. Her eyes narrowed and her lips pursed and a low-sinking weighed heavy in my gut.

There were plenty of terrible possibilities behind the current situation. There were *only* terrible possibilities. Someone had been killed already and the color green was vanishing. *Being eaten*, I amended, looking at the illustration in the book. But if what was plaguing the Canderfey campus had a place in *Gatekeepers* then our situation was even worse than I expected. And if Joanna had any special kind of connection...

My chest burnt with how hard my heart began to beat. I needed more information. Answers to questions and a collection of plans to study. I needed a solution to the problem and an action to take. I need Joanna safe and uninvolved.

"Callum," she whispered, and she tilted the book in her hands, brow furrowing. "There's...there's something-"

The front door on the ground floor shut and Joanna jumped up from the chair. I pulled the book out of her hands, leaving it open on my desk.

"That'll be them back with groceries," I said as Joanna watched the doorway. "Go down and fill them in? Let me do a little hunting for more information."

She was chewing at the corner of her mouth with worried eyes. I stood, drawing her into my chest and settling my lips over hers until she answered the kiss, rising up on her toes.

"As soon as I know what we're facing, I'll be able to start coming up with a solution," I said.

"I'll bring you up tea," she said.

Her fingers were fretting at the cuffs of the robe, and I wanted some way of soothing the anxiety out of her. But that was Isaac's skill and she would be better off downstairs in good company. And I would work faster alone.

❦

THERE WERE three drained cups of tea and the remains of a forgotten breakfast on my desk when the sun went out.

I looked up from the pages, squinting at the sudden darkness of the room, Joanna's gifted lamp the only shy source of light. Outside the window, the sky had turned slate gray, but soft clouds lay scattered across the sky as if it should have been a beautiful sunny blue day.

"Callum," Aiden called from downstairs.

I scrambled out of my chair, bringing half a dozen books with me. The stairs were pitch-black and I made it down to the first floor more by memory than by sight. Isaac and Aiden framed Joanna at the front window of the sitting room, the three of them staring up. I pulled up behind Joanna and found the glowing black orb in the sky where the sun should have been. I winced at the burn in my eyes and backed away.

"Don't look at it," I said. The words snapped on my tongue and I clenched my jaw to bury the barking command.

Joanna turned right away, her arms folded tightly over her stomach in a too-large sweater. Aiden's probably.

"Can it eat the sun too?" she asked me as Aiden and Isaac drew away from the window.

"The sunlight," I said. "The books call it things like the Hollow, Consumer, Devourer, Eater, etcetera..."

"Is this happening everywhere?" Isaac asked, glancing over his shoulder to the window.

"No, not yet. Canderfey and the Hand Woods for now. It's... been locked up for centuries, at least that long from what I can find. The library, the woods, Joanna's dreams, this is probably just its way of acclimating back to its appetite."

Joanna was pulling books free from my arms, taking them with her to an armchair in the corner where she curled up in the seat. "If it *was* locked up then it can be again," she said, as much to herself as to the rest of us.

"I told you we'd find a solution," I said, but she didn't smile, just began digging through the pages in front of her.

"There's a food shortage starting," Isaac told me. "I contacted the campus and they agreed to help any locals in whatever way they can."

"What's a true name?" Joanna asked, looking up from the book I had found most useful and swatting away a curl from her face. "This says '*The Hollow was caged by its true name*.'"

I pulled another chair over to Joanna's corner and Aiden and Isaac followed. "It's a name of power, one we're born with. Not the kind our parents give but one that holds the essences of our...our souls," I said. "There are supposedly rituals you can do to learn your own. But knowing someone else's true name gives you power over them."

"Power to trap something for centuries?" she asked. "Something strong enough to eat sunlight?"

"Given what that creature is capable of, the hold of a true name might be the key to keeping it contained," Isaac said. I nodded and Joanna lifted a hand to chew at her thumbnail.

"How do you learn the true name of something so old?" Isaac asked.

"That's the next thing I'll be searching for," I said. "If I can figure out who caged it, I might be able to find research of theirs that would help us."

"If it took the true name to cage the Hollow years ago, would you need the true name to open the cage?" Joanna asked.

I smiled a little, I had thought of the same thing. I wanted to push aside the current disaster and take the day to learn more about Joanna's magical instincts. She found patterns and errors in the world quickly. Once she had a better sense of what she was capable of, what other's magical traces felt like, she would be even faster and sharper.

"I don't know yet, it would depend on the cage," I said. "Whether or not the witch or coven that designed it trusted that it would be left locked."

"If it did take a true name then that means someone opened it intentionally," Isaac said.

"Or experimentally," I argued, thinking of the students. Thinking of the kind of student *I* had been growing up. I would have tested a lock to see if I could break it when I was younger. Consequences were a foggier concept than knowing my own strength at the time.

"We should go to the library," Joanna said, shutting the book in her hands and holding it to her chest. Her gaze was already on the front door and her face was missing any hint of expression.

Isaac and I met each other's eyes at the same time and I

could see the worry. Joanna had fallen into the deep end of magic in a very short amount of time. And while it was a revelation that *had* to come sooner or later, a part of me regretted that we had been the ones to lead her there.

"There will be books on true names," she said, looking at us finally. "And Gwen should know. Tatsuo and the others could help us."

I tried to wrestle the grimace off my face before anyone noticed, but Aiden laughed and I was caught out.

"Yes let's put Tatsuo Ito and Callum in the same room together and see who comes out with more research," he said.

"He's a hobbyist," I muttered.

"He's my friend," Joanna said lightly, rising from the chair and giving us her back. "And he's very helpful."

"Get dressed," Aiden said, grinning down at my still bare chest. "We're going to the library."

CHAPTER 21
JOANNA

If the tension of the two covens together in the staff library wasn't bad enough—in Callum's defense, Tatsuo *did* seem to be baiting him by voicing aloud every bit of useful information he found—I could feel my bones rattling under my skin. It had started in Callum's office, *Gatekeepers* in my hands and the imprint of the words almost shimmering on the page. An impression of letters scratched into the page like it had been drawn there with an inkless pen. Or a fingernail.

Let it out.

I couldn't focus on any of the books in front of me. I only saw the letters spelled out, a cruder version of my handwriting. Was it still writing without any pencil or chalk? I didn't remember making the words but I remembered the drowsy, drugged feeling while reading. I remembered the icy cold fear of waking, the itchy crawling in my head as I woke. The one I still had some mornings.

Isaac passed me, arms loaded with dark parchment scrolls, and I stirred in the window seat. The library lamps were turned up bright to combat the darkness outside. Aiden and Hildy were a couple aisles away, chatting about the city while they browsed books. I had been trying to read the same page for the past ten minutes. It was only information Tatsuo had already found three times in other texts. A true name might be a word, or a sound, or a symbol, or a color. Usually, they were some combination and the older the name the stronger they became.

Bryce rounded a bookshelf and came to sit at the far end of the window seat. They were empty-handed and watching me steadily. It was as likely Bryce had come to see me of their own volition as it was Callum or Gwen had sent them to check on me. I was snapping my thumbnail against my front teeth and Bryce arched an eyebrow.

"Sorry," I mumbled, stuffing my hand under my skirt.

Bryce leaned forward, taking my bag from where I'd stashed it against the window by my knees. I dove forward to grab it back but I was too late, they were already taking out the book I had smuggled from the house. They flipped straight to the illustration of the Hollow, setting it face-up on the bench between us.

I stared at Bryce's face and they looked up from the page to me, green eyes glinting.

"Your words," Bryce said, pointing to the slanted press of letters on the page. I could barely make out the *it ou* before it faded into shadow.

My breath caught in my chest and I exhaled, slow and shaky. "Is it a spell?" I asked, keeping as quiet as I could.

"Yes," they said.

The start of a sob cracked free, and I fastened my lips shut looking down at my lap while I blinked away tears. Bryce waited quietly for me to settle myself.

"Did you know?" I asked.

"I guessed," Bryce said. "Will you tell them?"

"Should I?" I asked. Bryce shrugged, and for a moment I thought they actually didn't care. But Hildy laughed somewhere in the shelves and Bryce's gaze twitched in her direction.

"Will you help me?" I asked, but Bryce had stiffened in their seat, turning to the stairs and back arching like a cat. There was a low sour note in the back of their throat, and then Callum was appearing between the shelves and the stairs, the same tension in his shoulders.

"It's on the campus," Bryce said, prowling toward the stairs.

"Stay with Joanna," Callum barked at the others.

Everyone shouted at once, Aiden and Tatsuo at Callum, Isaac at me, Hildy and Gwen at each other about which of them would stay with me. Bryce looked at me once over their shoulder, and I skirted around Callum following their footsteps quick down the stairs.

"Joanna!" Callum yelled.

"It's at the staff houses," Bryce said, just loud enough for me to catch the words.

I pressed my hand over my pocket, feeling for the case of chalk, and then lifted my skirt to run faster, hearing the footsteps pounding down the stairs after us. Callum caught my elbow at the bottom of the stairs, Tatsuo passing us both to chase after Bryce.

"Joanna," Callum growled.

"I helped the last time and I will again if I can," I snapped, yanking back on my arm. "But this thing is back on campus, and it's a waste of time and breath to argue about it."

"She's right," Aiden said, pushing us both forward as the rest of the group caught up.

"Everyone in the library," Gwen shouted, hands raised to her mouth. "Find your way to the staff lounge behind the circulation desk as quickly as possible and remain there until the staff calls the all-clear."

I ran to the nearest table of students, ushering them out of their chairs and shepherding them to the center of the building before running back to my...my... My thoughts stuttered at what to call Aiden and Isaac and Callum and I shook them out, focusing on the front doors.

There was a dark outline in the sky past the trees and buildings, over what must be the staff housing. Bryce and Tatsuo were already on the grounds rushing there and the rest of us followed quickly, Gwen leaving last and locking the library behind her, a few startled faces still staring out at us.

"If I tell you to run, you run," Callum said, his hand jamming into the air in front of him and drawing an enormous sword out as he looked back at me. The hilt curved back to his wrist like a pair of wings and half the blade gleamed bright and razor-sharp, the other half dark and heavy.

"I don't need to be your concern in this, Callum," I answered, my words biting out of my mouth.

"Stop," Aiden said to the both of us, jogging to walk between us, hands raised. "We are not having this argument right now. Joanna, you don't have a choice in Callum's concerns. Isaac and I want you safe as much as he does, as much as we want each other safe."

I swallowed and fixed my eyes past them, to the dark horizon, fighting back what I wanted to say. That I would have wanted them far away too. Because this was *my fault*. But they didn't know that yet, and it certainly wasn't the moment I wanted to tell them. If I told them.

Fingers trailed across my back, shoulder to shoulder, and I looked to Isaac at my side. There was a bright, clean glow resting over Aiden's red sweater, something shimmering and white.

"Just a little color magic," he said, eyes fierce on my face. "For protection."

"Thank you," I said, lifting his hand from my shoulder to hold it tight in mine.

A gust of wind carrying a bitter burnt stench swirled around us as we made it to the Burgess building. The ground trembled under our running feet and the shouting started in the distance. Callum and Aiden ran closely in front of us both, and for a moment I couldn't hear anything above the slaps of steps on the pavement. And then I realized that it was matching the cacophony of destruction on the far end of the campus. Dust and smoke were gathering in the air and echoes like thunder carried down the paths we ran.

My ears felt crushed under a heavy pressure that wanted to buckle my knees beneath me. People were streaking by us, others standing on their steps, screaming back at the darkness gathered in front of them, their hands raised to trace magic in the air. There was a storm whipping across the ground as we arrived, a torrent made from a smoke cloud and black shrouded fabric and a dark tear that ripped away the world to leave an empty hole, all swirling on the street in front of my little house.

And on either side of my house was wreckage, buildings turned to rubble and smoldering ash.

Bryce—small, delicate Bryce—was crouched in the middle of the street, shining a faint gold that the shadowy expanse skirted away from. Tatsuo stood at the edge, arms raised with short wooden staffs in either hand. Callum ran to join him, and the storm seemed to coil in on itself, and explosion in reverse. It was gathering into a shape, a figure, and the words fell loose from my lips.

"It came for me."

Isaac stirred at my side, as if he had heard and was about to look at me, when a tangle of darkness slithered across the ground in our direction.

"Look out!" Aiden shouted and both he and Isaac moved in front of me.

I dropped to my knees, chalk already in hand, and scrawled in heavy letters across the pavement.

STOP

The wind was gone from my ears, and the shouting was stilled, and the roar of what must have been the houses crumbling was quiet. Aiden and Isaac were frozen in front of me, Callum and Tatsuo and Bryce in the distance. Between us was the Hollow, something like a body under smoky gauze. A body in the right shape but wrong pieces. All I could imagine, all I could really make out through the shifting film of airy black, was a squirming, twisting split. A mouth waiting to surge forward and swallow.

I held my breath, waiting, hoping I hadn't hurt anyone.

I've waited for you, witchling, it said. The voice was something like Bryce's. Like layers and ringing, but this was more scratch and hiss in my ears than a sound. *You set me free and then you steal the food out of my belly. I wonder if you are friend or foe.*

I had put a stop to the fires in the remains of the houses, and a stop on my friends, but the Hollow was floating through the still-life scene as if it were a piece of refuse picked up by a breeze.

"Foe," I said. I meant to shout it, but it came out as a whisper, my eyes busy tracking its approach.

A brave answer, the Hollow hissed. *But you are not a foe when you are only a small, breakable thing that cannot hurt me. And you cannot hurt me, witchling. You can't even protect your belongings.*

Something like a hand reached out from the shadows, crawling through the air to Isaac.

"No," I whispered, and I tugged at the back of Isaac's jacket. "No, stop!"

Isaac swayed at my pull but stayed upright and held captive as the hand that looked more like a claw or a blade stretched closer. I stared down at the word on the ground, scrubbing my palm over it to try and smear it away and break my spell. But I had ground the chalk into the pavement and *STOP* stayed bright and unbroken, my hand scratched by the rough surface of the road.

I scrambled up to my feet, trying to place myself between Isaac and the Hollow, but I was too late. The smoke scratched over Isaac's right cheek, and into his hair. His eyes winced and a moan escaped his parted lips and his knees buckled. My arms were around him and he fell into me, the Hollow continuing to ooze over the ground on its way past us. It hissed and spat with laughter and the dark clouds over the sky cracked and drummed and rain came spilling loose as I sank down to the ground with Isaac gasping and groaning in my arms, red and gray and white streaking across his cheekbone.

"No, no, no, no," I whispered. "I'm sorry. I'm sorry."

His chest heaved and rain turned his white shirt translucent. I looked down at the ground beside us where I had wasted time, and my word was being spattered and spoiled under the falling drops. I dug my nails and fingers into the chalk, scratching and tearing until the word became nothing more than a white smear, streaks of red mingling where I had ripped at my skin.

"I picked the wrong word," I said, as motion stirred around me.

Aiden landed on the ground, warm hands on my cheeks, and I pulled away. My eyes were blurry with tears and my words came out in hiccuping sobs.

"I picked the wrong word. I'm sorry, I'm sorry."

"Callum!" Aiden shouted, but Callum was already reaching us, with Tatsuo and Bryce.

Bryce grabbed Isaac out of my arms with more strength than someone their size ought to have had and I shouted, reaching for him. Tatsuo stepped between Callum and Bryce and I thought it might come to blows. Isaac moaned in Bryce's hold and we all surged forward.

"Wait," Gwen snapped from behind us. "Wait, Bryce can help."

Bryce held him up, legs limp, and lifted one of their hands to his face, covering the marks made by the Hollow. They shined gold again, and there was a hum that felt like ringing in my ears, but I refused to look away. Aiden's arms squeezed around my waist and Callum strained against Tatsuo. Isaac's breath was ragged and he hissed and squirmed in Bryce's hold for a long moment. And then he went soft, relaxing and turning quiet.

Tatsuo released Callum and Bryce passed Isaac to him. "Take him to medical," Bryce said, green eyes bright and yellowy.

Aiden stood, his hand clasped around mine. I clamped my lips shut and choked down the remains of my sobs.

"Take her back to the house?" Callum asked.

I could see the way Aiden's shoulders drew in, but he started to nod.

"No," I said. I stood on shaky legs. "No, you should both go." Callum's forehead knotted and Aiden looked resigned, prepared to argue for Callum. "I'll stay with the others," I said.

"She's safe with us, you know that," Gwen said.

"Go," I said, flattening down tears that wanted to break free and the anxiety rioting in my gut. "I'll find you later."

I couldn't tell if Callum was angry or worried or hurt or if he simply didn't want to waste the time arguing when Isaac needed care. But he left with quick steps. Aiden pressed a hard kiss to my forehead that left me queasy with guilt and then hurried after him.

"This isn't your fault," Hildy said gently, taking my hands.

"It is actually," I said.

I felt numb with the truth of it. I had been curious and careless and even if it had all been an accident, it was my hands that let the creature out. And if I had not, Cecil Pincombe would have been alive and Isaac would have been safe and the woods wouldn't be dying and the sun probably would have been shining too for that matter.

"Joanna," Hildy murmured.

"Better get to the library," Bryce said, taking my elbow in their hand.

I sagged with a kind of relief. Bryce, at least, would not argue with me.

CHAPTER 22

JOANNA

IT RAINED FOR DAYS.

The campus kept busy coming up with magical means of keeping the flood at bay. And in the library we watched the rain break against the patched hole in the roof.

Isaac came back to the house sleeping, and I volunteered to keep the night shift of watching over him, shooing Aiden out of the room when he offered to sit up with me. I left early in the morning and came back late at night with excuses about the library. Callum and Aiden watched me passing through the house, but I found corners to hide around when I thought they might be looking for me.

At night I kept vigil in a chair by Isaac's bedroom window and wrote in my notebook. *Put it back. The Hollow is in its cage again and cannot come out. Everyone is safe.* But every morning the sun rose, dark in the sky, and the vise squeezed tighter in my chest.

Isaac slept like the dead the first night, the red mark bright on his cheek with the faintest glow above it, either from the healers or Bryce. The next night was fits and stirring, and I sat on the side of the bed, wiping sweat off his brow and letting him crush my hand in his grip. Finally, on the third night he settled, breath deepening. I leaned my head against the window, glass cool on my skin, and let myself drift off.

I woke choking on air, hands on my arms as I tried to fight them off.

"It's me, it's me, Joanna," Isaac whispered.

I reared back in the chair and caught my breath. Isaac's hands stroked at my sides, his eyes half-lidded with sleep and the scar on his cheek shiny but pale.

"Come to bed, love," he said.

"You should be sleeping," I answered.

"I will. Better with you next to me. Come rest."

I let him pull me up and then ducked under his arm as he swayed in step. "Do you want me to get Aiden or-"

"I want you to come lay down with me, Joanna," he said, words weary as we stumbled back to the bed together. "I just want to hold you." Isaac pulled me into his side under the covers, arm across my back and fingers in my hair. "Quit punishing yourself," he mumbled against my forehead.

I hummed and he squeezed me gently. Everyone had tried telling me similar things. Even Bryce had said, 'It's only a problem that needs solved.' It didn't soothe the heaviness at the back of my head or the clammy feeling under my skin or the guilt that lay bricks in my belly every minute. And Isaac's soft snores brought tears to the corners of my eyes rather than helping me drift into sleep.

Over and over in my head, it ran in a loop.

If I hadn't come here to Canderfey.

If I hadn't sent the charmed application.

If I hadn't met Aiden or Isaac or Callum.

If I hadn't called *Gatekeepers* back from whatever safe hole it had been moldering in.

Everyone would be safe. The Hollow would be in its cage and Cecil Pincombe would be alive and Isaac would never have been hurt.

It was my fault. And if it was a problem that needed to be solved, it was time I set about doing so.

HILDY ANSWERED the door in the morning before the dark sun had finished rising in the sky. I was already soaked through my coat and my boots, just from the short walk to the house.

"Joanna, come in," she said. Her face was clean and tired and she looked surprised to see me, but I thought it was probably beyond Hildy not to be welcoming when it was called for. "What do you need? Gwen is already at the library."

"I was hoping Tatsuo was home, actually," I said, ducking into the dry warmth of the house.

"Of course, we're just having breakfast."

"I'm sorry," I said, covering my hands over the sick clench in my stomach.

"No, don't be silly," Hildy said with a wave of her hand before gesturing me to follow her. "You're welcome at any hour, you know that."

Tatsuo was drinking tea, bare chest pale under his bathrobe, and his eyebrows raised as I entered the kitchen. Bryce sat opposite him and barely glanced over their shoulder at me, unsurprised by my arrival or simply not awake enough to care.

"I..." It seemed silly now, to have come while they were busy having breakfast. "I wanted to ask about...trance writing."

But Tatsuo's eyes lit up at that and Hildy snorted, going to her spot at the table while he rose up from his.

"Absolutely," he said as if it were a natural question for break-fast at dawn. "Come to the reading room and I'll show you some of what I've been working on."

There was a fire going in the reading room, dark daylight coming in through the windows and brightened quickly by Tatsuo turning on lamps. He offered me a seat and then fluttered busily around the room, gathering up stray pieces of paper and heavy books. He brought them back, pulling up another chair and laying it out over the table with a flourish. I glanced down at the scribbles, cryptic scrawling messages in strange directions, and bit my lip.

"I had a few...specific questions," I said.

Tatsuo clapped his hands together. "Yes, please, ask away!"

"The trance, is it hard to...to fall into?" I asked.

He leaned back in his chair, hand lifting to stroke at his chin and I could tell it pleased him to have someone here, asking him questions. It brought me something almost like cheer until I wondered if Callum would hear about this later, that I had come to Tatsuo to form a plan. And then I remembered that he probably wouldn't care after what I had done and I blinked quickly down at my lap.

"I suppose it may be, for a beginner," Tatsuo said. "It requires emptying one's head, making room for the openness needed in a trance. Sometimes though, Bryce will drone for me and then it takes no time at all."

"Drone?"

"Mmhm, it's like singing, but it leads almost directly to hypnotism for most people," he said. He took a breath and I realized he was about to launch deep into the new topic so I hurried to keep him on track.

"Is trance writing a way of discovering a true name?" I asked.

Tatsuo's eyes narrowed at me for a moment at that, the excited collector of knowledge replaced with someone shrewd and intelligent enough to know what I was fishing for.

"It could be. Certainly of the symbolic portion of a true name. But not of anyone or anything. It would have to be your own, or the name belonging to someone you share a connection with. And it is widely acknowledged as being the kind of thing better left unknown. Knowing a true name allows for the opportunity of it being discovered by the wrong hands."

"Of course," I said.

Bryce had not told him then that I already had a kind of connection with the Hollow. It was stealing my dreams and I had let it out of its cage. That may not be enough, but it was more than I wanted, and it was the best—or worst—anyone else could boast of.

I quizzed Tatsuo on the ceremony of the practice, filling in my real questions with aimless, harmless ones that sent him rattling in new directions. I kept him for an hour, saying goodbye to Hildy as she left for work. I hoped that he would forgive me later for pumping him for the information. I hoped that I would be around to receive forgiveness.

"I should get to the library," I said, as Tatsuo finished an explanation on different kinds of plant-based inks. "Thank you for humoring me."

"My pleasure, I love hypotheticals after breakfast," he said, gallant as ever, even in his dressing robe.

"I'll walk you." We both turned to see Bryce lingering in the doorway. "It's not safe out."

"Thank you," I said. I repeated the words to Tatsuo with a hug and then met Bryce in the hall. They walked me to the door, pulling a long black umbrella out of a stand.

"You can't do it alone," Bryce said as they shut the door closed behind us and passed me the umbrella.

I fiddled with it first, opening it out and waiting for Bryce to stand under the cover with me.

"I know," I said, quiet as if someone might be listening.

"I will help," Bryce said. The nerves in my stomach mingled with relief. They looked at me, eyes narrowed. "It is one of my kind, somewhat."

I had wondered as much. It didn't change the fact that I trusted Bryce completely to help. "Do you think it will work?" I asked.

"It will work or we will be eaten," Bryce said shrugging. "Does that suit you?"

I almost laughed, but it was laced with panic and came out like a squawk.

"I suppose," I said.

৩৮৩

I LINGERED late at the library, a queasy feeling hanging in my stomach at the thought of heading home. Home to the little staff house for the first time in weeks. And this time no one would come to fetch me back to the coven house.

Callum had explained that he had placed wards strong enough to keep the Hollow out of the small house before they managed to convince me to stay with them. It was why mine was still standing, unmarred, and my neighbors' homes were rubble.

But the neighborhood had made it out at the first sign of the sky turning dark. Isaac was the only one hurt that day.

I didn't want to go back to my house. It was small and empty and I had loved that it was mine and mine alone, but now the thought of it made me lonely. I wanted to put my cheek against lush fabrics and let my eyes soak up the color of bright walls. I wanted to fall asleep next to someone and wake up in a crowded bed.

It was a waste to crave that tall tower house, and the people inside, so badly now when I had given all of it up.

I snuck past Gwen to the main doors as the sun started to set. I didn't want to stay with her and the others either, not while where I really wanted to be was within easy sight.

The rain hadn't stopped once and the sidewalks were drowning, water up to my ankles that splashed and ran into my boots with every sluggish step. There was no busy traffic outside with me now. I wasn't even sure if classes were still in session or if students and faculty were in hiding together. I lifted my chin, shivering in my thin coat, and letting the tears wavering at my eyes roll over, mingling with the rain stinging at my cheeks. If Bryce and I were successful, would I leave campus? Quit the library and wander back to Bridgeston again? It would be too hard to see my...my men. Not that it was right to call them that now.

"Joanna!"

My heart skipped in my chest and my feet skidded in the water. But I clamped my eyes shut. "No," I whispered. Why hadn't I written *Forget me*. Or *We never met*. I didn't want to see them again. Didn't want to offer an explanation or—

"Joanna, stop!"

I didn't mean to listen. I didn't want to hear the crack in Callum's voice. I covered my face with my hands and my feet stilled beneath me. For a perverse moment, I wanted to be going a little crazy and imagining hearing him. Wet splashes pounded behind me, footsteps kicking through the deep puddles as they caught up to me. My street was within sight and I wondered if I could run there faster, hide in my small little house, and refuse to look back.

"Don't do this," he whispered, words blending into the whistle of rain. "Please don't do this to us."

I stifled a moan behind my hands as they slid down to my cheeks. I turned and he was there, getting drenched in rain, hair sticking wetly to his forehead. He pulled his glasses, spattered and wet, off his face and tucked them away, revealing the injured wince on his face. Aiden and Isaac were behind him, a little farther off, but Isaac looked pale and was leaning into Aiden's side.

Why? Why had they come? It had seemed like such a simple thing to do. Write myself out of their lives. It shouldn't have even mattered. Not to them.

"He shouldn't be out," I said looking at Isaac and his slow approach.

Callum looked back over his shoulder. "Tell him that. I tried. Joanna, why?" he asked stepping closer.

I stepped back, keeping the space between us. "Because it's true."

He pulled his hand free from his pocket, the note I had written and left under my pillow folded in his fingers. "Tear it up."

"I can't," I said.

"Of course you can. *I could.* I'm asking you to do it," he said.

I folded my hands under my arms to keep them from reaching out and smoothing away the furrow in his brow and the frown over his mouth.

"Why are you here?" I asked, my heart hammering in my chest. "I...I was never going to belong. This should be—It should be easy. Just go home-"

Callum stormed to me and I didn't have a chance to skirt away. "*Easy?*" he growled. "Joanna, tear it up, *please.*"

"It's my fault," I said, almost shouted, breaths ragged as the tears filled up in my throat. "I let the Hollow out. I wrote it in the book. I should never have come here. I shouldn't have magic in the first place. I'm just a stupid little nobody from the country whose absolutely in over her head and now everything has gone wrong!"

"It can be fixed, love," Isaac said. He and Aiden joined us at Callum's side.

"Cecil Pincombe can't," I said, voice cracking. "I know- I

know you wanted someone. You wanted me to be right. But I'm *not* and I can't be."

"If you weren't meant for us then you wouldn't need to write a spell to change it, Joanna," Aiden said, and he sounded angry but I could barely see for all the crying.

"Tear it up," Callum whispered.

"I won't," I said.

"Then you wrote the wrong thing," he said, and he pulled my arms free and stuffed the note into my hand before taking my face up in his hold. His face was blurry and close, but I could make out the blue of his eyes. "If I have to love you without you belonging in our coven then you've cursed me."

The sob tore out of my chest and the pain of it was more relief than wound. I folded forward with the force of it and Callum dragged me against his chest. The note, *I don't belong in your coven* printed inside, crumpled wetly in my fist as I struck it against him. I had told myself it would be enough. To erase whatever fleeting attraction that had fooled them in the first place. To make reality set in and break up all my romantic fantasies. Instead, every word had felt crooked and wrong to write.

"We knew something was broken today," Isaac said, and his voice was faint. "That you'd pulled away."

I wanted to get him somewhere warm and dry as much as I wanted to push them all away. *Thought* I wanted to.

"Callum was getting ready to find you at the library when I found the note," he said. "You can tear it up or leave it, but it won't stop me from *wanting* you with us."

"Tear it up," Callum repeated, a little sullenly. I could feel him nudging at the top of my head and I wiped my cheeks against his damp shirt before looking up. "Did you ever want it to be true?" he asked.

It was such a stupid question! I blurted without thinking, "Of course I did! From the start. But all of this was my mistake and I have to fix it!" Aiden was closing in at my side and I rushed to add, "And I can't stand that one of you might be hurt or worse again if I make another one. I...I thought, maybe, once it was all done..."

"Trying to do this alone is a mistake," Aiden said. He *was* angry. I could hear it now. It didn't seem like a good time to mention my plan.

Callum's eyes narrowed on my face. "You can't stop us from fighting for the campus or for you. We're already involved. Is that enough now?"

"Or did you think we wouldn't fight for you?" Isaac whispered. His hair was down, soaked like inky streaks running down the sides of his face, and his skin was almost as pale and gray as his eyes. But his gaze was sharp on me, pinpricks of heat that burned in my chest.

"Please, Joanna. No more," Callum begged. "If you meant it, if you really want us...tear up the note and come home."

I felt trapped under a weight of emotion I didn't understand and dizzy with confusion. Isaac was right. I didn't think they would come. I thought I could write the words and that would be the end. The only one left hurting would be me. But if what Callum said was true...I wouldn't be able to bring myself to write away those feelings. Not if they were real and I could have them, keep them and wallow in them. I couldn't carve them out of myself either.

The ink had all but washed away on the note, now soggy. But I lifted it between us and ripped through the middle of the words, and then again and again until it was pulp in my fingers. Callum took my wrists in his hands and kissed me, lips and teeth hard against mine, holding me close and still for a long stretch. I cried into the kiss and there were hands at my back until I was sheltered between the three of them.

"Say it," Callum said, drawing back.

"I'm sorry," I said.

"Not that," he said, pecking at my lips. "Say you belong in the coven."

My breath was shaky and nervous in my chest. But his eyes were fixed to mine and Isaac and Aiden were holding their breath on either side. "I belong with you," I said. "In the coven."

"We need to get somewhere dry before we have to swim home," Aiden said as Isaac pulled me from Callum, peppering kisses over both my cheeks.

"My house," I said, sniffling and wiping uselessly at my eyes. "I never got rid of the doorway into your room."

We were a cluster on the sidewalk together, walking as quickly as we could without having to be out of each other's reach. The street was desolate and I wondered how many staff were even still staying in their houses after what had happened on the weekend. There was a second, smaller wave of guilt and then Aiden's warm hand was at my back, leading me up the steps. I dug in my pocket for my key and let us inside.

The house felt abandoned, as if I'd needed further proof at how much more quickly I had settled into living with them than here by myself.

"Do you need anything?" Callum asked, glancing around.

I shook my head. "I left my case at the library and...and I never had much."

Isaac squeezed my hand and Aiden led us all to the pantry door in the kitchen and then back into their home.

CHAPTER 23

AIDEN

JOANNA'S STEPS SQUISHED IN HER SHOES AS SHE WALKED INTO my bedroom and she stopped abruptly before reaching the carpet. We were all dripping onto the floorboard and Joanna had a puddle around her from her boots alone.

"Get a bath going?" I asked Callum.

He looked between us, at Joanna fidgeting by herself, and Isaac shivering by the door. "Come in when you're ready," he said.

I knelt at Joanna's feet as they left, her hands landing at my shoulders as I untied her boots and lifted her feet free. They were like icicles and I resisted the urge to lift them to my lips to press some heat back into them. I looked up and she was already peeling herself out of her clothes, that flimsy, awful little slip of hers sticking to her skin and distracting me. I stood, stroking up her side as I went and she leaned into the touch. I took the clothes out of her hands and stepped back.

"Find something warm for yourself," I said, crossing past her to dump her clothes into the hamper and get out of my own.

"Aiden," she said, the sweet mellow syrup of her voice burrowing into my chest.

I wasn't sure if I wanted to be angry—that she had tried to leave, tried to shatter the possibility of being a part of our coven. Or to be grateful she had torn her note, her spell, up into dozens of little pieces. To prove to her once again that I could offer her something worth keeping. That I was worth keeping.

I turned back and she was waiting, holding out my robe and wearing my red sweater, the collar dipping low between her breasts. My lips quirked against my will. I didn't stand a chance. Not against her. She helped me into the sleeves and her arms followed mine around my waist as I tied the belt.

"I'm sorry," she said into my back, words mumbled into the fabric.

I squeezed her hands over my stomach and took a long breath before pulling myself free. She was anxious, wounded looking, eyes red and hair still running wet rivulets down her neck.

"Come sit with me," I said, keeping her hands in mine to lead her to the bed. She climbed up to the coverlet, knees disappearing under the hem of the sweater as she folded them under her. I faced her and kept our hands clasped, resisting the urge to pull her into my lap, to hold her face and kiss her beyond any thought of leaving again. "Tell me your plan," I said. She frowned and I added, "What were you going to do after you had successfully...kept us safe by leaving?"

Her fingers fidgeted in mine and she looked down at her lap, cheeks coloring. "Bryce Gast said they would help me. They... I went to ask Tatsuo about trance writing to find true names," she said.

"Is that possible?" I asked, feeling a panicked kind of temper rising in my chest. "Wouldn't you need-"

"A connection?" she asked, looking up. "I have one. I'm the one that let it out, it's eating my dreams at night from across the woods."

"And Gast was going to help," I spat.

"They offered, yes," she said and her words began to harden, shoulders straightening. "For their own reasons."

I released one of her hands to scrub at my face. "True names *aren't just words*," I said, breathing through my nose.

"I know, but-"

"While you've been hiding from us, Callum and I have been scouring for information. The Hollow's true name is made up of music, color, and…a word. We haven't found them yet, but don't you think that gives us the *right* to help you?"

"Yes."

I pulled my hand off my eyes to stare at her and almost immediately regretted it. She looked so fragile and aching still and it made me want to pull her up in my arms.

"Aiden, I'm sorry," she said, every word heavy with sincerity. She scooted closer and my arms twitched for her. "I *do* think it would have worked. Bryce wouldn't have agreed if they didn't think so too but– *but*," she said, raising her hand to stop my words and continuing quickly, "That doesn't matter. It was the wrong decision and I regret it. I… Aiden, I really didn't think you would all…" her breath hitched, eyes filling up, and my will broke.

I took her face in my hands and held it to mine, foreheads touching. "Haven't we told you? All we've wanted is for you to be a part of us, of this home."

"You have and I heard it and I just…I kept waiting for it to turn out to be a…cosmic trick on me," she whispered, tracing a kiss over my mouth. "I can still barely believe it."

"We need you to," I said, feeling the grip of panic at the back of my throat.

"I know," she said, hands soft on my back as she settled herself in my hold. "I know. I'm not going anywhere, I promise."

The panic shuddered out of me and I took her lips in mine, drawing deeply, holding her tight to my chest. Her hands squeezed at my shoulders before sliding between us to push away slightly, nipping at my lips in quick affectionate nibbles before leaning back.

"That doesn't change the fact that I am responsible for what's happening," she said softly.

"You cannot blame yourself for being manipulated into letting that thing out," I said.

"And you can't deny that I should be the one to put it back in its cage," she said, face steely. "I don't want to be guarded in the tower by three knights when it was my *mistake* that's led to this."

I huffed. For once, I needed Callum here to deal with the problem. If there was anyone who could talk Joanna out of self-punishment it would be him, and it might do them both good. In the meantime, there was something I could say.

"Joanna, we have waited for you for a *long* time. I know you know that. And I'm not saying that gives us the right to try and shield you. Although it's probably been a motivation for us, you're right," I said. I kissed her mouth before she could argue and then continued, "I'm just saying, we *all* try to shield each other. We've just already had the arguments over it, and you're playing catch-up. If it's any consolation Callum was walking Isaac home every night I escorted you back from the library."

She blinked at that, a faint smile appearing on her lips. "It helps a little."

"We won't let you try to fix this on your own," I said. "That's off the table as of right now. And Bryce Gast isn't enough help either, and if you argue that, I'll tell Woollard and the rest of their coven about the plan, and then the pair of you will both be in trouble. But I promise that we aren't trying to tuck you safely away. We're a coven, and we're doing this together."

"Are you going to tell Callum that?" she asked, smirking.

"I am," I said, raising an eyebrow. "If you're lucky, I won't even mention that you went to Tatsuo for help."

She was turning soft in my arms. I knew we should be finding the others, but there wasn't a cell in my body interested in moving. Not if she wasn't moving.

"I'm sorry, Aiden," she said again, simple and earnest.

"Don't ever do that again," I said.

"Never," she said, easily.

"Are you sure there's nothing you need at your house? You may be in for a long stay here," I said, wanting to ask it. *Stay, stay, stay.*

"I like it better here, anyway," she said.

"Right here?" I asked, grinning and looking down at where she was sprawled over my lap. I stroked my palms down her back to her waist and she rose to her knees, inching closer.

"Maybe...here," she said, pressing our chests together, a small smile growing in the corners of her lips. Her hands were between us, shaking with cold and untying the knot in the waist of my robe.

I teased my fingers down to the hem of my sweater, skimming them over the skin at the tops of her thighs.

"Are you eager for the bath?" she asked, voice tilting and teasing.

"Not especially," I said, trying to keep the growl out of my throat.

"And will Callum and Isaac come looking for us?"

"Would it matter if they did?" I asked.

Her eyes darkened at that and there was a needy clench in my belly. She liked the idea. I smoothed my hands up her skin and found her hips naked, my thumbs stroking over her bare mound. She hummed and closed her eyes, body leaning into the touch.

"My Joanna," I murmured, lifting the sweater to see a glimpse of the pink skin of her pussy before she was squirming down to nuzzle at my cheek.

"My King," she whispered in my ear and my cock jumped, stirring and aching, even as I laughed at her joke.

She kissed a wet trail over my jaw, rocking and twisting herself in my lap, drawing out a groan as I hardened against her. She pushed the loose robe off my shoulders, her hands roaming greedily over my skin as I pulled my arms free. We had both stripped down to nothing and I could feel her growing wet, sliding it over my length and working herself up in the process.

Her breasts were bouncing lightly with her movement, nipples turning to little points. I stroked my thumbs over them, grunting as she ground down against me. But there was something soft building in my chest watching her.

"I can't decide if I want to watch you in my sweater or out of it," I admitted.

She opened her eyes, raising an eyebrow at me. "Is *that* what you're thinking about? I wondered why I was doing all the work."

I barked out a laugh, and pulled the sweater up over her head, ducking to taste the skin I'd found. She rose to her knees again, and I grinned as a breast appeared conveniently before me. I wrapped my lips around a perfect, rosy nipple and then groaned against the skin when a small hand wrapped around me, pumping gently.

"I'm already there, darling," I growled into her breast, my hands gripping at her hips to draw her over me, teasing her opening with the tip of my cock.

"So am I, darling," she said, grinning. I looked up to watch her face as I pulled her down slowly, a fraction at a time.

I knew Callum and Isaac's bodies as well as I knew my own, and I knew that the girth of me would be a stretch for her. A stretch she seemed to appreciate if the way her face went lax and open with every gentle nudge deeper. I rolled her onto me, her hands clutching at the back of my neck.

"Oh, oh gods, Aiden," she said, high and breathy.

She was slick and hot around me and it took all my willpower to keep from surging up into her. I clenched my jaw, bouncing her, stretching and teasing at just her entrance until she was mewling, trying to push herself down farther.

"Darling girl," I said, wrapping an arm around her so I could free a hand. I stroked at her where we were joined and she arched, crying out.

"I want more," she pleaded, still squirming and trying to turn the small careful thrust of me inside her into something deeper.

"You'll have it, I promise," I said.

I sucked at the breast hovering by my lips and fumbled in her slippery folds until I found her clit, rolling and pressing. Her nails dug into my back as she shouted, squeezing in tight flutters around my cock as I finally drew her down. I seated myself fully, swallowing my groan and tensing my thighs to keep from bucking as she quivered around me with small aftershocks. I wrapped my arms around her back, a pleased rumble in my chest as she settled, and kissed my way up to her neck.

"Do you always get your way?" she grumbled against my ear, and then nipped at my lobe, a bolt of pleasure shooting down my spine.

I laughed again, as she pushed me backward into the mattress, and then the laughter died and turned to moans as she took revenge for my teasing. Her hands were braced against my chest as she rose and fell, clasping and dragging over every inch of my cock. She squeezed around the tip of me before sliding down again and grinding our bodies together, broken sounds falling from both our mouths. I braced my feet against the edge of the bed, bucking up to meet her and holding her steady.

"Aiden," she whispered, turning it into a chant as her head drooped.

The pace turned quick, her thighs shaking around me, and every dive and drag of her body pulling straight from my gut. My hands felt hot and an electric current was jolting up my spine in time with Joanna's torrid rhythm. She surged up, back arching and hands moving to my knees, body leaning back and putting me at a new angle inside of her that had her singing. I gentled our movements, pressing in slow, strong strokes until she was trembling with every small brush between us.

"Come again, darling," I begged, needing it as badly as she did in that moment.

She shook, abbreviated little cries and babbling praises, and she was slippery and hot around me, trying to milk pleasure out of me in return. I gathered her to my chest and rolled her onto her back, her legs and arms wrapping around me as heat burrowed at the base of my spine and exploded outward. There was a roar in my ears and a dense blanketing warm rolling out into my muscles. She had me enveloped, sweet heat still clenching around me and hands fluttering and kissing over my back.

Joanna hummed small happy sounds in my ear, kissing the corner of my jaw, and she held me tight to her as I tried to draw back.

"'M too heavy, I'll crush you," I said, squeezing gently at her shoulders while my arms were still trapped beneath us.

"Just one more minute," she said.

She loosened her hold around me as I softened. Her hair was rumpled and damp around her face and she was flushed red over her chest.

"Hello," she said, smiling and biting her lip. I leaned down to pluck it free with my own.

"Hello," I said. I drew back and she squirmed, a little whimper at the back of her throat as I pulled out. "Alright?"

"Yes," she said, grinning. "But I'll have that bath now, I think."

I scooped her up off the bed and ran us down the hall and into the bathroom. The room was warm and misty and Callum and Isaac were both already submerged in water. There were candles lit on the counter and glasses of wine waiting for us. I set Joanna down and she hurried to the water, Callum moving aside to put her between him and Isaac, drawing her against his chest. Isaac was pink-cheeked, warmed in the water, and leaning back against the lip of the tub with his eyes closed. But he lifted Joanna's feet and set them up on his knees, thumbs digging into her soles and drawing a purr from her lips.

He had looked stricken, almost green when he came down from his room with her note in hand. There had been actual defeat in his expression and I had let it dig into me too, rejection thorny in my chest. It was Callum, of all us, who had refused the words, the spell, the gesture completely. But Isaac seemed content now, if maybe a little reserved. He and Joanna would have their time later, she was watching his face.

Isaac's hand reached back for me and I took it, letting him drawing me in on his other side. The water stung with heat, burning at the lingering chill of the rain and the dark.

"Say it again," Callum whispered and both Isaac and I turned to look at Joanna, reclined in his arms.

She met our gazes. "I belong with you," she said, reaching up to cover Callum's hand on her shoulder. His answering smile was light and simple, a pure kind of pleasure he rarely showed. Joanna was still staring back at Isaac. "Can I see my room after the bath?" she asked.

Isaac exhaled heavily, leaning into me. "Of course you can," he said, words soft.

Joanna smiled, no nerves or shy hesitation on her face. There was a giddiness building up in my chest. A wild delirious feeling that threatened tears at the back of my eyes and made my throat swell shut. She belonged with us and she *would* stay this time. I had my coven, my family.

Now I—*we* just needed to keep each other safe.

CHAPTER 24

JOANNA

My bedroom was on the fourth floor of the house. My bedroom *was* the fourth floor of the house with an ensuite bathroom as nice as the one the men shared. The ceiling was high and domed, wood beams dark and exposed and there was a large round window at the far end of the room. An enormous bed sat in front of the window, wide enough to be shared by four, I realized, staring at it.

The men were at my back and I could hear them shifting, waiting for my reaction. And I couldn't come up with one because I was too busy being overwhelmed.

There were cream bookshelves lining the walls and I wondered if they had been added after they had met me, or if they had known they would find an avid reader. Or if they simply had been there when Aiden bought the house. Five small windows hung in the roof, and later, when everything was settled and safe again, I would see the stars out of them at night. There was a set of armchairs over a rug, by a small fireplace, with a low table between them.

"Do you like it?" Callum asked, standing close to my back and resting his hands on my hips.

"It's beautiful," I said, and then realized that wasn't the right kind of answer I added, "I love it. It's so big though. I won't have to stay up here alone will I?"

Aiden laughed and moved over to the fireplace, pulling logs from the rack. We were all fresh from the bath and I was back in his sweater with Aiden and Isaac in their robes and Callum's hips wrapped in a towel. The room was a little chilled, and smelled dry and dusty, unused for too long. But everything was clean and there was a painting of a field of wildflowers on the wall that made me ache with sweetness.

"Not until you get sick of having us in your hair," Aiden said. "This was designed to be the master suite. I just wanted to save it until..."

"Until the coven was full," I said and he looked back at me from the fireplace, eyes bright and crinkled with a smile.

"You mean it," Isaac said. I turned and he was behind Callum, hovering near the door, face shadowed by the stairwell.

"I mean it," I said.

Callum bent his head, fingers tugging at the sweater to pull it down and expose my shoulder to his mouth. Isaac stepped up close, his hands layering over Callum's on my ribs, nose brushing mine.

"I'm sor—" I started, happy to say it as many times as they wanted to hear. Happy to be in the house again, happy to feel stupid for ever trying to leave. But Isaac swallowed the word with a kiss, tongue delving and stroking into my mouth, licking at the back of my teeth and curling over my own tongue.

I moaned into the kiss as Callum's teeth scraped over my shoulder. He traveled up my neck, sucking and licking, hips pressing into my back. Isaac crowded me at my front, lips turning soft and teasing. I wished for more hands, more ways to return their touches as I arched and curved between them.

Callum's fingers stroked over the tops of my thighs, sliding between my legs to brush and pet, dancing away as I tried to chase them. Isaac drew away from my lips and then he and Callum were kissing, one long smooth caress into each other. I was surrounded by them, swallowed up in the embrace and feeling every inch of them against me, cocks stirring against my belly. Their hands gathered up the sweater, dragging it up over my head.

"Take her to the bed," Isaac said. Callum lifted me up, arms around my hips and I squeaked in surprise.

"I can walk!" I said, laughing as Callum layered kisses on my shoulder.

Aiden was grinning from in front of the fireplace, a small flicker of flames already started. He winked at me and offered no help.

Callum kicked the towel away as it fell to the floor in front of the bed. I bounced on his lap as we landed on the mattress and then he dragged us back to the headboard. My back was to his stomach, the start of his erection bumping into me as he spread his knees inside of my thighs, exposing me to the air. He caught my hands before I could cover myself, drawing them back and kissing them both.

"Let us see you," he said against my ear and then kissed at the corner of my jaw.

I shivered and even I didn't know if it was the cool air or the sound of Callum's voice in my ear or the sight of Isaac and Aiden watching us.

Isaac was prowling to the bed, eyes caressing over my skin as he crawled up the mattress. He nuzzled into my belly button, flicking his tongue out briefly and making me gasp at the touch.

"The pair of you are art like this," he said, glancing up.

"You are not allowed to sketch this," I said, but my words were weak and breathy.

Callum's hands were tracing over my ribs, barely brushing across my ribs. His tongue lapped over my neck until the skin was hyper-sensitive and I wanted to beg him to stop or bite. Instead, I just stretched it, exposing more flesh to the treatment.

"Maybe from memory," Isaac said, grinning.

Isaac's palm cupped over my pussy, rubbing the pads of his fingers across my clit. The tip of Callum's cock was peeking between my legs, just under his hand and Isaac dipped his head down, sucking it into his mouth. Callum arched under me, bucking me up into Isaac's hand while his chest rattled into my back with a groan.

"Tell her," Isaac mumbled, pulling away from Callum and moving his hand away. He nibbled at my lower lips and Callum arched forward to swallow my whimper in a kiss. "Tell her, Callum," Isaac said again and I rolled my hips up to try and draw him back to me.

"We...we talked about you," Callum mumbled into the kiss. "While we were fucking, we talked about how we wanted you."

I moaned and he pulled at my mouth again, Isaac rewarding us both by lapping avidly at me. Callum stretched my hands back around his head, banding an arm over my ribs to hold me for Isaac's efforts. The bed dipped at our side and a large warm hand stroked down from my neck all the way to the hair just above my folds, a finger toying at the top of my slit. Aiden's mouth landed at my breast and suddenly there was too much at once and I couldn't think of what I wanted next, only that I wanted more.

Isaac licked, swirling over my clit, and a finger and then two slid inside of me, testing, before drawing out again. Callum's breath hitched in my mouth and then he was pushing into me, guided by Isaac's hand.

Callum cursed into my neck, knees spreading wider and hips thrusting beneath me. Whatever word I meant to say fell apart into nonsense. He released my hands and they fell into Isaac's hair, tangling and gripping at the strands.

Isaac lay flat on his belly and I watched his back, the planes and knots of muscles working as he mouthed wetly over where Callum and I were joined. He groaned against us as my fingers tightened in his hair and moved up to flick and lap and swirl at the bundle of nerves stirring heat and ecstasy into my blood.

Their names were falling out of my mouth, tangled together in the wrong order. Callum bounced me over his length, mouth panting grunts against my neck as Isaac toyed with us both. Aiden's hands were everywhere while his lips pulled steadily at my breast.

I crested quick and hard, a bright shout echoing out of me as stars lit up behind my eyes, and my thighs clamped around Isaac's ears. I wanted to fix him in place to me and push him away at the same time. Callum fucked through my orgasm, extending and deepening it until I was twitching and boneless and my whole body felt fevered and charged.

Isaac pushed my thighs apart and stole me out of Callum's

hold, his hips kicking in chase and a ragged growl breaking out of his throat.

"Not yet," Callum snarled.

Aiden laughed, drawing away from me and pulling Callum to his chest. His hand wrapped around Callum's cock and sliding evenly over it, coated in my juices, and Callum grasped onto Aiden's hold with a grateful moan. Isaac scooted up to my back as I curled up on my side. He pulled my hips into his and raised my right leg up over his, fitting himself inside of me from behind.

I whimpered, twisting my neck to hide my face in a pillow, but Isaac pushed my hair back, hooking his fingers under my chin. He lifted my chin up and kissed at my pulse.

"Watch them," Isaac said in my ear. He was fully seated, hips barely pumping, and free arm stroking over my side and belly. "Watch them with me."

I caught my breath in little puffs and opened my eyes. Isaac settled his chin into my shoulder and we stared at Callum and Aiden in front of us, curled together like a mirror of our own position. Aiden was peppering kisses over Callum's shoulder, one hand stroking softly at the base of Callum's cock and the other working behind. Callum's mouth was opened wide on a soundless cry. I reached out, running my hand down his chest and into the hair trailing down from his navel. His stomach trembled under my touch.

Isaac nudged us closer until Callum and I could reach each other, mouths latching hungrily to one another. Aiden rumbled at Callum's back and the sound echoed out of Callum into the kiss. Aiden pushed forward and then Callum was sliding against me, cock twitching and leaking fluid against my thigh. Aiden's knuckles brushed over my sex as he squeezed and dragged his hand down Callum's length, both of them bucking closer.

Isaac braced himself up on an elbow, one hand holding me open at my knee, hips swirling and thrusting, hitting at my front walls. Wet sounds filled the room and noisy cries. I could feel the echo of them in my throat and mouth, but I couldn't pick the voices apart in my ear. Just like I couldn't keep track of who was touching me and when and where. Only that every part of me was full of hunger and a dreamy kind of satisfaction.

With every rutting push, Callum and I tangled closer, Isaac struck deeper, Aiden's hands were harder against me. I felt frenzied and calm at the same time, riding a torrent that was pounding in my ears and blood. The drumbeat was heaviest between my legs, where Isaac was rutting into me and Callum was bumping and Aiden was nudging.

The first wave of pleasure was slow, had overtaken me before I realized I was under it. I pulled free of Callum's lips to cry out as the crashing warm feeling buried me, catching my breath. The second, as Isaac's rhythm turned erratic and desperate inside me, was sharp and sudden, a stab of pleasure bolted through me leaving me tense, squirming away from the touch. There was a wet splash, hot and sticky against my belly, and then Callum was panting on my throat. Aiden's arms wrapped around us both, tight, as he shouted.

The four of us were limp on the bed, hiccuping breaths punctuating the air. I felt like a sticky, stretched out mess, but a giggling bubbly sensation like champagne was rising up in my chest.

"Someone grab that towel," Callum grumbled, face pressed into my neck.

Isaac's hand slid up my leg, making it twitch, and dipped into the fluid cooling on my stomach. "I'll get it," he murmured, kissing behind my ear.

I hissed as he pulled out of me, and he kissed my hip, stretching to the edge of the bed and digging on the floor for the towel.

"Remind me why we took the bath first," Isaac mumbled after cleaning away our mess and passing the towel to Aiden.

"We were too cold for the necessary blood flow," Callum said. He hadn't moved an inch yet, but he reached up and grabbed at Isaac's shoulder drawing him back down to the mattress, and tight to my back.

"Are you alright?" Isaac asked me.

One of the giggles broke free, and then a second, until they were all loose and I was shaking between him and Callum. Aiden sat up, eyes soft on me and smile only a little concerned.

"I'm fine," I assured them when I caught my breath again. "I'm perfect. Exhausted and possibly bow-legged, but perfect."

There was a collection of kisses laid over my skin where they could reach, Callum pressing several to the bridge of my nose, and then we were all settling. Someone found the edge of the blanket to draw over us. Having them all around me as I fell asleep was like being nested, and it was a feeling I was coming to crave. My skin was still tingling, and I was a pleasant kind of sore, but relaxed and drowsy.

I drifted down to a chorus of breaths in my ear, eyes blinking slowly up at the ceiling of my bedroom.

૭૪૭

CALLUM WAS WAITING for me as I got out of the shower the next morning. Out of *my* shower. That felt like warm rainfall and was the size of the entire bathroom in the little campus house.

There was a stack of clothes on the bed next to him.

"Aiden went to the library to get your case," he said. "And they sent me up with these in case you objected."

I scrubbed a small towel through my hair and flipped through the clothes. It looked like they had come from Hildy and my only real question was *when*. How long ago had Aiden started picking out new clothes for me? But they were only nicer versions of what I usually wore, things I had already been saving up for.

"What were you supposed to do?" I asked, passing him my towel and slipping into the underclothes. "Wrestle me into them?"

"I will if you need me to," Callum said, watching my skin vanish. "But it's that they think we match for stubbornness."

"Well then we better tell them I was extremely uncooperative," I said. I slid the new slip, heavier and softer, over my skin.

Callum laughed and lifted the dress, a rusty orange with long sleeves and a full skirt, up from the bed and held it up for me to step into.

"I came to talk to you," he said, quieter than before. "About the Hollow. And Cecil and Isaac."

I froze in place and Callum finished dressing me, drawing the zipper up my back, fingers gentle over the nape of my neck.

"I know you want to tell me not to feel guilty or—" I started.

"I only want to tell you the facts, I promise," he said, kissing where his fingers lingered before going back to the bed. He moved to sit against the headboard and patted the spot next to him.

I crawled in slowly as if it were a trap. Callum waited, an arm held out for me to fit against his side. It was an easy trap to fall into when presented that way. His hand wrapped over my shoulder and we sat together in quiet for a moment.

"I know better than anyone how impossible it is to let go of guilt for responsibility," he said and I turned into him to see his face better. His focus was distant and his free hand reached out to fiddle with mine over my lap. "I'll get to that later. I just want you to know I'm not trying to talk you out of your feelings. *But* there are things you should know."

He glanced at me and I nodded for him to continue. "*Gate-keepers* was taken off-campus for a reason. I wasn't aware, no one was. The magic used to write it seems to contain some kind of... preservation of the beings it describes. And in the case of the Hollow, the proximity of the book works like an echo. Or a microphone, even. And if you hadn't been the one influenced, *I* might have been."

"Or the student who requested it," I said, thinking of the younger girl looking for research materials for a paper.

Callum paled a little at that. "Probably the student. Either way, the Hollow would have found a target."

"You *are* trying to talk me out of my responsibility," I said. Because there was a tangled knot loosening in my chest and a part of me—the stubborn part—*did* want to hang onto it.

"You are no more responsible for Cecil Pincombe's death than I or Isaac are," Callum whispered, hands tightening around mine. "We were on the ground floor with him. And he did what he could to protect a student, but nothing and no one was going to be fast enough to protect him. You saved dozens of lives that night."

"Isaac," I said.

"Isaac is fine. He has a little scar and a few gray hairs now. Honestly, he could do with being a little less handsome," Callum said, trying to stifle a grin.

I pushed at him. "He is *not* less handsome. It isn't *funny!*"

Callum sobered with only a small roll of his eyes. "I know. I do."

"I got him hurt," I said. "I don't know what I'm doing and I can do..."

"So much?" he asked, raising an eyebrow. "With just one word."

"And that was the wrong word."

"We don't know what would have happened if you hadn't written it, though," Callum said. "What if Bryce and Tatsuo and I had tried to battle the Hollow then? I didn't know half of what I know now. It might have gone better and it might have gone worse. But Isaac *is* safe. And you should speak to him."

I winced. Trying to abandon three lovers meant owing three lovers a sincere apology when you'd realized your own stupid mistake. And while Isaac seemed to accept that I was here now, that didn't keep my actions from being hurtful. He and I had been closest from the beginning with how much we had in common.

"There's something else I need to tell you," Callum said after a stretch.

His arms and hands and chest were tense all around me. I twisted in my spot to sit close, facing him and keeping our hands tangled together.

"About the war," I said.

He nodded, eyes fixed to where my thumbs were stroking the backs of his hands. "You've heard about the Toy Soldier?" he asked.

"The general on the front lines at the end of the war," I said. Callum looked up, his eyes going flat with anxious lines appearing between his brows. It sank in slowly. "But...Callum you were...you can't have been. You were so young."

"Sixteen," he said.

"How on earth?" I murmured.

"My father, he was- is a general," Callum said, taking a deep breath. "His older sons, my half-brothers, are all in the army. And we're from northern parts so he was home a lot during the war. And at the time I was his last son. He brought me into his office, tried to teach me about war. But I was...I was already learning about it. I'd been listening to him talk about it my entire life, that was all we had to read about and I was..."

"Natural," I said, thinking of what Aiden had mentioned.

"My strategies were crude but effective," Callum said darkly. "He took them with him to the fronts and won battles. So then he took me too. I think it was meant to be a bit of a joke at first. A way to show off to the other officials. They ended up being impressed. And I was an idiot and thought I was a genius. I wasn't seeing the results of my plans, I only heard the news. Battles won, armies defeated. It sounded like a game."

It had sounded like a game in the south too. I was younger and by the time I really knew what was happening, we were winning. There was no chance of the war coming to Bridgeston.

"My mother had died, and the others in the coven...it was different than ours is. And I was making my father proud which was all he or I cared about the time." Callum grimaced and then shrugged. "No. I cared about winning. I was proud of myself."

"You were too young," I said.

"I was. They gave me a brigade and advisors and put me in a tent on battlefields and I...I devised the strategies that would win fastest and by the largest numbers. And they kept bringing me more men because...because I was..." he went quiet and I held my breath, already knowing what would come. "I was having them slaughtered. Just a fraction less than the enemy. I saw it at the end. What I had done to them. And they sent me back home because by then..."

"You'd won the war for them," I said. It was what we had heard at home. The Toy Soldier had won the war. I wondered how many people had known that the Toy Soldier was a boy.

Callum nodded faintly. My hands rose up from our laps, wrapping over his cheeks and his eyes met mine, dull and exhausted and wary. Everything I thought to say I threw out again. I could not say that I was sorry, or that it wasn't his fault, because they were true but they weren't *enough*. And they wouldn't change anything. So I kissed him, pressing my lips gently to his and holding us there as his hands clutched at my back.

"You said your mother was from the north," he said as I leaned back. "She'll know what I did to her people."

I blinked at that. "My mother died a few years ago," I said. "And she was Vermenian." Callum's eyes widened. "My father met her while he was in the army in the north, before your war. And they said that was where she was from, like it would explain the accent. I don't know how she felt about the war, not really. But she talked about it like everyone else in town. Saying nasty things about her own people. Praising our soldiers, *you*. So my brother and I did too. Even though we knew. She spoke Vermenian when she was angry, if we were alone."

Callum's brow furrowed again and I gave him another swift kiss. "You should not have been a general," I said because that was simple and it was true. "And no one is their best self during a war. My mother would have forgiven you."

He studied my face, maybe looking for the Vermenian pieces, and then nodded briefly.

"My mother would have loved you," he said, with the trace of a smile.

His father and I would not be getting along, that much was for sure.

CHAPTER 25
JOANNA

"HERE...HERE IS SOMETHING," HILDY SAID, LIPS TWISTED thoughtfully as she leaned away from the book in front of her.

Midterms were put on hold, classes were canceled, and the Library was locked. Hildy and Aiden, apparently trustees of the university, had gotten access to the President's private library. Callum had pulled all the relevant books and brought them back to join us, clustered in the sunroom of Gwen's home.

"It's about the history of the university," she said. "*The Hand Woods, designed and cultivated to contain magical forces*," she read, "*Became an ideal location to foster growth in students. In addition, the University would act as a line of defense.* It's very vague but-"

"The woods is the cage," Tatsuo said.

Callum and I glanced at each other, our expressions a mirror of puzzlement, and then it struck us both at the same time.

"The Hollow isn't the only thing out there!" I exclaimed as Callum said, "The woods is a prison, Joanna only unlocked one cell."

"Which is why it hasn't left the area," Gwen said, pulling the book to herself from Hildy's lap. "It's still trapped. In here, with us."

"The cage is built of sigils, that's easy enough," Callum said, books open in front of him on the floor of the other coven's sunroom. "But we guessed partly right. There's a coded melody and a swatch of color here. Pieces of the true name. But the word was never written down for safety's sake. And we need the whole name to keep the sigils in place."

"But I have the connection we need to get that word," I said. "Tatsuo said—"

"It's not safe," Callum said without looking up from his texts.

"Neither is trying to solve this with a missing piece and if I can do it, then that's what we have to do." I watched Callum's shoulders draw in as he reached up to adjust the glasses on his nose and acted as if he hadn't heard me at all. "You're being unreasonable," I started again.

"I'm not sure that he is," Gwen said from the loveseat, and Hildy was looking studiously into her own lap. "You've never tried trance writing. You're still so new, Joanna."

My cheeks warmed and I looked at the others. Aiden was studying the page Callum had handed him with the melody and Tatsuo seemed to be avoiding my gaze. Only Bryce and Isaac were looking back at me, and both of them were too inscrutable for me to puzzle out in my embarrassment.

"I can put you in the trance," Bryce said, words slow and cautious.

"No," Callum snapped, looking up.

"If she practiced," Tatsuo tried.

"With whom? Herself? It's something entirely different," Callum said, voice snarling on the words. "Or were you volunteering?"

Everyone stiffened at once, Gwen and Hildy staring at Tatsuo with wide eyes.

"No," Tatsuo said slowly. "And Joanna and I don't share the necessary connection. I was thinking of someone in her own coven."

Callum paled at that, face dropping back down to the floor. Even Aiden's expression became shuttered at the suggestion. Isaac was as quiet and wary as he had been since I'd tried to leave them. He didn't withhold physical affection, but the distance remained clear.

I couldn't blame a single one of them. If it had been my choice to offer up the most vulnerable piece of myself to another person—give them power over my will—I wouldn't volunteer either.

"I'll do it," Isaac said. The whole room stared at him and he stared back at me.

"You don't have to," I said.

"I know," he said, and what had seemed wary now appeared steady and centered. "But I'll do it."

I glanced at Callum and Aiden, expecting them to argue with him. To at least warn him what a terrible idea it was. Callum looked frustrated, but he didn't say a word. Aiden only reached out to squeeze Isaac's hand and then turned to smile gently at me.

Isaac pushed away from the fireplace to come stand in front of my chair. "Come on, let's talk."

I took his hand and followed him back through the house into a small study stuffed with books and smelling faintly of tobacco.

"Are you sure you want to do this?" I asked.

"I am," Isaac said, facing me. "I think you're right and that you have the best chance of finding that missing piece to the name. And I know you writing it will make it the strongest cage possible. But that's not why I'm volunteering."

"I know that it's such a risk and I swear to you I would never abuse the power. I'll never even *use* it, I promise!" I said.

Isaac smiled, faint and flickering, and his hands squeezed at mine. "I need you to know that...I'm still hurt. That you left us," he said and when I opened my mouth to answer, apologize, he darted forward and pecked quick and soft against my lips. "I know you regret it and I...I do forgive you."

"I won't leave again, Isaac," I whispered.

"I believe you," he said, and then he winced a little and added, "I will. Time will prove it. I'm telling you that doesn't change how I feel. I trust you. Even if you had left us and said you didn't want to be a part of the coven, didn't want to belong with us. I would still trust you with this."

"I love you," I said, quick and clumsy because I was afraid he might say it first. And I wanted him to know that I meant it, and it wasn't just an answer.

His eyes brightened and his cheeks dimpled and I jumped forward into his arms, kissing him fiercely. His arms wrapped around my waist, lifting me to my toes, and a weight in my chest lightened.

"I love you, Joanna," he said, pulling away and we both grinned. "I love you and I trust you to know me. Every bit."

It was probably wrong to feel so giddy, walking back into the sunroom hand in hand with Isaac. Especially given how grim Callum still looked, sitting on the floor staring blankly into the books. Aiden was busy transcribing music onto a piece of paper, tracing the notes in the air and grimacing as he worked through them. Tatsuo and Bryce looked up as we entered, and Tatsuo's expression brightened at seeing ours.

"With Bryce leading the trance, it accelerates the process. You'll need to be focusing entirely on Isaac or the results will be aimless," Tatsuo explained, placing a pencil in my hand and notebook in my lap.

"Gast," Callum interrupted, looking up at Bryce. "Is it safe for them?"

"If it doesn't work, I will stop," Bryce said shrugging. "But what happens in the trance is up to Joanna."

"It's just a practice," I said.

"A test," Isaac hedged. "To see if it's even possible."

Callum's jaw worked, but he nodded once. He and Aiden and Gwen and Hildy all cleared out of the room to the kitchen, leaving Isaac and me with Tatsuo and Bryce.

"Now Isaac, you're more of a prop in this situation," Tatsuo said, taking Isaac by the shoulders and leading him away from me to the rug to sit. Bryce guided me over to sit across from him.

"If Joanna were experienced in this, and with a few years under her belt in the coven, she could probably manage this without you. But having you here will help with the focus," Tatsuo explained. Then he came to me and knelt down. "I'm going to leave in a minute. The fewer distractions the better. It's important that you stay as relaxed as possible. You'll want to direct the trance, but it will flow best when you let it carry you. What's important is maintaining your connection to Isaac."

I nodded, trying to fight the grin on my face as I met Isaac's gaze. But he was looking at me with those dimples in his cheek and the shade of his eyes had just gone the blue right before he kissed me. I couldn't imagine *not* feeling connected to him in the moment.

"She'll be fine," Bryce said, smirking at me.

"You may not realize at first when you find his name," Tatsuo said. "It isn't a label, it's portions of our soul. Just be open to what you find."

"I will," I said and Isaac's lips twitched again, mine resisting the urge to answer his. "What happens if I don't find his name?"

Tatsuo glanced at Bryce and they both shrugged at me. "Nothing," he said. "We'll think of something else."

Tatsuo coached me into a slow, regulated breathing to help with Bryce's drone. I watched Isaac's chest rise and fall steadily as he followed along, and that was its own kind of hypnotism. I didn't notice as Tatsuo tip-toed out of the sunroom. And at first, I didn't even notice as Bryce began to hum by the fireplace. It was all white noise, and I had given my attention to Isaac completely.

My heart squeezed in my chest and our eyes linked over the space. The room around me dimmed as if to give Isaac my focus. The hum in my ear became a buzz and then a roar burrowing into my thoughts more than lingering in the air. Isaac was larger and closer in my vision with every second and every echoing wave of sound in my head. Bryce's drone was overwhelming. For a moment, I wanted to tear away and ground myself again, in the sunroom and in myself.

But Isaac's eyes, the familiar dusty blue, were locked to my face. And it was a color I had grown fond of, felt safe surrounded by. The room shifted, blurring into that blue, and I settled. My heart thumped evenly, the beat joining the persistent burn of noise in my ears and head.

In one breath the rug scratched at my ankles and I felt the

wood of the pencil between my fingers. In the next breath, I was bodiless. I wasn't in a room *with* Isaac, but I could feel him all around me. The taste of paint was on my tongue and the sharp bite of the woods in my head. The droning was gone and replaced with something that sounded like the ocean, a twin rhythm of waves.

Heartbeats, I realized. Mine and Isaac's.

The gray-blue I was surrounded by fragmented in time with the beats. A flicker of new color appeared here and there until I was in a prism, hues flashing and spinning around me. They tangled and reshaped and overhead, a blinding brilliance shined into a glare.

When it cleared I was in a wheat field, bright golden and shimmering with sunlight. There was no sound and no temperature and no taste or smell in the air, but the colors were strong and abstracted. The sharp yellow-brown of the grain, the near white-blue of the sky, and a trim of green along the horizon.

The sun flared overhead, and a sweep of dark rose up, like a hand shielding my eyes. The field twisted and the brown deepened and the scene shifted into a small kitchen. One like my own in Bridgeston, close and hot from the stove, with a small window and the sunset shining in. There was a faint whiff of cookies and a little melody, one my father had known, but in a sweeter voice. A woman's figure, monstrously tall—no, just large like adults were to a child—and distorted in shadow, passed at my side. She wore a vivid blue apron, and the fabric outshone everything in the room. Its color was saturated and crisp, and it made me feel immediately safe.

She went to the fireplace, back turned, and the blue vanished and the room went dark. The flare of the sun became the red glow of a dying fire. There was a scratch of splintered wood nipping at my palms and knees. A low growling sound rumbled from beneath the floor under me and there was a shattering crack on the stone floor. Bottle green glittered and sparkled by firelight. The color was stark and queasy and made the pain of the wood splinters sharper. A coal hot anger rose up in me as the green gleamed and the room went blue-black with night.

More of Isaac passed through me. A secret stash of paper and pencils kept under his mattress. Heartache for the girl living down the lane *and* the boy who courted her. The blinding, glittering, first moment of stepping onto Canderfey, a blur of colors and so many of them *new*. Gawky, clean-shaven Callum, barely more than a teenager and hiding behind a stack of books. Aiden's hands starkly dark against the white keys of a piano.

White sheets and three bodies in bed, sunlight bouncing off their skin, throwing a pinkish-brown halo into the hair. I ached as the color burned through me, a sweetness so painful it made the outline of my heart in my chest clear again through the trance. It was Callum, Aiden, and I in the bed, legs and arms tangled together. There was a dent on the mattress next to me where Isaac had just risen from. It could have been that morning or sometime in the future but the dawn pink light stretched over us like a fresh canvas until we were lost in the glow.

The pink flushed into the ruddy red skin of a screeching baby, and the noise was high in my ears, ringing like an alarm. The baby was wrinkled and still wet, inky black hair matted down to its head in tufts. It swatted one red fist and there was an emotion I had never known, something beyond love or ferocity or safety. It swallowed me up until my sight blurred.

The tears were hot in my eyes, streaking down my cheeks and my legs were numb underneath me. I blinked and the room cleared around me. Isaac had moved close, sitting knee to knee to me, and he reached up and swiped at the wetness over my cheeks. There was a little frown at the corner of his lips and I leaned forward at once, kissing it away, kissing him just for the sake of it.

"Are you alright?" he asked.

I nodded, swallowing and hunting for my own voice.

Bryce beat me to words. "You didn't write anything down."

I glanced down. The pencil was still in my hand, the page blank.

"We can try again," Isaac said.

I realized that they assumed the trance hadn't worked and shook my head. "I'm fine," I said. "It's fine, it worked. I didn't write anything." Bryce's eyes narrowed and I thought I probably sounded like I was babbling. "Can you give us a minute?"

They stood and left and Isaac's fingers wiped away the last of my tears.

"Do you feel alright?" he asked again.

I sat up on weak knees and wondered how long we had been sitting together. It was dark outside, but with sunlight missing it was hard to tell evening from midnight. I moved into Isaac's space and he made way for me, pulling me close to his chest.

"I love you," I said and his smile flickered back. "I'm fine. I didn't write anything because there was nothing to write. Just color."

Vivid blue, bottle green, rosy earth, squalling red.

Isaac's eyes lit up at the news. "What—Well, maybe I shouldn't know. Really?"

"Really," I said, grinning.

"And nothing to scare you off?" he asked, a note wavering in the question.

"Nothing," I said, drawing him in for a slow and thorough kiss. "What did it feel like? Did you notice anything?"

"It was like...having you close," he said, smiling. "As if you've known me my entire life."

The others came into the sunroom, and I knew by the relief on Callum's face that Bryce had told them I had failed.

And then Isaac spoke.

"It worked. She found it."

And Callum's face fell.

৩৵৩

He didn't come to bed when we returned to the house. The trance had taken hours, another point in Callum's argument against it, and there was exhaustion in everyone's expressions. I didn't fight against his refusal and no one else continued the discussion, but it was clear that he knew it was only a matter of time. They would end up needing me in whatever plan we formed against the Hollow, and Callum would be outvoted.

"I don't disagree with him," Aiden mumbled in my bed as we lay down with Isaac to sleep. "I just think we all know he's wrong."

I huffed a laugh at the time and then lay awake until Isaac and Aiden fell asleep. Then I crawled out from the bed with a pillow under my arm and snuck down to Callum's office. The glittering lamp I had written him was lit on the table and he was hunched in his armchair, dark circles shadowed under his eyes.

"If you've come to argue your case," he growled, "I plan on being unreasonable."

"I was thinking," I said, dropping the pillow to the floor. I took a seat in front of the bookshelves and grabbed a discarded book from the pile around his feet. "What do you think would happen if I wrote 'the Hollow is back in its cage and the cage is locked and cannot be unlocked?'"

Callum blinked at me over the rim of his glasses. "I think...we should have tried that already?"

"I did," I said, passing my notebook full of the anxious scribbles of Isaac's sickbed. His expression fell. "Now, since that didn't work, what do we try next?" I asked.

Callum stared at me for a long stretch of silence and I waited. "Did you come down here in the middle of the night to strategize with me?" he asked, the angles in his face softening.

I nodded and waited as he took a long breath and sighed it out. He gathered up a collection of the books in front of him and then slid down from the chair, moving over to sit next to me. He passed me one of the books and flipped it open on my lap, something like sigils staring stark and black up from the page at me. One looked like a crescent moon with a jagged edge of teeth, and the other was twisted like a knot but with no sign of a beginning or end.

"This is an ancient alphabet, supposedly one belonging to gods. Or god-like creatures. I thought maybe they might be... helpful," Callum said, grimacing. "Except I'm not really sure what any of them mean."

"I could try one out on the paper to see what happens," I suggested, hiding my smile.

Callum took his glasses off and rubbed at his eyes. "I'm too tired to tell if you're joking and I'm desperate enough to consider saying yes. Let's talk about what parts of the caging spell we *do* understand."

I left any further writing to him for the night. But we discussed phrases I might try to help stall for time or keep everyone safe. And slowly, and very late at night, we talked about how I might find the missing piece of the Hollow's true name.

CHAPTER 26
JOANNA

WHEN WE OPENED THE CUPBOARDS THE NEXT MORNING ALL the porcelain had been turned to dust. Hildy arrived an hour later to tell us the pack of campus stray cats had been found, injured but whole. Tatsuo was nursing two of the older tom cats who had been injured, and there was a litter of three kittens in need of a home. Aiden made one attempt to object, and I cut him off before he could finish the sentence.

Callum found me and the kittens—an orange and white, a black and white, and a calico—by the fireplace in my bedroom. They scattered under chairs and, in the case of the orange and white boy, my skirt as he sat down with me.

"We shouldn't wait," I said.

He and I had barely made it to bed before dawn and the fresh round of bad news.

"We have a little time left," he said, tapping his fingers on the rug and making the kitten under my skirt peek its head out. "Bryce says the Hollow probably never chose a name for itself which is why we call it by these spook titles. Nothing for your spells to pin down."

Callum held still as the little tuxedo cat rushed bravely out and attacked his pant leg. He reached one finger out, scratched at its tail bone, and the kitten flopped onto its side with a roaring purr.

"What do we try next?" I asked.

He waited to speak until all the kittens reemerged, using him as a playful obstacle to climb and conquer.

"I'm afraid that if you use your connection with the Hollow it will make you more vulnerable," Callum said. "That it may be able to manipulate the connection as well."

"I'm afraid of that too," I said. "But I trust you, the three of you and the others, to keep me safe."

Callum stretched his hand out to mine, linking our fingers loosely, and the calico went tumbling down his leg to paw at our wrists. I smiled in spite of the conversation.

"I think instead of setting sigils, I should be focusing on hexing...distracting the Hollow," Callum said. "Keeping it busy while the rest of you work."

"Gwen and Hildy and Tatsuo can handle the sigils," I agreed. It was what we'd been saying for most of the day before.

Callum nodded loosely and then looked up at me. "If anything does happen, I'll get you out."

"I know," I said, squeezing his hand.

❧

It took another day of discussion and planning and Callum's wired pacing through the house. But we set into the woods by full daylight, as distorted as it was, armed in every way we could be. Aiden carried his latest handmade violin, stained black for battle. Callum had a knife that looked as deadly sharp as it did heavy with power and runes. Isaac carried the rough slate tile I would write on and the others were all armed with ceremonial wands.

I had a dense stick of chalk waiting in my pocket and it felt as comforting as being left naked in a thunderstorm. I didn't say that to the others.

Storm clouds gathered at our backs the deeper we walked into the woods. The path back to the clearing I had met Isaac in weeks ago was silent, dull and gray and devoid of life.

"What if it doesn't come back?" Isaac whispered as if to avoid shattering the hush of the woods. "Why would it walk back into the cage we let it out of?"

I *let it out of*, I thought. "That's what I'm here for," I said. "To lure it back."

Callum looked over his shoulder at me, eyes flinching at my words, but it was true. It was one of the things we had talked about in the dead of night in his office.

I thought I wouldn't recognize the clearing a second time. That I would rely on Isaac or the others to tell me when we had arrived. But it couldn't be mistaken. The ground had been scalped down to a barren mudscape, already our feet were squelching in the wet earth. In the colorless landscape, the trees ringing around the clearing really did look like bars on a jail cell.

We walked into the cell in silence, my covenmates sticking close to my side. Bryce remained near us and Gwen, Tatsuo, and Hildy continued on to the three farther points, like the ends of a compass. The sky darkened in a ring all around the tops of the trees and I knew we were being watched, tracked. I just wasn't sure if the Hollow saw us as a predator or prey.

"Are- are you sure?" Aiden asked before I could kneel, the neck and bow of his violin in one hand and the other reaching out to me.

Callum's plan, the order of actions, and all the different variables he and I had argued and pored over in our planning rattled through my head. I went to Aiden, pressing myself to his chest and feeling Callum and Isaac at my back. Aiden's arm folded around us and we held each other for several deep breaths.

"I'm sure," I said, starting to pull away. Aiden gave me a hard swift kiss, Callum leaving a softer one at the back of my neck.

Isaac bent as I knelt into the mud; cold, wet earth clasping around my knees. He left the stone in front of me and a long, soft kiss to my temple.

"Be careful," he said, standing again.

It wasn't a careful thing we were doing. I didn't answer him. There was a sound in the distance like a tree trunk splitting open, and it seemed just as likely as a crack of thunder.

I looked over my shoulder and Isaac's hands were held out in front of him, the space between wavering darkly. He had said he didn't need paint or ink or canvas to work color and I hadn't understood what he meant till now. Color was pooling in the air between his palms, the sickly gray-green of the woods around us growing dense and rotten. It was a stagnant, dying shade, the color of the Hollow. It clogged the back of my throat and left a pungent smell in my nose.

Aiden raised the violin to his shoulder and with the first stroke of the bow over the strings the sound was a tear in the air. I turned back to the clearing, closing my eyes and finding the spoiled color behind my eyelids. The melody Aiden had dragged off the page was a slithering, rasping piece running talons through my head.

My stomach rolled and when I blinked my eyes open, the clearing was spinning around me. I slammed them shut again, trying to push past the twist of music in my thoughts and the pounding dark color that hammered through me. I dug for the headache I woke up with in the mornings, right at the base of my skull. It was there, dull and pulsing in time with the Hollow's melody. When I found it, everything tangled together into one blurring, burning cacophony.

And then it was there, lurking inside the headache, coiling around itself like a snake. I opened my eyes, finding the clearing around me, but with the feeling that I was somewhere else. Bryce was watching my face and we nodded at the same time.

As Bryce began to hum, the color squatting at the back of my head spread across my vision, flattening the stone gray of the woods. Hildy in all her rich blues faded away, swallowed up by rotten green. The droning buzz of Bryce's voice joined the music and goosebumps rose up on my skin until I was one tingling, vibrating nerve.

And then I was nothing.

I remained that way for what seemed to be *too* long. There was something at the edges, something crawling in a perimeter circle. Pacing at a horizon of a color that stopped being a color and a song that had no beginning or end.

I tried to hold onto what Tatsuo had said, to let the trance carry me. But I was afraid now of being left here, rotting in a color gone bad.

Then there were shadows, rising up over my head. My knees were cold and my skin was clammy. The space around me sharpened, the foggy edges of darkness grainy in my sight. I looked up and the shadows became impenetrable. I looked down and saw the faint trace of my own feet, now standing, and a cluttering tangle of dark around them.

That was a very stupid thing to do.

I spun and stumbled back, my feet catching and tripping over uneven ground. The words were in my head, but the language was foreign on my ears, like the thunder of rocks breaking against each other.

The Hollow was behind me. Unshrouded, a naked pale thing that wasn't human or animal, only horror. Its flesh was greasy, body elongated as if it had made an effort to become *something* and then gave up. There was a distended belly, and the suggestion of a face, and pieces that were *like* limbs but were not.

"Where are we?" I asked, and the words echoed, my voice small and useless.

I've been building you a cage, the Hollow said, voice a spider's crawl up my skin. *To keep you in my belly with all the tasty things.*

"This isn't your belly," I said. "You haven't swallowed me down. I've come for your true name. You'll be back in your prison before nightfall."

You think like a human, witchling, the Hollow hissed. *I ate my true name too. And I'll eat your coven and your friends, but I won't keep them. Not for you. I'll spit them out into the dirt after I've chewed them bloody. I'll eat the woods and the brick mountains they built to gate me in and the hills and I'll keep you here to watch it all slide down my gullet.*

The Hollow grinned or snarled and its mouth was a fresh rotting rip in the moon white flesh. And then it was gone as I was catching a sour, humid breath to answer it. I gagged on the taste of the air as it clung to my tongue. My breaths stuttered in my chest and my eyes watered as I waited, hoping for the scene to shift like it had with Isaac. But the space was still and quiet and my heart hammered in my chest.

I fumbled in my pocket and found the stick of chalk still there. I shifted my feet over the floor until the right slid back and forth over something smooth and hard. I bent down and wrote blind.

I have a lamp to light the way.

There was a lamp, a little glass and oil one, yellow flame flickering and spitting at my side. The words were written on a piece of smooth dark wood, half-swallowed in the muck beneath me. I stood, raising the lamp, and shivered. Mountains of refuse rose up around me, bones and brick and glass. There were books, walls, pieces of what looked like an old ship, and more gruesome images I shied away from. I lifted the lamp above my head.

I was in a cavern, dark and massive and held up by spiraling stone gray that resembled something like a belly. My belly heaved and I covered my eyes, breathing into my palm.

It had to be a trick. It *had* to be.

But how long would it be before the others realized I was getting nowhere in my search? Could I leave the vision if the Hollow didn't let me out? Or worse, had I come waltzing into a trap I'd built for myself?

My stare fixed to a scrap of bright yellow fabric snagged on a shard of wood, a carved wolf's face broken into, as panic flooded through my veins. But the wolf was familiar, the yellow fabric too. It was the same yellow as Cecil Pincombe's shocking necktie, and it was flecked with a rusty brown. And the wolf had been one of the animals carved into the desk of the library.

I ate my true name too.

If that was true...and I was in the Hollow's belly...

I released a slow, shaking breath. My grip tightened around the handle of the lamp and the flame brightened. Vision or not there was something I could do while trapped here. I crawled to the top of one of the mounds of churned up wood and glass, picking up the books as I went, balancing as carefully as I could. I held my breath at the top, afraid of falling in an avalanche of trash, and looked around.

What surrounded me seemed to be from the campus. Several mountains deeper was the ship, and beyond that my lamp glanced off the window panes of a steepled church. The cavern went on and on, and I wondered how far in I would have to go, digging through waste and wreckage to find the word.

I lifted the lamp higher, squinting to see what was dangling from the steeple of the church. Firelight glinted above me and I tore my eyes gratefully away from the shadowy figure hanging. There was a glitter of warmth overhead, tracing over the bone of a rib, and I swung the lamp in an arch, watching more lines glitter.

There were symbols carved into the bone, worn and polished into the twisting arch. One flickered in the glow, a knot that tangled endlessly. I stumbled over trash, wincing as my foot caught in something sticky, but I kept my eyes up, following the pattern of symbols. Most of them were familiar, foggy in my memory, but from Callum's ancient alphabet.

In my head, they made the heavy crashing sounds of the Hollow's language. The sound looped, inverting in on itself. Like the knot letter and the melody. I practiced it silently on my tongue, working out the shape.

"Gvesdrasveg," I tried and everything rattled around me, the hill I stood on grumbling and scratching at my legs.

"*Gvisardrasivg!*" I said, louder and lower, the notes of the word clawing at my throat and grinding on my teeth.

And then the glass and wood and bone dropped out beneath me and swallowed me up.

I was braced, one hand in mud as the clearing reappeared around me. Night had fallen and stars winked overhead and my legs felt frozen in the cold underneath me. My right hand was poised over the stone, my palm sweaty around the chalk in spite of the chill. Books I had rescued lay scattered around me in the mud.

"Joanna!" Callum said, palms on my shoulders.

"*Gvisardrasivg,*" I hissed and a ring of storm clouds snarled in above us, swirling together like a tornado and dropping to touch down in the heart of the clearing.

"You have it?" Callum asked.

"*Gvisardrasivg,*" I shouted and Bryce echoed it, the word stronger on their tongue and sounding closer to the right word.

"Sigils, now!" Callum shouted, standing up at my back.

I drew the knot at the top of the stone as the Hollow, Gvisardrasivg, The Belly of Nightmares, poured itself out of smoke and storm cloud, shrouded again and as tall as the trees.

Aiden's bow was screeching over the strings of the violin and Isaac had turned the world the sick gray-green. Bryce shone yellow in the strange light, bellowing the word I had found into the sky. The Hollow bent, lunging at my coven, and there was a flash like orange fire. Callum was behind me like a blaze at my back, the tingling warmth of his protection charm multiplied by hundreds. He was chanting and there was a slice of metal in the air above my head, his knife tracing a ward.

My legs burned and my bones throbbed as I added the next letter, a mass of points like a bursting star. It was like the library all over again, my head pounding and my body screaming in protest. My writing slowed as my hand began to shake while I tried to make the smooth rounded edge of an empty moon. The next shape zigged and zagged and my teeth ground together through a scream. My back bowed and my vision blacked as the sensation of my bones shattering and splintering rocked through me.

"Callum," Isaac shouted. "What are you-?"

"Joanna's failing," I heard him say. "Hold the circle as long as you can."

Arms that burned like fire wrapped around my middle and I writhed against them.

"I have you," Callum said in my ear and there was a cool touch at the back of my neck that smoothed the rough, tearing feeling under my skin.

"The others," I whispered. But my body had calmed enough, making an X at the bottom of the stone and then crossing at the top and bottom, like an hourglass.

Across the clearing, a tree tore up from its roots, crashing dangerously down to the ground in front of Hildy. But the woman didn't even flinch, tracing a vivid blue sigil in the air that looked like a lopsided clockface.

"Finish the word, Joanna," Callum said, and I could hear the strain in his voice, feel the sweat sticking us together at my back.

My hands felt numb as I worked and out of the corner of my eye, I could see the Hollow thrashing. More trees came crashing, shattering on impact into jagged pieces that scattered in all directions.

The entire world seemed to shake, threatening to break apart, as I finished the second starburst, the last letter. The chalk crumbled against the slate as I joined the last point. Bryce was joining me in the dirt, placing small glowing hands on either side of the name. The letters burned bright with Bryce's touch turning from chalk to fire to scorched carvings on the stone

The Hollow screamed and the sound reverberated at the back of my head like a white-hot poker. My throat burned as I screamed with it, my body seizing and my sight swimming into a blind, bright, burst of empty color. Callum's lips were on my cheek, moving with a word, but I was falling under.

CHAPTER 27
JOANNA

EVERYTHING WAS GRAY AND FOGGY AS I OPENED MY EYES. MY head still felt split in half and my vision pulsed like a drumbeat for a moment before clearing. The plaster above me was cracked and stained, a familiar bowing moon white circle above a narrow and lumpy bed.

I took one breath, mildew and charcoal and fresh bread, and I knew. I was back in Bridgeston.

I sat up and my head swam, the room blurring to a cloudy smear and then back again.

The house was quiet and my heart sank, knowing the inherent wrongness of the silence. I teetered out of the bed in bare feet, mud brushed away from my knees so they were still dusted in dirt. I looked out the window by the bed and there was a low morning fog hanging over the yard, hiding the rest of the town.

I stumbled to my bedroom door and out into the hall. The house seemed to have faded since I'd left, like the life and charm had been leached out over time. That or the cheerful pale yellow of the walls was now dull to me in comparison to the saturated colors of my coven's house.

Where were they?

There was a choking panic in my throat. What happened in the woods? Why was I in Bridgeston and not with my coven?

My legs were weak and my feet barely felt the grain of the floor underneath me. But when I made it down the hall to the stairs I saw gleaming black shoes under the rickety kitchen table and for the first time since waking I took a full breath.

"I was afraid- afraid you weren't here," I said, coming down the stairs and finally seeing Aiden, Callum, and Isaac crowded together in my family's kitchen.

Their faces turned to me in unison, but instead of relief or smiles, their expressions were smooth—a placid smile on Aiden's mouth, a sneer over Callum's. Isaac only blinked at me.

"Why are we here?" I asked, at the bottom of the stairs. "What happened with the Hollow? How are the others?"

"The Hollow is caged," Isaac said, and there was nothing in the words, no joy or feeling.

"Come sit, darling," Aiden said. "You must be tired."

I wanted to go to them, fold myself between the three of them. But there was no room with the way they linked together, Callum sitting in the chair with the others framing him, hands on shoulders like the twist of a knot. And Aiden was pointing to the seat across from them. I walked to the table, trying to catch my feet on the ground to settle myself, but instead left wading in a murky dread.

I made it to the free chair and then stopped, hands grasping onto the back of it. I didn't want to sit, I wanted to resist the weight sinking into my gut.

"Why are we here?" I repeated.

Their faces turned to face each other, something so synchronized in the movement. They had been together so long, it was as if they were a single unit. And I was still an outsider.

They looked back at me and it was Callum who spoke, head tilting and eyes squinting at me through his glasses.

"You were right. About everything."

I stared back, my breath locked in my lungs as I waited, feeling that dread shaping underneath me. A familiar fear that I had tried to give up as if it were an addiction.

"It's so much clearer, seeing you here," Isaac continued. "You're such a simple creature. So small."

"Canderfey was swallowing you up," Aiden said. "And here you look so at home."

"I'm at home with you," I whispered, because it was a promise they had given me.

"Do you think so? Or did you just want to be more than you really are?" Callum asked, voice gentle and poisoned.

I swung around, facing the small stove where dented pots were hanging overhead and a ragged, stained towel was dropped carelessly on the counter. I squeezed my eyes against the tears and pressed my hand to my chest where my heart was trying to crack open.

"Joanna."

I spun again, fixing my eyes to Callum, hearing the urgent plead in his voice, but he only looked bored. My head panged and the room darkened, the three of them blending together into one dark and menacing shape, and then the pain faded.

"You're an awful lot of trouble, darling," Aiden said, his grin cruel.

"Writing is an... unusual gift, but it doesn't mean you suit us," Isaac said.

"You don't belong in our coven," Callum said, firm and final.

My lips parted and I didn't know what would come out, a scream or a sob or protest...or an agreement. I stared at them, vision watery and body feeling trembly and useless. Plain and small and pathetic.

"There you are girl," my father said, coming in from the back garden, hands dirty and face distracted. "This kitchen is a mess. What have you been doing all day?"

"I—" My brow furrowed. I had only just woken up.

My sister-in-law, Rose, came rushing down the stairs, two squalling children in her arms. "Could you take Aggie for just a minute? She's got a tooth coming in and she's impossible and Donny needs changed."

"Quit gaping and daydreaming, mouse," my brother said, appearing through the front door.

My niece was screaming and wiggling, arms reaching out to be held and bounced and my father was frowning at me and my brother was rolling his eyes. And through it all my coven sat, watching me with narrow eyes and patient smiles as if to say 'See? This is what you are.'

"No!"

The activity in the room paused, my family's eyes wide as I dug my nails into the chair in front of me and braced myself.

"No. This is not what we agreed," I said. "We fight for each other. We do belong together. It's as much my coven now as it is yours."

"You can't be in a coven, honey, you're not a-"

"Not *now*, Rose," I hissed, without tearing my eyes from Aiden's face. "And it isn't up to any of you whether or not I go back to Canderfey. I have a job there."

My coven looked at each other again and there was something strange in the movement, the pace slow and smooth and regular. Callum turned back to me, a twist of annoyance in the purse of his lips.

"We really don't know you well enough to be sure you're worth it," he said.

But he had said so, from the start. They had all said so, even when I refused to listen.

"You do," I said, but the protest was weak.

"You would have to prove it to us, darling," Aiden said.

My stomach was twisting around itself and my knees were shaking. These were not the men I had found too easy to fall in love with. I didn't understand what had changed, but I felt needy and desperate to change it back.

"How?" I whispered.

My family was hanging back by the stairs, the children gone quiet in their mother's arms, and all eyes fixed to me.

"Your true name would tell us," Isaac said, the usual sweet rasp of his voice now honeyed.

"My... I don't know it," I said. My gut stopped rolling and turned to stone.

"You could find it," Callum said. "If you wanted us, you could find it around here somewhere."

"Around...around here?" I stepped back from the chair and Callum rose up, Aiden and Isaac's hands still on his shoulders.

"Just look, darling," Aiden purred.

I blinked at them and then let my eyes wander slowly around the room, thoughts scrambling.

These were not my men...these were not...

"I can't find it," I murmured.

"*Look*," Callum snapped.

I bit my lip and avoided their gazes. The fog was still hanging outside the window, dense and dark.

"Gvisard-" I started.

"Stop!" The room shouted as one, my coven in front of me and my family behind.

I should have felt afraid or threatened, but instead there was only relief. I looked directly at the men, not into any of their faces, but at the twisted, hulking shape of them together.

"You were too impatient," I said.

"I can find it myself now that I'm here," it said from a half dozen voices.

I backed up another step and the table and chairs vanished between us, the image of my covenmates starting to congeal together at the shoulders. I had seconds.

"Gvisardra-"

Callum lunged and pulled the bodies of Aiden and Isaac with him. I scrambled back, spine hitting the edge of the stove as six hands—dark and tan and pale—wrapped around my throat, choking off the sound.

Joanna, breathe.

Callum. They were with me. Not here in the vision the Hollow conjured to torture me, but out there in the woods, waiting.

"Gvisardravig," I said, or tried to say, air squeaking out of my lungs. Aiden's face was smashed to Callum's, eyes bulging together as Isaac's jaw fell loose, and looser, long and gaping and grotesque with too many teeth.

The room was going black and my voice was strangled but I kept my lips moving even as nails clawed at my face and neck.

"Get into your cage and *rot* there."

Fingers punched into my throat like blades and I choked on on blood or air or nothing.

I thrashed as voices shouted in my head, too many voices. My hands swiped through the hair and were caught up in a firm grip.

"Joanna! Joanna, it's us. It's us. It's alright."

I tried to lunge back but arms were banded around my waist. A cool hand brushed over my forehead and the black cloud in my vision washed away. Callum and Aiden and Isaac were surrounding me and I screamed, the shout burning in my abused throat.

Callum reached up to my neck and I flinched away. But his hand was gentle where it landed.

"You're safe," he whispered. "You're safe. It's over."

I was gulping for air, finding that I could breathe again, and the sudden introduction of oxygen made white stars burst behind my eyes. I sagged in Isaac's hold and Aiden's worried face leaning forward to leave a warm kiss on my cheek was the last thing I saw.

※

I WOKE up in Isaac's bed, an emptiness in my head. And in my stomach. There was a kitten sleeping on my shoulder, the orange and white one, and the calico was snuggled against my side. Callum was asleep in the chair I had taken vigil in while Isaac was ill. I froze at the sight of him, panic and relief warring in me, afraid to find myself under a new trick.

There was a little mewling chirrup from the end of the bed, the tuxedo kitten, and then Callum stirred. His head lolled in my direction and for a moment he only blinked at me. Then he was out of the chair, tripping in his bare feet on the way to the bed.

"Is it you?" I asked, and the words came out sticky and slurred. I pushed myself up on the pillow and the orange kitten growled and rolled away.

"Here," Callum said, pulling over a little mug of cold tea and lifting it to my lips as he climbed onto the bed with me.

The tea was sweet and icy on my aching throat, carrying away some of the burn and parched dryness.

"You kept kicking and pushing at us while you slept," Callum said, with a goofy smile on his face. "The healers said to leave you to it."

I 'hmm'd and then reached out a hand, brushing my fingers over the rise of his cheek. It felt right, the warmth and softness instead of the hot and sticky fever of the Hollow. I tugged him closer by the front of his shirt. He laughed and scrambled up to the pillows, tucking me into his side. I felt a little stiff and a little weak, but none of the lingering pain that had struck me unconscious.

"How long's it been?" I mumbled into his shirt, smiling as I heard the house groaning with running footsteps up the stairs.

"Just a day," Callum said.

I blinked at that and then realized that the sun was shining and there was blue outside the window. "It really worked?" I asked. "It's...is it gone?"

The door to the bedroom opened and Aiden was charging in, straight for the bed. I stretched and arm out for him and he slid underneath it, heavy over my stomach and face pressed to my neck.

"It worked," Callum said. "The Hollow is locked up tight."

"Hello, love," Isaac said from the doorway, carrying a tray in his arms. "How are you feeling?"

"Okay, I think," I said. I waved a hand towards the back of my head. "A little like I'm...missing a headache I've grown used to?"

Callum's fingers combed through my hair and I let my eyes drift shut at the touch. "That'll be the connection gone now."

The connection that had let the Hollow into my head, my fears.

"'S a relief," I murmured. Aiden shifted up to my side, an arm joining Callum's over my shoulders. I folded my legs, up making room for Isaac and reaching out for the tray of food. I was starving. "How are the others?" I asked.

They hesitated for a moment and I froze, a muffin halfway to my lips, stomach sinking. Aiden sighed and spoke first.

"They're alright, really," he said, trying too hard to be reassuring. "Tatsuo was hit by a piece of tree falling. Got a nasty shot through his left leg. But he's healing, quickly if Hildy and Gwen have anything to say about it. And Bryce was a little wavery at the end yesterday, but I expect they're rested up by now."

"Altogether, nothing serious," Isaac said, hand stroking at my leg over the blanket.

I eased and Callum kissed at my temple as I took another bite of food. "So...what's next?" I asked, looking at each of them.

"You take time off, a week according to Woollard," Aiden said, fingers tracing a pattern on my belly.

"What?" I snapped, sitting up and jostling him. "No, I'm fine—"

"A week," Isaac said, tone firm.

I sulked back against the headboard. "I'll play it by ear." I hurried on before they could correct me, "And what I meant was I've agreed to be in the coven so now...there's supposed to a series of trials right?"

Callum grinned at me. "Those are old traditions."

I fidgeted. "I only read about them. And I wasn't *expecting* to practice them. But I remember that there was an Invitation and..."

"A Union and a Trial?" Isaac asked, head leaning to one side. "I think we covered those, love."

"Isaac issued a formal invitation," Aiden rolled onto his back to look up at me. With a sly grin, he said, "We've had unions. And if locking the Hollow back up wasn't a trial, I don't know what was."

"I assumed we covered that when you tried to leave," Callum said shrugging.

"So...that's it?" I asked.

"There are formal commitment ceremonies, coven marriages," Callum said, watching my face. He glanced at the others and back to me. "When you're ready, we can talk about that."

"For now," Isaac said, squeezing at my leg. "I would like to simply enjoy the company of my coven, complete and safe as it is now."

And strangely enough, there was something thrilling in the suggestion. Without the threat of danger, and with my promise to stay and be open with these men, a relationship seemed suddenly exciting. And I had agreed to move into the house.

I pushed the tray aside and Isaac immediately leaned in closer, stretching forward to kiss me. "I may get bored at home for a week," I mumbled against his lips.

He leaned back, eyes rolling, and Aiden laughed.

"I'm sure we'll find ways to entertain you," Callum said, voice dry and eyes hot on my skin.

EPILOGUE

CALLUM

I stood in the doorway of Joanna's bathroom with a forgotten book in my hand, watching as she and Aiden kissed under the falling water. I'd come upstairs to show her notes I'd found on Scribes, a rare breed of witches whose magic centered around their writing, but the new information wasn't half as interesting as the sight of the pair of them. Aiden's dark arms twisted around Joanna's narrow waist, her soft hips rolling forward, seeking friction. His hands skimmed down her back, over her ass, and his mouth trailed down her chest to her belly as he dropped to his knees.

Joanna's small cry echoed against the stone of the shower walls.

I was ready to drop the book and join them when a hand settled on my shoulder.

"This came in the mail for you," Isaac said.

It took a minute for the hungry fog to clear out of my head before I could tear my eyes away from Joanna arching back as Aiden held her against his mouth. Isaac was holding out a letter in his hand.

My stomach sank and the desire fled my blood. The writing was my father's.

"Did you tell him about Joanna?" he asked, voice lowered.

"I don't tell him anything if I can help it," I said. But he might have heard by now. It'd been almost a week since we'd put the Hollow away. Joanna's part in it—and her place in our house —was no secret on campus.

"Probably news of war," Isaac said. Because it was almost always news of war with my father.

"Or a summons," I said.

Isaac and I looked at each other for a long moment. "If it is, Aiden and I will come too."

A little bit of tension leaked out of my shoulders. I knew what it cost Isaac to offer, but I would need him if I had to go North. *Joanna* would need us all if she had to meet my father.

Joanna was calling from the shower, not for us but for release, and Isaac's attention shifted, a dark smile replacing his frown.

I flicked my hand and the letter vanished. If I was lucky, I would forget it ever arrived.

Isaac pulled his shirt over his head. "Come on, Aiden looks like he could use a hand."

I snorted. Aiden seemed to be fine. It was Joanna that was begging. I started to strip.

I didn't want to think about war or monsters, and my father crossed both categories. I just wanted to lose myself in the touch of my coven for another day. The book I'd been carrying dropped to the floor with my pants. I would tell Joanna about the Scribes after.

Isaac was walking into the shower, steam billowing out from the glass door, and I followed quickly. Joanna reached for me, face tangled with pleasure and frustration, and I banished my worries with her kiss.

CONTINUE WITH THE COVEN IN WARRIORS!

Warriors, Book Two of the Librarian's Coven

Joanna just wants to spend the holiday curled up with her coven of handsome professors, but family obligations wait for no one. Instead of wintery cuddles, she's up to her neck in the Pike brothers and their wives, a cast of political figures invited to their dinner parties and, worst of all, Callum's father, Duncan. Duncan Pike is a nasty piece of work--not only did he place a young Callum in the heart of an ugly war, he disapproves of Isaac and Aiden.

Duncan claims a new war is coming, and it looks like he might be right. As if that weren't enough, the infamous warrior Sabine York is showing a marked interest in Callum--is she after revenge? Or does she want to add Callum to her coven of soldiers?

When trouble strikes and Callum is separated from the rest of the coven, Joanna, Isaac, and Aiden must travel from the library to the capitol to Vermenia, desperate for their reunion. And, on his own for the first time in years, Callum must tread carefully back into the waters of war he's spent decades avoiding.

Can they fight through the people and the miles standing between them and return safely together again?

CONTINUE WITH THE COVEN IN WARRIORS!

Warriors is available now!

ALSO BY KATHRYN MOON

COMPLETE READS

The Librarian's Coven Series

Written - Book 1

Warriors - Book 2

Scrivens - Book 3

Ancients - Book 4

Summerland Series

Summerland Stories, the complete collection plus bonus content

Standalones

Good Deeds

Command The Moon

Say Your Prayers - co-write with Crystal Ash

The Sweetverse

Baby + the Late Night Howlers

Lola & the Millionaires - Part One

Lola & the Millionaires - Part Two

Sol & Lune

Book 1

Book 2

Inheritance of Hunger Trilogy

The Queen's Line

The Princess's Chosen

The Kingdom's Crown

SERIES IN PROGRESS

Sweet Pea Mysteries

The Baker's Guide To Risky Rituals

ACKNOWLEDGMENTS

Endless thanks to my family and friends for listening to me obsess and fret since the day I started this project. Your support and patience has meant the world to me. Mom, I won't let you read this in its entirety but I love you so much and I hope to be half as awesome as you someday.

Thank you to my beta team; Megan, Polly, Krysti, Rachel, Maria, Britts, Carmen, and my fellow Kathryn! I appreciate all your help in shaping and polishing that early draft!

To BloomBloomBoomBoomBBNut, you're a one woman cheering squad and I couldn't be more grateful to have found you! You're so talented and I can't wait to buy all of your books and fangirl over them. Love you, bb!

Ariel Bishop, the incredible artist who made my gorgeous cover and helped me with promotional graphics! What you do is magic, end of story.

To the amazing writing squad who answered incessant questions from me and witnessed an embarrassing amount of whining. Dresupi, Pink, Dizzy, Cherie, Stancey, and Aenaria, thank you so much for bringing me into the fold.

Britts. Lady. This would not have happened without you. Thank you so so so much for the nudge and all the help and back-up and cheering you gave along the way. I hope to repay it tenfold.

Karen Dailey and Sara Box helped me edit and polish this book and they were probably gentler than I deserved but I hate to think of what you might be reading if not for their help. They are amazing women and I am a lucky duck to know them.

Hey Waffles. If it weren't for you I would probably be staring at a blinking cursor right now waiting to finish this book. Thank you for the pompom waving and the dirty inspiration. Thank you for being The Actual Best ™ no exceptions. Oh look it's in print now, so you can't argue. Ha! I love you.

ABOUT THE AUTHOR

Kathryn Moon is a country mouse who has been trying to write reverse harem since The Backstreet Boys had their first album. When her hands aren't busy typing they're probably knitting sweaters or crimping pie crust. She definitely believes in magic.

You can reach her on Facebook, hang out in Kathryn's Moongazers, and contact her at ohkathrynmoon@gmail.com!

Printed in Great Britain
by Amazon